KNIGHTS CORRUPTION MC SERIES

RYDER

S. NELSON

Ryder
Copyright © 2017 S. Nelson

Editor
Hot Tree Editing

Cover Design
CT Cover Creations

Interior Design & Formatting
Christine Borgford, Type A Formatting

Ryder/ S.Nelson.—1st edition
ISBN-13: 978–1546957294
ISBN-10: 1546957294

This is a work of fiction. Names, characters, places, and incidents are a product of the publisher's imagination. Locales and public names are sometimes used for atmospheric purposes. Any resemblance to actual people, living or dead, or to businesses, companies, events, institutions, or locales is completely coincidental.

Elmarie—I dedicate the final ride of this series to you, someone I'm honored to call a friend. I adore your enthusiasm for my stories and truly appreciate all of your wonderful feedback.

PROLOGUE

MY HAND COVERED MY INJURED cheek while my lips moved in silence, praying to be saved from the monster who'd attacked me. Again. I wished for his death, and sadly, even at the tender age of seven, there were moments I wished for my own.

Still whispering my pleas, I finally opened my eyes. That was when I saw him standing in the doorway to my bedroom, huffing and puffing as if he'd run a hundred miles just to get to me.

Words formed in my throat, but when I opened my mouth to plead for him to leave me alone, only silence sounded. His black eyes stared me down, the intensity enough to make me cower on my bed. With my hands clutching the superhero blanket beneath me, I closed my eyes once more and tried to escape what was going to happen next. Unfortunately I knew all too well the pain I was about to endure in the next few minutes, although it would certainly feel like hours.

"Look at me, you little shit!" he thundered, pounding the doorframe for emphasis. When I refused, I heard him shuffle his heavy feet across the wooden planks of my bedroom floor. "What did I tell you about interrupting me and your mother?"

I'd woken to the sound of my mom begging him to stop. I knew what was happening and, although I was terrified, I had to help her. After racing from my room, I'd flown down the steps and found her crumpled on the living room floor, clutching her belly with one hand while the other was raised in the air to try to stop his next attack, blood dripping from her nose. As I ran toward her to try and protect her, I was hit so hard I flew across the room and crashed into the far wall. I was a small kid, weighing nothing at all, especially compared to the man terrorizing us. She tried to crawl toward me, but he stepped on her back, pinning her to the ground. With defeat in her voice, she told me to go back to my room, promising that she'd be all right. I didn't believe her but I didn't want her to watch him hit me again, so I scrambled to my feet and ran back to my room.

I heard him getting closer so I squeezed my eyes tighter, but my loss of sight didn't stop my mouth from opening.

"You're hurting my mom," I cried out.

"That's none of your business," he spat.

I tried my hardest not to appear scared, but I was. When I pried open my eyes, I saw him standing directly next to my bed, his hand on his belt buckle.

"I'll teach you not to interfere," he slurred, his stinky breath making me sick to my stomach. He'd been drinking that brown liquid again. He took another step closer, the belt loosening and sliding through the loops of his pants. Instead of holding on to it, however, he tossed it on the foot of my bed. "You'll learn your place in this house," he threatened as he unzipped his pants, a stranger than normal look in his eyes as he snagged my ankle and yanked me down the bed. Without much effort, he flipped me on my belly and knelt across my lower legs to keep me from getting away. "Don't fight me or you'll hurt yourself." I didn't understand what was about to happen.

Why wasn't he hitting me?

Why was I on my stomach?

Why was he taking his pants off?

Before I formed another silent question, I heard my mom screaming at him to get away from me. When the pressure on my legs lessened, I turned around and I saw that he had ahold of her hair, her arms swinging wildly, trying to hit him. "Don't you touch him, you bastard," she gasped, her breath coming in short spurts as she winced with every movement. She didn't care that she was bleeding, that bruises were forming on her face and arms, that some of her ribs were probably bruised or broken.

Her only concern was for me.

He shoved my mother to the ground, grabbed the belt that had been tossed on my bed, knelt down next to her and wrapped it around her neck. Everything happened in slow motion and yet at a frenzied pace all at the same time. Her green eyes bulged wide, while her fingers scratched at the rough leather robbing the breath from her lungs.

"Noooo," I screamed as loud as I could, watching the life slowly start to drain from her face. Finding my last bit of strength, I launched off the bed and flew toward her, trying to loosen the belt, but it was useless. He was too strong.

When all of the fight had left my mom, he let go of the belt and stumbled backward, mumbling something only he could understand before disappearing from my room.

Burying my face in her neck, I cried harder than I ever had before, praying she would start breathing again. Hoping this was all a nightmare and I'd wake up any minute.

But it wasn't a nightmare.

My mom had just been murdered, a tragedy that shaped the person I would eventually become.

CHAPTER ONE

Ryder

THE MUSCLES IN MY HAND burned, the ache intensifying with no sign of relief. My knee was wedged into his back, holding him steady against the gravel beneath me. Rage bubbled inside me, overtaking any sense of rationality I had left, which was but a frazzled thread. Words tried to escape, but nothing passed my lips except my harsh breaths, panting like some kind of rabid animal.

Fury.

Revenge.

I felt it in spades but I couldn't move from the spot I was frozen in. I tried so hard to exact my kind of justice, but my mind was spiraling out of control, ensnaring me deep in its tight grasp.

"Ryder." I heard my name as if it'd been whispered. I'd been staring into the face of the man who'd changed my world forever, but his lips never moved. "Ryder," I heard again, that time a little louder. Before I could shout out and ask who said my name, the man I'd been pinning down vanished, as if he'd never even been there.

All of a sudden a sharp pain radiated through my leg. "Ryder!" A female voice captured the letters of my name, shouting out in fear and anger, both emotions mixed together to form a jolt that thrust me from whatever world had dragged me under, trapped in the deepest recesses of my mind. My eyes were already open, but as my vision tunneled and then expanded, I realized that Braylen was lying on her back . . . and I was pinning her to the mattress. Her legs were spread wide and flailing, my knee wedged between them to keep them apart. I'd captured both of her arms with my large hands, trapping her so she was utterly defenseless. That was until another wave of pain shot through my calf again.

"Fuck!" I yelled, staring down into the face of the woman who'd been sharing my bed for the past five months. Her wild blonde hair was fanned out on the pillow, the look in her eyes telling me she was gonna lay into me as soon as I fully came back into the moment.

"Get off me," she cried out. "You're hurting me." She bucked beneath me and, although she didn't possess the physical ability to budge me, her show of strength was enough to tell me she meant business. Before I could move, however, she kicked me again, that time the heel of her foot grinding into the tensed muscle of my calf.

"Goddamnit, Bray, stop fuckin' kickin' me."

Of course, she didn't listen, as was evident when another surge of pain hit. Knowing she wouldn't stop until she was released, I rolled off her and hit the mattress on my side of the bed. For as much as I wanted to massage my leg, I remained still, doing my best to catch my breath, trying to understand why I was on top of her in the first place.

"What the hell is wrong with you?" She sat up straight, scooting down the bed to put some distance between us. "I can't deal with this much longer. Your nightmares are getting worse, this time affecting *me*." It wasn't until I saw her clutching her forearms that I tried to move closer. I glanced from her arms to her face, cursing silently when I saw the first tear fall. I reached for her, but she moved back. "Don't touch me," she rasped, more tears falling down her reddened cheeks.

"I'm sorry." It was the only thing I could think of to say, although I knew those two words weren't enough to tell her how much I hated myself for hurting her, even though I had no idea I'd been doing it. I'd been trapped in another nightmare, helpless because I had no control when the past came to claim me.

Several minutes passed, allowing both of us to regain some sense of calm. When she finally cast her gaze toward me again, I saw her red and puffy eyes. Her breaths were still short and choppy, but not as erratic as when I'd first released her. I hated that I'd marked her, bruised her tender flesh while in the throes of my darkness.

"I'm sorry," I repeated, hoping she could see from my expression that I meant it. I was used to being guarded, keeping my past from everyone around me, including all of my brothers at the club. I figured if I told anyone it would make it real. I knew how ridiculous it sounded, my reasoning beyond irrational and fucked up, but it was how I chose to deal with my mother's death—keep it close and private. It was the only way to protect the last piece of myself.

"Why won't you ever tell me about your nightmares? Maybe I can help you," she whispered, already preparing herself for the anger she knew was coming, even though I knew damn well she didn't deserve any of it. Not that time, at least. Braylen certainly knew how to press my buttons, challenging me every single time she found an opportunity, but right then she was simply concerned.

An attribute I both appreciated and loathed.

Inhaling deeply, I clenched my jaw before shouting, "I told you I don't remember my fuckin' nightmares, so how the hell are you gonna help me?" I hopped off the bed and strode toward the bathroom, slamming the door before she could even respond. I knew she knew I was lyin', but I didn't want to give her a chance to call me on my bullshit.

After a hurried shower, I walked back into my bedroom only to be greeted with an empty space. Braylen left. I wasn't surprised, though. Not in the least. I'd been a real ass, first by bruising her, then yelling at her as if she was at fault for my fucked-upness.

I should've chased after her.

I should've called and attempted some sort of half-assed apology.

I should've told her what haunted my dreams.

But I couldn't do any of it. Instead, I collapsed on top of my bed, hoping she wouldn't curse me out too bad when I finally did contact her.

CHAPTER TWO

Ryder

SLAMMING BACK MY THIRD BEER, the alcohol did nothing to soothe my nerves. It'd been two days of silence from Braylen. Normally, I'd give her the time she needed, especially since I was usually the cause of her anger. Although for some reason, this time was bothering me more than normal. Was it because what I felt toward the woman had been intensifying over the past month?

But safety lived in silence and denial. It was how I'd survived this long, and I refused to change because of a woman.

Trying to push aside all thoughts of Braylen Prescott, I focused on gettin' piss drunk and passing out. And since Trigger refused to serve me hard liquor, knowing damn well what happened when that stuff coursed through my veins, I had to drink what he offered—beer. But as long as it did the trick, I wouldn't complain. Not too much, anyway.

"You're unusually ornery tonight," Trigger acknowledged. "What's up your ass?" Slinging a towel over his shoulder, he went about cleaning up behind the bar. Trigger was the club's resident bartender, lending an ear to those who needed it and givin' shit to those who deserved it. Apparently I was the latter. Tucking strands of his graying hair that had come loose from his ponytail behind his ear, he locked eyes with me and waited for me to engage.

"Ornery? Since when did you start breakin' out the big words?" I swallowed the rest of my drink, tapping the bar to indicate another. "Did you get one of those 'word a day' calendars? Deciding to test out your fake smarts on the likes of us?" My laugh was humorless. Giving someone else a hard time helped to take the attention off myself.

"Just because your dumb ass has a limited vocabulary doesn't mean we all do," he retorted, sliding a fresh glass my way.

I never let on that I was a smarty in school. High honors and all that good stuff. School came easily to me, numbers and theories the easiest. It was how I was able to help invest a lot of the club's earnings years back, setting us all up for life with the returns.

"Whatever." Focusing on losing myself to the suds in front of me, I zoned out and thought of nothing except becoming sloshed enough to barely keep my head up. But I should've known it wouldn't be that easy, not planting my ass on a barstool at the club. When I'd arrived earlier, only Trigger was present, the rest of the guys out taking care of what they needed to before gathering back together.

Most days I loved the company, even though I was more on the quiet side, sittin' back and takin' it all in. But right then, I wanted nothing more than to be left alone.f Those hopes were dashed as I heard Breck, Cutter, Jagger and Tripp stride through the entrance.

"Holy shit!" Tripp shouted. "What brings you here, stranger?" The nomad of the club strolled toward me, clasping me on the shoulder once he closed in on me. "Where the hell you been?"

"I was just here the other day," I gritted, keeping my simmering temper in check.

"Last week," Cutter said as he walked toward the kitchen. If I thought I was a quiet one, Cutter had me beat, usually only speaking when he wanted to call people out on their bullshit.

"He's too busy wrapped up in Braylen's pussy," Breck taunted, taking the seat next to me. *Does he have some sort of death wish?* "Tell us, Ryder, does she have a magic cunt?" He laughed, but it was cut short when I jumped up and hauled him off his chair by the scruff of his neck. There was a quick flash of fear in his eyes, but it was gone seconds after glancing at my drink of choice. Had I been drinking hard liquor, he probably would've pissed himself because he knew what I was capable of when it passed my lips. They all did. They'd seen it. Hell, they'd had to beat and restrain me to get me to calm the fuck down. Or pass out. Whichever came first.

"What?" Breck laughed. He was the complete opposite of his father. His unkempt shoulder-length brown hair and beard were way past due for a trimming. The biggest difference, however, was his ability to spout off at the mouth and irritate the fuck out of most of us because he never knew when to shut up. "It's an honest question. We all wanna know." He brought his drink to his lips even as I held him tightly in my grasp, spilling the contents down his front when I shoved him away from me. "Fuck," he mumbled, wiping the dots of beer off his cut.

After chugging down the rest of my beer, I attempted to leave but Tripp stopped me, stepping in front of me and arching a brow. "You good?" Two simple words. Too bad he had no idea how complicated his question really was.

"Yup."

"Good, 'cause you're up tonight."

"For what?" I racked my brain to try and figure out what he was talkin' about, but I came up short.

"Jagger's fight. It's you and me, brother." A slight smile curved up the corners of Tripp's mouth, trying his best to lighten my darkened mood. The nomad knew I had secrets, a mistakenly shared word here and there during our convos, but he had no idea what I'd been through before becoming a part of the club. None of them did, and that was how I wanted to keep it. I didn't need anyone's sympathy or pity. That would only make it worse.

"Fine," I agreed, sidestepping his large frame. "Send me the time and location," I shouted over my shoulder as I approached the door to leave.

Straddling my bike and kicking over the engine, I couldn't help but be annoyed at the fact that I had to attend Jagger's fight that evening, simply because I wasn't in the mood. But before I let the thought rattle me too much, I remembered there was a good chance Braylen would be there, seeing as her sister, Kena, was Jagger's woman. And far be it from Braylen to let her little sister out of her sight for too long.

CHAPTER THREE

Braylen

THE LAST THING I WANTED to do was attend Jagger's fight with Kena, but I hated leaving her alone, even though I knew at least two of the other guys from the club would be there, protecting Jagger and his winnings, even though Jagger could take out anyone who challenged him. There was more to their show of support, and while I didn't know the full story, I knew it was serious. Something coded spoken once about the Savage Reapers.

Ryder and Jagger sheltered my sister and me as much as they could, which sometimes seemed a bit too much. I fought Ryder when he made ridiculous demands, but somehow he always won. It was quite infuriating, to say the least.

Usually I was the last person who would shrink away from confrontation, but I'd been deliberately avoiding him. Well, his phone calls, to be more precise. Surprisingly he hadn't shown up at the salon where I worked, giving me time and space instead. And while I had no idea whether or not he'd be at the fight that evening, chances were good that he would be.

Why don't you wear this? Kena signed, a tentative smile on her beautiful face while she waited to see if I'd give her any sort of resistance.

My younger sister had developed a viral infection when she was an infant, damaging the nerves in her larynx which prohibited her from ever speaking a single word. My family had learned sign language, even though many times we chose to speak since she could hear us.

"I'm really not up to going. I'm tired," I lied, walking past her to grab my cell from the charging dock. Checking to see if I had any messages, even though I wouldn't respond even if Ryder had contacted me, I busied myself unlocking the device. I kept my head down since that was a surefire way of avoiding my sister.

Strands of my blonde hair flew around me as fabric suddenly covered my vision. Swiping at the material, I realized it was the top Kena had just presented to me. The bitch had thrown it at me. Normally my sister was docile, but apparently not then.

"What the hell?"

Stop avoiding him. Besides, don't you want to make sure nothing happens to me? The smirk on her face told me she knew damn well what she was doing—drawing on my need to perpetually keep her safe. Normally, Kena hated my overbearing ways, but right then she played on my fears that something would happen to her if I wasn't around to protect her. My fears weren't all that irrational, however. It wasn't long ago that she'd been kidnapped right along with Adelaide, the VP's woman. They'd been taken by the Reapers but thankfully had been retrieved unharmed, except for some physical bruising. The mental aspect of the incident, however, was something my sister chose to keep to herself, even with all of my incessant prodding.

"I'm not avoiding him. I've just been busy." I saw from the quirk of her manicured brow that she didn't believe one word of my careless untruth. "I'm not," I repeatedly lied.

I'd told her about what happened with Ryder, how he'd held me down while trapped inside some crazy nightmare, essentially scaring me half to death in the process. While she'd been concerned about me, she'd also been worried about Ryder. Kena had become fond of the brooding man, explaining that any guy who could periodically render me speechless had to be someone special indeed.

You and I both know you're hiding from him, but if you really don't wanna go tonight, then don't. I'm sure I'll be fine. She pouted, telling me she didn't want to go by herself, for whatever reason.

After several very long seconds, I relented. "Fine, I'll go, but I'm not gonna enjoy myself."

We'll see about that.

"I guess we will," I mumbled, more to myself than anything.

After I finally finished dressing, I glanced at my reflection in the mirror, making sure I looked appropriate enough for public view. I wasn't vain by any means, but I did care about how I looked when I stepped outside. My highlighted tresses fell just below my shoulder blades in soft waves. As far as my makeup went, I chose to keep it simple with two coats of mascara and a lightly tinted lip gloss.

You look great. Dressing up for anyone in particular? Kena teased, plopping down on the edge of my bed.

"What are you talking about? I'm not wearing anything special." Looking down, I was confused as to why she thought I'd put any extra effort into the clothes I'd chosen. A simple black tank top that scooped low in front to show a bit of cleavage, paired with my favorite dark skinny jeans and my go-to red heels were oceans away from being special. While I believed I looked good, my outfit wasn't anything out of the ordinary.

My sister smiled wide. She loved to get me going, probably paying me back for all the times I aggravated her. Ours was a special sisterly relationship, both of us caring for the other deeply. But there were times, like right then, when one of us couldn't help but razz the other. It was all done in good fun, so I smiled back and released most of the tension pent-up inside me.

"You look nice too," I said, playfully shoving her shoulder as we walked toward the front door. Holding my phone tightly, I chanced a look at the screen once more before the night air hit me.

CHAPTER
FOUR

Ryder

THE SMELL OF BODY ODOR, piss, and cheap cologne drifted to my nose as I positioned myself against the farthest wall, waiting for Jagger to emerge from the back room. His impending bout started in five minutes, the screams and shouts from numerous groupies making my ears ring they were so damn excited.

Surprisingly Kena and Braylen hadn't arrived yet, an odd fact since Jagger told me they were coming. I hadn't asked him—he'd volunteered the information, mumbling something about some goddamn look on my face, how it was sad and pathetic. I'd ignored him, choosing to focus on what would happen once I saw Braylen. Would she continue to ignore me? Would I ignore her in turn?

Shaking my head to rid my brain of the back and forth, I lifted my chin toward Tripp when I saw him enter. A few strides and he'd sidled up next to me.

"What the fuck is that smell?" he asked, grimacing as he pulled the top of his shirt over his nose. "It smells horrible in here. Jagger really needs to find other places to fight."

"Who cares what the place smells like? As long as he wins and gets paid, nothing else matters."

"Still. . . ."

Dropping the material shrouding his nostrils, Tripp opened his mouth to say something else when Jagger came bursting out of the back room, searching the area before settling his eyes on us. Stomping forward, he reached us in record time, looking worried and frazzled.

At first glance, the guy looked in control. Fierce even. His dark blond hair was shaved on the sides, the top strands longer than the rest. Slicked back and in place, the style was enough to ensure he could see his opponent without obtrusion. It also enhanced his etched features, which were pinned with worry for some reason.

"Where is she?" he asked, looking past us into the adrenaline-filled crowd.

"Who?"

"Kena. She's supposed to be here. She said she'd be waiting for me before my fight. It's not like her to be late." His fists clenched at his sides, the sign that he was subject to blow in a few seconds if he didn't find what was keeping his woman.

Kena was punctual, though her sister was always late. If they were coming together, it could explain her absence.

I couldn't deny that Braylen had somehow burrowed inside me, alighting on my nerves in both aggravation and intrigue. Passion and annoyance. The woman was something else, a firework in the darkest of nights.

I would've loved to say there was a quiet innocence and grace about her, but anyone who knew Braylen knew that wasn't entirely accurate. An embellishment of the highest degree, to be more exact. Every time she entered the room, she lit it up with her presence, her fierceness and undeniable sex appeal. Although the last trait was for me and me alone. She'd shoot off at the mouth at the drop of a hat, misinterpreting situations quite often. She ranted and raved first, then asked questions, but only after she'd calmed down enough to allow me to speak. And by speak, I mean kiss the hell out of her until she had no other choice but to calm down.

"Here they come," Tripp announced, pulling his phone from his pocket and taking a step toward the aisle. "You got this?" He cocked his head toward the two women fast approaching.

"Yeah."

"Be right back." No doubt he was checking in with Reece, his woman, who was pregnant with his kid. It seemed everywhere I looked lately the guys were knockin' up their ol' ladies. First Stone and Adelaide, and now Tripp had fallen down that rabbit hole. I didn't have anything against kids—I had one of my own—but I sure as hell didn't want to start all over again at thirty-four.

Jagger pulled Kena toward him, wrapping his arms around her and giving everyone quite the show. Damn, the guy was smitten, but I couldn't blame him. Kena was pretty damn cool, never seeming to give my friend much of a problem. Not like her sister with me.

Speaking of . . .

Braylen shot me a warning glance before trying to shuffle down a nearby aisle, squeezing past a few guys who seemingly didn't want to keep their hands to themselves. As I pushed off the wall, intent on wiping the floor with the asshole who dared grab her ass, my steps faltered when I saw her whip around and slap the guy across the face. Even over the roar of the frenzied crowd, I heard the impact.

Thankfully, for her and for me, the fucker seemed embarrassed enough to mouth something before looking down at the ground. Was it because he feared another smack from the feisty blonde, or could it have been the death daggers I shot his way when he looked around to see who'd witnessed the assault? While I was proud of Braylen for sticking up for herself, she had no idea how much danger she'd just put herself in for slapping that bastard. Had I not been present, would he have snatched her up and hurt her? I knew how the world worked, about all of the evil contained within, but Braylen was clueless. For as ballsy as that chick was, she lived in a bubble. Something we fought about on occasion.

I was always right, and she hated when I pointed it out.

Peering over at me, she looked away as soon as our eyes connected. She wanted to appear unaffected by my presence, but I saw the way her body reacted when she knew I was looking—no, staring. Her taut muscles locked up tight and the heave of her chest increased; it was slight but noticeable. Her tits looked amazing in that fuckin' black top, her ass round and delectable in her painted-on jeans. If I wasn't so intent on playing aloof, I would've approached, snatched her up and taken her back to my place right then and there. But because I wasn't entirely sure she wouldn't sting my cheek with a smack, I stayed planted against the wall. Not that I didn't encourage a bit of feistiness in the bedroom, but it wasn't the time or the place.

I knew Braylen well enough to know that if I pushed her too far, she'd continue to give me the cold shoulder. And while her silence gave me the room to try and come to grips with the shit I'd been dealing with—or pushing back down for my subconscious to bury again—I needed to be with her. To feel her against me. To taste her.

I could toss it up to simply being horny, but even though I knew it was more than hormones, I refused to acknowledge the fact that I was becoming more and more attached to her. My survival was key, emotional as well as anything else.

Entirely consumed with my own thoughts, I hadn't even seen Tripp approach, grumbling to himself as he came to stand next to me once again.

"Fuckin' women," he muttered, shoving his hands in his pockets while looking off into the distance.

He'd just given me the opportunity to focus on someone other than myself for a moment. "Reece okay?"

"Yeah, she's great. Just ask her." Sarcasm dripped off him. Tripp looked a little more than put out, and even though he'd be the first to poke fun at me, he'd also be willing to lend an ear.

"What's the problem? She not givin' you any now that you knocked her up?"

Cocking his head, he narrowed his eyes before flashing an arrogant smirk.

"No problem there. In fact, she's all over me." Bending his leg, he braced himself on the wall behind us, his smirk fading as quickly as it had appeared. "She told me she wasn't feeling well before I left, so I convinced her to call off from work. But when we just spoke, she told me she decided to go in after all." He stopped talking, looking at me as if I had a fuckin' clue as to what the problem was.

"So?"

"What do you mean 'so'? She's fuckin' pregnant. Every time she goes to work she puts herself and my kid in danger. I've told her I want her to quit, and she agreed, but she keeps pushing back the date. First it was gonna be last month, but then she told me that Carla needed to keep her on until she found her replacement. I spoke to Carla. Reece lied to me. Problem is I have no idea why." Becoming more upset the longer he spoke, he released a barrage of curses before slamming the sole of his boot against the concrete wall.

"Maybe she's pissed you're makin' her quit," I blurted, not entirely believing what I was saying. I couldn't even imagine how much my ears would be ringing if I ever tried to convince Braylen to quit her job. Granted, the salon where she worked was worlds different than Indulge, one of the club's strip joints, but Braylen still had male clients. Customers who wanted in her pants. I was positive of it.

"*She* agreed with me. So why would she be pissed?"

"That's like asking me why the sky's blue, my brother. I'm as clueless as you are when it comes to understanding how chicks think." Tearing my eyes away from Braylen—who continued to ignore me, even though I saw her look in my direction every now and again—I gave Tripp my full attention. "From what you've told me, your woman's been through some shit. Maybe her job is some kind of security or somethin'. And now that she has to give it up, it's messin' with her." I sought out Braylen again. "My guess, anyway."

Before we could continue our conversation, Jagger stepped into the cage, cracking his neck from side to side and bouncing on his feet. He'd never been the showboater the other fighters were, but he seemed to steal the audience's attention each and every time.

The next fifteen minutes passed with the both of us just watching everyone else, on guard in case any unwanted guests showed up. Ever since Koritz, the crooked DEA agent, showed up at our club—and with Rabid, the Savage Reapers' VP, no less—an unsettling awareness shrouded everyone involved with the Knights Corruption.

The men were uneasy, just waitin' for shit to pop off, and the women were affected by our moods, even though they had no clue what was really going on.

We thought we'd put the war to bed between our two clubs when we took out Psych, only to find out that his club was hell-bent on finding out where he was and what had happened to him.

Too bad they'll never know . . . or find his rotting corpse.

As Jagger was declared the winner, he strode from the cage and barreled toward Kena, snagging her hand and pulling her toward the back of the room. Lifting his chin toward me before kissing his woman, he pointed toward the office on the second floor. It was code for "Watch my woman while I get my money."

Tripp flanked me on my left side while the women stood on my right. Braylen had still made no move to talk to me, and after another five tense minutes, I deemed enough was enough.

CHAPTER FIVE

Ryder

"WATCH HER," I INSTRUCTED TRIPP, referring to Kena, and seized Braylen's wrist, pulling her behind me toward the Exit sign. At first she didn't fight because I'd caught her off guard, but as we entered the night air, she tried to pull her hand from mine.

"Let go," she shouted, yanking her arm back a few times before I finally released her. "What is wrong with you? You can't just manhandle me whenever you want to."

Ignoring her question, I fired off one of my own. "Why didn't you respond to any of my texts or take any of my damn calls? You can't still be that pissed at me for the other night." As soon as I asked the question, I knew my fuckup. What I referred to was when I balked at her before disappearing into the bathroom, not the memory of pinning her to the bed beneath me.

"Are you kidding me?" she yelled, taking a step backward. I reached for her but she shook her head. "I wake up to you lying on top of me, bruising my arms because you were holding me down while you were dreaming. You had no idea I was even there until I shouted your name."

"And kicked me," I reminded her. A half smirk found its way onto my lips.

Not the right time.

"It's not funny, Ryder. You could've choked me to death."

"My hands weren't near your neck," I rebuked.

"But they could've been. What happens next time when you decide to wrap your hands around my throat?"

"I wouldn't do that."

"You had no idea what you were doing the other night, so how can you be so sure?"

"Because I would never hurt you." Scratching at the hairs covering my jawline, I did my best to convince her I believed the ridiculous words spewing from my mouth.

"Not intentionally," she whispered, the breeze stealing her words and swirling them around me like a tornado. Braylen put another foot of space between us.

"Stop moving away from me like you're scared of me, Bray. I don't like that shit." My head ached, all muscles in my body suddenly becoming too sensitive to the anxiety coursing through me. I hated the look of doubt shadowing her eyes, as if she wanted to come to me yet refused to move because she wasn't sure she should.

Hell, I didn't know if she should either.

I'd battled with the fear that I could've hurt her that night. I could've snuffed out her life, all the while having no fuckin' clue I'd even done it. Not until I woke up. Then what would I have done? How would I ever explain something like that to the club? To her family?

Dangerous.

The only word to describe what I was when it came to Braylen sleeping next to me, innocent and unknowing.

Silence drifted between us because neither of us knew what to say at that point. I hated the physical space separating us but I understood it, although I'd never let on.

Don't show any vulnerability. It was my motto since I was a kid, and in that moment it was being put to the motherfuckin' test.

As her lips parted to finally speak, a rousing burst of noise erupted behind us. A large crowd of people emerged, halting any thoughts that I'd get any further with Braylen right then.

"Come back to my place," I said, clenching my hands at my sides in preparation for her refusal.

"No." Blunt and to the point.

"Why?"

"Because there's something going on with you, and until you can tell me what it is, I can't help you." She bit her lower lip, averting her eyes to behind me every few seconds, no doubt waiting for her sister to join us.

"It was one night. One incident. Let it go," I rasped, pissed that I had to defend my fucked-up dream once again. I didn't want to delve back into my past, and that was exactly what would happen if I entertained telling her.

"It wasn't just one night." Her voice rose over the shouts of the people milling around us. "You've been acting weird for at least two months."

Dammit! That was about how long it'd been since the nightmares had returned.

Again, I refused to acknowledge what she said as anything but crazy talk. Before my brain could formulate a response, however, the back door to the building flung open. Tripp, Jagger, and Kena appeared, laughing and looking like everything was peachy fuckin' keen.

Well it wasn't.

Not for me, and apparently not for Braylen either.

One look from her sister and Kena rushed to her side, pulling her farther away from me and signing frantically, glancing back at me a couple times. Realizing I'd lost the battle, I gave up trying to convince Braylen to come home with me and joined my buddies.

"What's up with those two?" Tripp asked, slapping me on the back before removing his phone from his cut. Putting the device to his ear, he gave me a sideways glance while waiting for whoever he'd called to answer.

"Who the fuck knows," I grumbled. I had no desire to talk about it right there in the middle of the goddamn street. Jagger walked toward the women, watching the back and forth between the two of them before turning his head to look at me. He smirked, no doubt lovin' that I was the one in hot water. I hated that he could understand everything they were signing while I stood there like a dumbass, completely ignorant.

Finally, Jagger walked back toward me, grinning and shaking his head.

"Fuck off."

"Hey, I'm not the one givin' you shit." Jagger chuckled, slinging his black bag over his shoulder.

"What was she sayin'?" I didn't want to ask, but the need to know gnawed at my insides like some kind of insect.

"That she really wishes you would open up and let her in. That she's really concerned about your emotional sanity and wants to be there for you, to help you through whatever drama has you trapped in such a state that you shut down and lash out whenever something happens."

At first, I thought Jagger was telling me the truth, that she'd really said all that stuff, until he burst out laughing.

"What the fuck?" I growled, flashing him my most menacing look, but apparently I was losing my touch, or Jagger knew me well enough to not be afraid of me.

"Sorry, I couldn't resist, man."

"What. Did. She. Fuckin'. Say?"

"She said you're actin' like an ass, and that if you don't start talkin' soon, you can forget about her . . . or somethin' like that." Jagger walked away before I could ask him to repeat what he'd said, laughing at my misfortune of having to deal with Braylen's stubborn ass.

I knew Jagger was heading back to their place, so I straddled my bike, turned over the engine and took off down the street, not once looking at Braylen as I passed. I couldn't. Otherwise, I'd toss her over my ride and kidnap her, kicking and screaming.

And something told me that wouldn't go over too well.

CHAPTER SIX

Braylen

ALL I COULD THINK ABOUT while lying in bed that evening was Ryder and how clueless he was to just how detrimental his actions toward me had been. And how he refused to tell me exactly what was going on with him. He played it off as no big deal, as if it was normal to attack someone while in the throes of a nightmare. But it sure as hell wasn't.

Ryder had been acting funny for a couple months, although I couldn't pinpoint exactly how. It was a gut feeling, a warning that something explosive would erupt soon enough, and I wasn't entirely sure I wanted to be around to help pick up the pieces.

While I cared for him—more than I wanted to, honestly—I feared that he'd destroy me if he continued to keep me in the dark.

If secrets festered long enough, they would devour a person's soul, leaving them black and dying on the inside, blocking the smallest glimpse of healing light.

———◆———

"WORK YOUR MAGIC, SWEETHEART." TAKING a surprised breath, I lowered my arm to my side, the lightweight shears almost slipping from my fingers. I'd been lost in thought yet again and had completely ignored the client sitting in my chair. Taking a step back, I tried to gather myself, but it was too late. He'd seen my loss of focus. "Are you okay?"

"Um . . . yeah. Sure. Sorry about that. Now where were we?" I plastered on a big fake smile and turned his chair to the side so I could better assess the length of his hair, which hadn't grown too much since I'd seen him two weeks prior.

George had become a regular client of mine, his incessant need to make sure his hair was trimmed every couple weeks kind of amusing. But hey, I wasn't complaining. Besides, he was a great tipper.

I had the good fortune to work at my best friend's salon, Transform. Sia offered me a job as soon as I graduated cosmetology school, promising me a lucrative career with her clientele. I not only worked with all things hair, of course, but I was also certified in nails, waxing, etc. Name it, and I did it, which put me a leg up from most of the other women who worked there.

After only a year, Sia offered me the manager position, telling me she was desperate for someone with my organizational and people skills. And while the offer, complete with generous salary, was indeed tempting, all I wanted to do was come in, handle my shifts, chat with my clients and perform the magic on them they'd come to expect from me.

Sia was disappointed but understood. She ended up hiring a string of interim managers, none of them having what it took to help run an upscale salon. Because I felt bad and wanted to help her out until she found someone more permanent, I agreed to assist with some of the duties if she handled the rest—mainly dealing with the staff. I took care of inventory and bookkeeping while she dealt with scheduling, the stylists and whatever else popped up that required her attention.

"Just the usual today." He smiled at me as I turned his chair back toward the mirror.

"You know, I might start to think you have a crush on me," I teased, snapping the black cape closed that I had draped over him to protect from hair shavings.

"Who says I don't," he replied, winking at my reflection before flashing me his pearly whites. "Why do you think I come in so often?"

"I thought you had an agenda." I returned his smile as I ran my fingers through his short tresses. There wasn't much for me to do except clean his edges and polish him up. After ten minutes, I'd done all I could, turning him from side to side to make sure everything looked even.

I walked around his chair to stand in front of him, bending down to check out the front of his hair. My eyes were glued to his blond strands while his were glued to my breasts. My V-shaped top certainly showed a bit of cleavage, nothing obscene, although apparently the display was enough. Clearing my throat, his green eyes popped up to mine, a wolfish grin on his face at the knowledge that he'd been caught, although he didn't appear embarrassed by it. Not entirely, at least.

I figured there could be worse things in life than having the attentions of a handsome man. George appeared to be close to my age of twenty-four, although he could've been a couple years older. He looked young but distinguished. During one of our conversations, he'd told me he was a corporate lawyer of some sort. He stopped talking about his job when he saw my eyes glaze over. I'd apologized, telling him I didn't understand anything he'd tried to explain. He didn't seem put out by my lack of interest, thank God, as was apparent with the fifty-dollar tip he left me, and when he returned time and time again to sit in my chair.

On top of being successful before the age of thirty, he was stereotypically handsome. A full head of thick hair, light green eyes, and a sculpted jawline. His face was clean-shaven, giving him that younger appeal. The only thing not symmetrical on him was a tiny bump on the bridge of his nose, but it did nothing to detract from his good looks. But for as handsome as he was, he just wasn't my type.

Apparently my type was a dark-haired, rugged-looking, stubborn biker who was a pain in my ass as of late. Oh hell, who was I kidding? Ryder had been a pain in my ass since the first day I met him. Since he'd so eloquently told me that I needed a good fuck to calm me down.

"So, tell me, Braylen. Do you have a man?" George's words drew me back into the present. He was staring up at me, waiting for me to say something, but when I opened my mouth to answer, a rough voice cut me off, shutting down any reply I had. Stealing my choice to tell him I was indeed involved with someone, although we were kind of going through some stuff at the moment. Of course, I would've censored my response.

"Yeah, she does." Whipping around, I saw Ryder standing ten feet behind me, glaring at George's reflection in the mirror, looking all intimidating and . . . sexy.

Oh for the love of God, stop lusting after him while he's embarrassing the hell out of you.

"What are you doing here?"

"Apparently interrupting something." His mood was sour. His tall, broad frame was drawn tight, the muscles of his bare forearms dancing under the weight of his obvious displeasure. Ryder stood there in all his stubborn, infuriating glory, dressed in dark-washed jeans, a white T-shirt, and his Knights Corruption leather vest—or cut, as he often referred to it. He'd just witnessed another man openly flirting with me; I knew it was only a matter of seconds before he snapped. I had to do something and fast before the situation escalated out of control.

"I'll be right back, George," I offered, giving him an apologetic smile before removing his cape.

"Sure thing. I'll wait right here." What he said was innocent enough, but Ryder jumped all over him anyway.

"I think it's best you get outta here before I toss you out on your ass." Ryder took a step forward, but I stepped in front of him, blocking his advance toward my client. Pushing on his chest, I tried my best to move him back, but he continued to shoot daggers at the guy. I thought I heard George snicker, but I couldn't be sure. Either way, I had to remove Ryder from the salon before he really caused a scene. As it was, a few of the other employees and their clients were casting wary glances toward us.

"Go outside," I rasped, unable to contain my anger any longer because of the embarrassment he'd caused me. "Now!" I whisper-shouted as I shoved at him once more. The man was like a goddamn marble statue, unyielding except for the flicker in his eyes telling me he'd comply.

Reaching for my hand, he clasped it tightly and practically dragged me from the salon, walking briskly down the sidewalk until we were out of sight from any onlookers inside Transform. Thankfully there weren't too many people milling around outside, everyone locked up inside the shops and spending their money.

"What the fuck, Braylen?"

"What is wrong with you?" I asked, choosing to ignore his question. "What are you even doing here?" My back faced the concrete wall between a high-end boutique and a fancy shoe store. I kept my eyes pinned to his, and for several seconds we entered some sort of deranged staring contest, both of us trying to mentally overpower the other.

Ryder eventually broke. "What are *you* doing?"

"Working. What does it look like?"

"It looked like that guy was hitting on you and you were lovin' it," he snarled, the veins in his neck protruding with every spoken word. *I walked right into that one.* "Tell me I'm wrong. I dare you." His dark eyes turned black in his self-induced delirium.

I couldn't believe he thought I was interested in George, or any other man for that matter. He had to know that, even though I was upset with him and needed some time, I only had my sights set on him.

"Yes and no," I answered, huffing out a breath when his nostrils started to flare. "You need to calm down, Ryder. That's not what I meant."

"What the fuck did you mean, then?" He took one step closer, the warmth from his body igniting my own. He looked savage, and although I chastised myself for even feeling this way . . . I was undoubtedly turned on.

"George is harmless."

"*George* is not harmless. That guys wants to fuck you."

Our conversation wasn't going as planned. Not at all.

"Maybe he does." Ryder flinched, his hands curling into fists at his sides. *Wrong thing to say.* "But does that mean he gets to? No, of course not. I'm not interested in him. I only engage him because he's a great tipper."

Without hesitation, he growled, "Well I got a fuckin' *tip* for ya: stop flirtin' or you'll never see him again. Got it?" His fists uncurled, and his flattened hands ran the length of his jeans as if he was somehow self-soothing, doing his best to calm down. He took another step toward me like some sort of feral predator. Anger danced behind his eyes, along with jealousy, but I knew he wouldn't physically hurt me. Not while he was awake, at least.

As I opened my mouth to reply to his outlandishness, Sia approached us, her hands on her hips as she took in the scene. "You okay, Bray?" My friend and employer was all of five feet two with short pink hair. She looked whimsical and fierce all wrapped into one. She could be your best friend, as she was mine, or your worst enemy.

While I loved her concern, she was the last person I wanted to deal with. I had enough on my plate.

"She's fine," Ryder answered for me, not once turning to look in her direction.

"Well, I'm not asking you. I'm asking my friend," she shot back, taking a few steps closer. "Do you want me to call the cops?"

That question had Ryder whipping his head toward Sia, glaring at her as if he wanted her to crumble into pieces in front of him.

"No, of course not. It's all just a misunderstanding," I lied. "Ryder was just leaving." I held eye contact with her, silently pleading with her to return to the salon so I could convince Ryder to leave without further incident.

Tapping her foot, she narrowed her eyes before turning around and walking back toward her livelihood.

As far as I knew, Sia had no issue with Ryder. She'd met him on a few different occasions, and the main thing she'd uttered was that he was hot. But then he went and messed with her business, potentially scaring off one of her clients, which she undoubtedly took personally. And I couldn't say that I blamed her.

"You have to go." My back was pressed against the cool wall, my hands coming up in front of me to ward off Ryder's attempt to pull me close.

He ignored my nonverbal communication and advanced, regardless of the hesitant look he saw on my face. Or at least I hoped that was the look I portrayed. Because there was another one—lust. For as maddening as the man standing before me was, he was everything I'd ever dreamed of in a partner.

Well, mostly. I'd prefer him without the secrets and the potential danger following him everywhere. While he swore his club was no longer involved with anything illegal, that they'd gone legit a while back, it didn't assuage my feelings that something bad could happen where he and the rest of the Knights Corruption were concerned.

Refusing to give life to all the random thoughts firing around inside my brain, I tried my best to focus on one thing at a time—specifically

Ryder and his incessant need to drive me crazy, of both the good and bad persuasion. The silent battle of wills wore on me, to the point that I was the one who caved that time around.

"You need a haircut." I had no idea why I said what I did, but it seemed to relax him, all while doing the opposite to me. The last thing I wanted was to be in such close proximity, touching him, staring at him to make sure my work was impeccable. Ryder naturally kept his hair short, but as of late the strands were a little longer than normal, hitting his collar. I thought he looked sexy no matter what style he chose, so I suppose my offer was my way of extending an olive branch. Of letting go of the need to keep the distance between us, even though I was uneasy and on guard with the way he continued to exclude me from certain aspects of his life. I understood the need for privacy with his club, but what I couldn't wrap my head around was why he wouldn't share anything about his past with me.

He never spoke of his family. I asked him once, and he shut me down right away. I figured I should consider myself lucky he'd told me his real name, Roman, although he asked me not to use it. When I asked him why, he shook his head and never answered. From his demeanor I knew not to pry again, or at least for a very long time. Maybe as the months passed, he would become more comfortable with me and want to open up, but as of yet, the topics were off the table.

"Why don't you come back to my place and give me one, then?" His fingers danced over my side before pulling me close so our chests were touching. I could feel his muscles, even beneath the thin white fabric, hard and chorded, twitching and warm.

"Why not just come in the salon and we can do it right now?" I countered, focusing on his full lips while waiting for him to answer me.

"Because if I see that guy, I'm gonna put him flat on his back. Besides, I don't think your friend would appreciate it."

He was right. Sia would definitely disapprove if Ryder waltzed back into the salon.

"Fine."

"Fine?"

"Yeah, fine. I'll come over when I'm done here."

"How about I pick you up?"

"How about you don't push your luck?"

He gave me a tight smile before releasing me and retreating, shoving his hands in his pockets as he waited for me to make a move. Only after I'd turned and started walking back toward Transform did I hear the roar of his bike before he raced off down the road.

CHAPTER
SEVEN

Ryder

AS I WATCHED BRAYLEN ROLL out her little black bag across my kitchen counter, I couldn't help but stare at her ass. I mean, come on, it was right in my direct line of view. The way her jeans cupped her cheeks was enough to make me want to tear them from her body. Her legs looked killer, even though they were covered by dark fabric. They seemed to go on for miles, even when only wearing her sneaks.

"Are you staring at my ass again?" she asked, looking over her shoulder just in time to catch me in the act.

"You know damn well I am, woman. Your ass is one of the things I love about you." I hadn't meant to say *love*; it popped out of my mouth before I could stop it. Braylen noticed as well, judging by the stiffening of her shoulders as she turned back around.

We weren't there yet, expressing our feelings and shit. Yeah, I cared about her and wanted to be around her more often than not, but I sure as hell wasn't in love with her. Hell, I'd never been in love with anyone before. I wasn't quite sure I even knew what it felt like.

I'd been involved in a long-term relationship many years back, but thinking about it now, I was never in love with Rose. She'd gotten pregnant a month in and I did the right thing by sticking with her. In the end it just didn't work out, the danger surrounding the club too much for her, which I completely understood. I wanted her to take my daughter and move far away, outside any reach our enemies would've had.

Which brought me to another point—Braylen didn't know I had a daughter. I'd meant to tell her a few weeks after we started hanging out, but it just never seemed to be the right time. And now . . . fuck, too much time had passed for her *not* to know. Or so I'd been told by Jagger, Tripp, and Stone, Jagger being the one person I feared revealing my business before I could. After all, his woman was Braylen's little sister. But he assured me it was my news to tell, so he promised not to say a word to Kena.

"Okay, let's do this." She walked toward me with a pair of scissors in one hand and clippers in the other. She looked like a woman on a mission, pointing toward the chair she'd set in the middle of the kitchen, silently instructing me to take a seat.

Braylen shocked me from time to time, either with her sass and stubbornness or her ability to hold a grudge and give me the cold shoulder. During the time we'd been together, I could safely say she kept me on my toes. Life certainly wasn't boring where she was concerned. I just hoped her intentions were on point that evening.

"You're not gonna shave my head because you're pissed at me, are you?" My thoughts immediately flew to when Hawke's woman, Edana, shaved his head when she'd found out he'd been cheating on her. She did the deed while he was sleeping, cutting off his long hair like Delilah did to Samson.

Hawke was no damn biblical figure, though. He was a guy who couldn't keep his dick in his pants, until his woman had unfortunately been attacked—raped and beaten, to be exact—by some of the Savage Reapers a while back. Since then, he'd been towing the straight and narrow, watching over Edana like never before, glued to her hip whenever she left the house. It was a side none of us ever thought we'd see, but unfortunately it took a devastating incident to wake him the hell up.

"No, not unless you give me reason to," she teased, spraying my hair with a water bottle. "Now keep still or you're gonna end up with a funky do." She smiled, and it was the best sight in the world—next to her lying beneath me, of course.

Braylen was the most beautiful woman I'd ever seen. And sexy as fuck. She knew I lusted after her, and if she didn't know just how much I'd be sure to remind her very shortly.

We'd started off a bit rocky, me running my crass mouth and her telling me exactly what she thought of me. "Arrogant" and "cocky" were the two descriptive words she used the most, but after being around her a few times, I'd managed to wear her down enough to convince her to give me her number. A few phone sex sessions later—me always initiating because I couldn't stop myself from picturing her naked—and she'd agreed to come over to my place. To be alone. Just the two of us.

I happened to be a pretty good cook, so the first time she came over, I made her spaghetti and meatballs. I knew it didn't sound like anything too fancy but it was tasty, and she agreed.

She'd gotten a splash of sauce on her chin, and when I leaned over to wipe it away with a napkin, I couldn't help myself. I'd used my tongue instead. Remembering the first time I'd kissed those pouty lips of hers was enough to make my dick hard, a happenstance that occurred on the regular whenever she was near me.

"Almost finished," Braylen whispered, the warmth of her breath tickling my earlobe, a strand of her hair gently brushing my neck. She was inspecting her work, leaning in so close I could smell her shampoo, some kind of mango scent. Closing my eyes, I sucked in a breath while she clipped away here and there, the buzz of the clippers jolting my gaze from the darkness and back to her.

"Be careful with those damn things," I warned, nervous she was gonna exact some kind of revenge because I'd embarrassed her earlier.

"Stop being a damn baby. I'm just trying to clean up your sideburns." Her tongue snuck out from between her delectable lips, wetting the bottom one and teasing the fuck outta me. When she was done with the sides, she circled me until she was standing directly in front, moving closer until she full-on straddled my lap.

"What are you doing?" Surprise and excitement filled my veins, thickening other parts of my body as the realization hit that she was sitting on me.

"I need to get close so I can inspect the front of your hair."

"You better not sit like this with your clients. So help me Christ, Braylen." I couldn't help it, the words tumbling outta my mouth before I could even think to stop them as my imagination ran wild. My heart picked up pace, ramming against my ribs like it wanted to break free from my chest altogether.

"Oh stop it. You know damn well I don't."

"Do I?" I couldn't stop.

"Do you want me to have an accident with the clippers? Because that can certainly be arranged."

A stare off ensued, both of us vying for dominance with raised chins and narrowed eyes. Eventually, she continued her work, turning my head from side to side multiple times. Finally, she blew out a satisfied breath and placed the clippers and scissors behind her on the table, all while still sitting on my lap. "There. All done." Our eyes locked again and although only a few seconds passed, it felt like a lifetime.

I lived in the brief silence. I existed there, reveled in it.

Looking deep into her eyes made me nervous. Not from what I saw, which was something deeper than lust, but because I knew my feelings for Braylen were stronger than I let on. To her and to myself. It was my place in the club to try and keep the peace, to make sure everything went off without a hitch. Granted, I'd done a shitty job as of late, but I continued to try. Whatever was happening with Braylen and me, however, was making me second-guess myself, questioning how I saw the world and the people around me.

Maybe I was losing my mind. Or maybe I was just desperate to get Braylen naked and fuck her until neither one of us could move.

When she finally did make a move to stand, I grabbed her waist and pulled her back, thrusting upward as she came down. The friction of our bodies connecting, albeit still covered in clothing, elicited a shiver of maddening desire. Far be it for me not to explore the possibility that she'd feel the same and give in to what I had planned. She had to know this was where we'd end up as soon as she stepped foot in my house. Especially when she straddled my lap, feigning it was part of her hair cutting process. *I call bullshit.* She knew exactly what she was doing, taunting and teasing me with her body, the way her thighs clamped on the sides of mine, the way her eyes drank me in when she thought I hadn't been paying attention. The way her tits pressed against my chest as she ran her fingers through my hair.

Yeah, she knew what she was doing all along. Probably had this whole scenario planned out on the drive over.

"Don't do that, Ryder." Placing her hands on my shoulders to hoist herself back up, she struggled against my hold. I refused to let her go until I knew she was completely over being upset with me. Not only for earlier but for the other night when she'd left in a huff.

"I'm not letting go until you kiss me."

"Not gonna happen, so you may as well let me up." She tried to remove herself again, but again I stopped her. "Ryder," she said threateningly, "let me go." She was so cute when she tried to be authoritative.

"Nope. Not until you plant your lips right here," I said, tapping my mouth with my index finger.

"One kiss? Then you'll let me up?" She looked skeptical. I didn't blame her.

"Uh-huh." A smirk found its way onto my face. I tried to hide it, but I failed big-time, causing her to cautiously study me.

"Fine."

"You like that word, don't you?"

"Do you want me to kiss you or not?" I nodded. "Then zip it," she said, a twinkle of mischief lighting up her brown eyes. The corners of her lips tilted upward, a secret only she was privy to, right before she leaned in and pecked me on the mouth.

Quick.

Chaste.

No emotion.

She drew back and tried to stand once more.

"What the fuck? That's not a kiss," I growled. Wrapping the thick strands of her hair around my hand, I tightened my grip and pulled her close. "This is." Crashing my lips to hers, I teased her mouth with my tongue, begging for entrance into her warmth as my free hand disappeared down the back of her jeans, pressing her closer to create the contact I needed.

It wasn't long before she opened for me, tangling her tongue with mine as a deep groan escaped from the deepest part of her. It was matched only by one of my own.

I bit her bottom lip.

She sucked on my tongue.

I cupped her ass.

She stroked my cock through my jeans.

Fuck! This was more than a kiss, and we both knew it. Rising from the chair, I kicked it behind me and walked toward the kitchen table, planting her on top of it before breaking away from her mouth. "Goddamnit, woman! You drive me crazy. Do you know that?" I tugged at her shirt, pulling it over her head with ease when she offered no resistance.

"You're just horny," she whispered breathlessly, fumbling with my belt buckle and pulling me toward her as she tried to unhook the leather strap. When she finally freed it, she unbuttoned my jeans and hastily unzipped them, pushing the material, along with my white boxer briefs, over my hips until my cock sprang free. I was painfully hard, and I feared if Braylen was just messing with me I'd lose my shit. If it was all a joke, her sick way of getting back at me for making her angry earlier, I'd beg to fuck her if that was what it took.

I grappled with whether or not to restrain her, tease her until she pleaded for me to fill her. Thankfully I didn't have to do anything, losing myself and all of my reason when her delicate fingers circled my thickness, stroking me from base to tip over and over again.

"You better stop or I'm gonna come before we even get started."

She rolled her eyes and shrugged, as if what I'd warned couldn't possibly happen. Granted, my stamina was pretty impressive, if I did say so myself, but we hadn't had sex in a few days, and I was more than amped up to blow.

Cupping the back of her head, I brought her mouth to mine again, kissing her so deeply I felt it in my goddamn toes. She tasted so sweet, her lips, tongue, and teeth enticing me to strip her bare and claim her until she begged me to stop.

"Let's get these off you." I reached for her jeans, practically ripping off the top button and tearing them down the front. As soon as the fabric parted, I pushed her onto her back, hooked my fingers into the waistband and shimmied her jeans over her hips, much like she'd done with mine. Only I took them all the way off her, tossing them over my shoulder before tearing off her white lace panties.

Pulling her back into a sitting position, I reached behind her back and unhooked her matching bra, flinging that somewhere behind me as well. All the while, Braylen continued to stroke me, softer than before because she didn't want me to come yet any more than I wanted to.

"I'm still upset with you," she said, smearing a drop of precum over the crown.

"I can live with that," I rasped, mentally counting to ten to calm myself. "Just as long as I get to bury myself inside that sweet pussy of yours." She loved when I used that word—pussy. It turned her on beyond all reason.

"Say it again," she whimpered, moving toward the edge of the table and spreading her legs. Her arousal glistened between her thighs, the sight enough to almost make me lose it right then and there.

Leaning closer, I nipped her earlobe. "Pussy."

She shuddered, her fingers tightening around my cock.

"Careful, sweetheart." Braylen flashed me a wicked grin before lining me up at her entrance. "Do you want me to fuck you now?" She nodded, lowering her fingers to cup my tightly drawn balls. I groaned into her mouth as I seized her lips once more, thrusting inside her in one quick motion, joining our bodies before either of us could take our next breath.

We'd stopped using condoms a month prior; we were both clean and she was on the pill. Taking her bare was the best feeling in the entire world. No barrier, just skin on skin. Heightened pleasure for us both.

She gasped, her own moans swallowed by our kiss. "Ryder!" she screamed, bracing herself on the table as I withdrew before roughly plunging back inside. There was nothing sweet and calm about how I took her. Braylen loved it rough and so did I. We both needed the aggressive sex more than ever, anger still simmering inside both of us for various reasons.

The legs of the table screeched against the tiled floor, the back-and-forth rhythm matching the erratic beat of my heart. I wanted so badly to fuck her with wild abandon, but I toed the invisible line between having rough sex and eviscerating her.

As soon as I hit her sweet spot, she threw her head back and arched her tits in my face. Without a second thought, my teeth grazed one of her nipples, my fingers pinching the other hardened bud. "Oh my God!" she cried out. "Yeah . . . right there. Yeah . . . yeah." She pumped her hips toward me as I drove into her, neither of us giving in to the other. We were both chasing our high, the sweet bliss of release that was inevitable.

"I love fucking you, baby," I roared, moving to bite down on the tender flesh of her throat, running my tongue over the affected area to soothe away the bite of pain.

I marked her.

I claimed her.

I fucked her until her pussy started to clench.

"That's it. Come for me." I pushed her body to the limits, forcing her to look at me while she came all over me. Her body squeezed my cock, shooting tiny spasms down my shaft until I was barely holding on.

Braylen shouted my name as she came, her fingers diving into my hair and yanking while she rode out her wave of pleasure. Tinges of pain erupted at the roots of my hair follicles, but it only drove me to fuck her faster, stretching her orgasm out as long as possible.

When she was finally sated, I chased my own climax, my bruising grip on her waist crushing her to me. "Oh fuck!" I shouted over and over until my balls drew tighter, the all-too-familiar pull starting at the base of my spine.

I wanted to last longer but her body demanded so much from mine. I gave her greedy pussy everything, spilling every last drop inside her as my orgasm threatened to pull me under and never let go.

CHAPTER EIGHT

Braylen

STILL SITTING ON THE TABLE, Ryder's face buried in my neck and his cock still jerking inside me, I realized there was no other place I'd rather be. Call it hormones, or the high from my orgasm, but something pulled me toward this man time and time again. I couldn't pinpoint exactly what the connection was, and after trying to dissect it for weeks—months even—I came to the conclusion that it was inexplicable.

All I wanted to do was melt into the man pinning me in place, but I couldn't release all of myself. Not completely, without reservation. Especially since there were so many things up in the air between us. We were like oil and water, and other than a few rare moments sprinkled in between, the only times we meshed as one were when we were having sex. Or leading up to the utterly delicious act.

As the pace of my heart steadily slowed, my eyes roamed around the space of Ryder's home. His place exuded masculinity, rustic décor everywhere, yet I found it cozy. A hearty fireplace took up the center wall of his living room, a few pieces of camel-colored leather furniture surrounding the focal point. His kitchen was small yet updated, all the latest stainless steel appliances glimmering in the condensed space. One of my favorite areas of his house, however—beside his bedroom, of course—was his en suite bathroom. The antique claw-foot tub called to me each and every time I spent the night. Although I wasn't sure I'd be sleeping over again anytime soon, not with the threat of him possibly maiming me in my sleep.

Hell, possibly worse.

From what I understood, most of the men in the club lived close to the compound, yet on their own parcel of land, with top-of-the-line security installed to deter any unwanted guests. Ryder's house was no different. Sitting on three acres of land, he was housed in solitude yet close enough that he didn't live in the middle of bum fuck Egypt.

"Let's get you cleaned up," he mumbled before lifting his head to look at me. Several seconds passed of looking into each other's eyes before he placed a chaste kiss on my lips. It was almost as if he wanted to tell me something but thought better of it. Ryder fell from my body, pulled up his boxer briefs and jeans and tucked himself back into place. He reached for a box of tissues sitting on the counter.

"What?" He pushed my legs apart to wipe himself from my inner thighs.

"Nothing. I just like when you take care of me after sex. It's nice."

"Nice?"

"Yeah."

He mirrored my expression, his smile melting my heart. Ryder was a tough guy, his appearance matching his personality. It was only during these tender moments that I glimpsed another side to him. A more intimate side I cherished because I knew it would disappear soon enough. I realized that sounded odd, seeing as how the act of sex was intimate, but sometimes sex was just sex. Primal urges between two people. It was the aftermath that could sometimes be more rewarding.

After he finished, he hoisted me off the table and helped to steady me until I found my footing. Grinning widely, he turned and moved to retrieve my clothes. Normally, I'd be self-conscious standing naked in front of a man. I had a little more junk in the trunk than I'd like, and my belly wasn't as flat as it used to be—I was a sucker for sweets—but the way Ryder stared at me made me feel like the most perfectly shaped woman in the world. I felt sexy and confident whenever his eyes raked over me, clothed or otherwise.

Walking back toward me, he held my clothes but made no attempt to hand them over.

"Can I get dressed now?" I asked, extending my hand so he could pass me my bra, panties, and outfit.

"What's the rush?"

"*You're* dressed."

"I kinda like you naked, though. You know, you can stay that way all night if you want. No complaints here."

"Nice try," I replied, snapping my fingers. With a loud sigh, he passed them to me, and within a minute I was fully clothed.

When I came to his house to cut his hair, I hadn't planned on having sex with him. Not really. I knew it was always a possibility, but I thought my smoldering anger would've blocked my lust.

I guess that didn't work out too well.

Ushering past him, I took a seat on his couch, crossed my legs and leaned back against the cushion. "We need to talk." I tried like hell to appear as if fighting was the last thing on my mind, but the reality was we would most likely end up there.

"The four magic words every man loves to hear," he griped sarcastically. Fiddling with the television remote, he clicked on a sports station before giving me his full attention. "What's up?"

His question was guarded, and I couldn't say that I blamed him. We still had a lot of unfinished business to discuss, and no doubt our conversation was going to turn heated. We were both stubborn, neither of us ever wanting to give in. When our fuses were lit, there was no stopping the explosion.

I wasn't a submissive person—not outside of the bedroom, at least. And Ryder sure as hell was domineering. He'd said on multiple occasions how he wished I'd just do as he asked without issue, but he'd been with me long enough to realize that was not how I was wired.

Crossing my arms over my chest, I braced for impact, ripping off the Band-Aid and blurting out, "I want to know what caused you to do what you did the other night."

His chest expanded as he inhaled a deep breath. Then his lips parted, expelling the air in the form of a shout.

"Jesus Christ! Are we goin' over that again?" Pacing in front of me, he ran his hand through his newly cut hair. "I told you I don't wanna talk about it. Look, I'm sorry for holding you down while I was dreamin', but it won't happen again." The vein in the middle of his forehead bulged, his breathing increasing the more aggravated he became.

"You can't say that."

"Yes I can," he gritted, tossing the remote on the couch next to me.

"If you talk about what's bothering you, you'll feel better."

"Nothing is fuckin' bothering me. Let it go, Bray." The rasp of his demand should've halted any further discussion on the matter, but of course, I just had to push.

"You need to let me in if we're gonna continue doing whatever it is we're doing."

"Fuckin'?" A look crossed his features so quickly I didn't have time to dissect it. Was it disgust? Uncertainty? I just couldn't be sure.

His choice of words hurt. Ryder was guarded, and I feared he always would be. If I was a sane woman, I'd just walk away, wish him well and move on. But I never claimed to be in my right mind when it came to the infuriating man.

"That's what we're doing? Nothing more than fucking each other?"

"Yeah. No." He planted his ass on the arm of the sofa at the far end. "I don't know. What I *do* know is that I'm not delvin' into my deep-seated feelings about what may or may not be bothering me. And if you can't deal with it, you can leave," he said, pointing toward his front door.

My lungs seized, taking in air seeming too difficult a task. He kept spouting off at the mouth, hurting me more and more with every syllable. The muscles in my chin started to quiver, so before he bore witness to the tears that would surely follow, I rose from the couch, grabbed my keys and bag from the kitchen counter and hustled toward the door.

But not before tossing "Fuck you" over my shoulder, then disappearing outside and slamming the door behind me.

CHAPTER NINE

Ryder

"SHE JUST HAD TO FUCKIN' push, didn't she? Couldn't leave well enough alone," I mumbled, whipping my beer bottle into the hearth of the fireplace, the shattering glass doing a less than stellar job of releasing any of my pent-up fury. "Fuck!" I roared, adrenaline coursing through me with no end in sight.

My cell rang, vibrating on top of the end table and cutting through the expletives I continued to yell into the silence around me.

"Hello," I shouted into the receiver.

"Hey, it's Stone. No time to ask what's up your ass, man." No break between words before he asked, "Do you know if anyone visited Braylen at work? Or approached her on the street? Anything weird?" His words were clipped and quick.

"What are you talkin' about?"

"Are you with her right now?"

"No, she just stormed outta here a few seconds ago. What the hell is goin' on?" I'd begun pacing again once I answered the call but I halted, fear of the unknown freezing me in place.

"Addy and Sully were approached on the street by some guy, telling them that they would get what was coming to them soon enough. The whole club would. Same fuckin' thing happened to Reece and a few of the strippers at Indulge and Flings."

"Who was it?"

"Don't know. He wasn't wearin' a Reapers cut, although that doesn't mean anything."

"I'll call you right back." I hung up on Stone while he was still talking, ran out the front door and raced down the steps toward Braylen's car. Thankfully she hadn't left yet; she was sitting in the driver seat texting someone.

Whipping open her door, I grabbed for her hand to pull her out of the car. Startled, she dropped her phone, but when she realized it was me, she shot me daggers before leaning farther into the vehicle.

"I don't have anything to say to you," she yelled, bending over to retrieve the fallen device. Her blonde hair looked disheveled, as if she'd been tugging at it, and her eyes were red, almost like she'd been about to cry. No time to feel bad about upsetting her, though. There were more pressing things to deal with right then.

"Did anyone strange approach you recently?" My forearm hung over the top of her door, refusing to budge in case she tried to slam it shut.

"What?"

"Just answer the question, Bray. Did a man approach you recently? Spouting off at the mouth about getting what's coming to you?"

"No." Worry etched deep around her eyes. The last thing I wanted to do was freak her out, but I needed to make sure she was safe.

"Listen, put everything else aside. I need you to trust me. Don't go anywhere alone. I mean it. Not to work, not back home. Nowhere."

"You can't seriously think you're gonna tell me what to do, especially after what you just said to me in there," she spouted, angrily pointing to my house. "Because I'm not listening to anything you have to say."

"You can be as stubborn as you want, woman, but I'm fucking serious. There's a possible threat out there and I'll do what I have to in order to keep you safe. Even if that means being your goddamn shadow."

Unlocking her phone, she frantically started typing a message, biting her lip in concentration while waiting for a response. "Where's Jagger?" she asked. "Is he with Kena? Is *she* safe?"

"I'm sure he's with her. He won't let anything happen to her."

"I need to go. I need to find out where she is. She's not texting me back now." She said something under her breath before turning the key in the ignition. Grabbing the door handle, she tried to close it, but I still had it braced open.

"I'm following you home," I instructed, my tone deadly serious.

"Fine. Hurry up."

As I removed my arm from the door, she slammed it shut, threw her four-door sedan in Drive and peeled out of my driveway.

That woman was gonna be the death of me yet.

CHAPTER TEN

Braylen

FIVE DAYS HAD PASSED SINCE Ryder freaked me out with his sudden and random interrogation. I'd asked him later that night, when he insisted on following me home and then walking me inside, if I was in any real danger. He said no, but I couldn't help but feel that he was lying to me.

Against my wishes, he'd continued to show up at my house to follow me to work, then at Transform to follow me home, making me promise to call him right away if anyone strange tried to talk to me. I'd wanted to ask him to define "anyone strange," but I had a gut feeling he wouldn't be too happy with my lack of concern about the situation, one I was still left fumbling around in the dark about.

Ryder and I weren't any better off than when I'd rushed out of his house the previous week. He refused to open up and I refused to keep quiet about his lack of sharing. Maybe because there wasn't anything in my past worth shielding, I didn't fully understand the ramifications of guarding secrets. And I would've been okay with allowing him to open up when he was good and ready, but then he basically attacked me in his sleep. He could've killed me. If he ever wanted me to share his bed in the foreseeable future, he'd better start talking.

Then again, maybe I didn't mean anything more to him than someone to *fuck*, as he so eloquently put it. The thought alone had my chest tightening, but if that was how he felt, there wasn't a damn thing I could do about it.

So why try and protect me?

And men say women are confusing.

———— ◆ ————

"ARE YOU SURE YOU DON'T mind me hangin' out with you two tonight? It's been a long day and I could use the company." Tucking my leg underneath me, I plopped down on the couch, wineglass in one hand and a bowl of popcorn in the other.

"It's your place," Jagger said, smiling at me before wrapping his arm around Kena's shoulder and pulling her closer. "Besides, I need a witness to prove that your little sister does indeed fall asleep during movies." Jagger laughed, but not before Kena slapped his thigh for making fun of her.

It was in fact true; I couldn't recall a movie I'd watched with her where she'd made it all the way through to the end. That wasn't the case for me, however. I was always up for a good flick. If it held my interest, I was in for the long haul—or the typical hour and forty minutes, give or take.

"What did you put in?" I asked, throwing some air-popped goodness in my mouth while watching the opening credits. The lights were dimmed low, and we were all sitting comfortably on the couch, Kena between Jagger and me. No doubt, my sister would be lightly snoring in T minus thirty minutes.

Far from the Madding Crowd, Kena signed, flashing me a smile before resting her head on Jagger's shoulder. He groaned, earning him another playful tap on the leg. Maybe it'd be more like T minus fifteen minutes before she passed out.

The way Kena and Jagger snuggled on the couch made me think about Ryder. I tried to stop it and focus on the film, but his image kept popping up in my head.

He'd obviously made his decision not to integrate me further into his life, and while it hurt because I'd grown fond of the broody, arrogant man, I took the opportunity to gain some space as well. Though that didn't stop Ryder from continuing to follow me to and from work or calling me multiple times throughout the day and night.

The man was infuriatingly confusing.

After two hours the movie finally came to an end. Exhaling a breath of satisfaction at seeing what I deemed a wonderful film, I stretched my arms over my head and groaned out a hearty yawn.

"My damn leg's asleep," I bellyached, untucking it from underneath my body and straightening the appendage, pins and needles in full force.

"And so is your sister," Jagger teased.

"How long did she make it this time?" I was so engrossed with the movie right from the beginning, I hadn't taken notice of exactly when Kena fell asleep.

"She made it forty minutes," he replied, shifting slightly so as not to wake her. "I'm impressed."

"Me too." Rising from the couch, I stretched once more, tugging down the hem of my yellow cami before striding toward the kitchen. "Do you want something else to drink? Another beer?"

"Nah, I'm good. I should be going."

"Oh. You're not staying over?" Even though Jagger slept in Kena's room with her when he stayed the night, I felt safe knowing he was under the same roof.

Scratching the light dusting of hair on his jaw, he cracked his neck from side to side. "Wish I could but I can't. Have to deal with something at the club." Gently picking Kena up from the couch, he rose and tucked her back into him before walking out of the room.

A few minutes later he returned, yawning and doing a bit of stretching himself. Jagger's hair was sticking up in the back and a little bit on the sides, but he somehow still pulled off the tough guy look. I'd come to enjoy his company, even though I hadn't been his biggest fan in the beginning. Scratch that. I was, then I wasn't, and then I was once more.

Pulling on his club's vest, he snagged his keys from the coffee table. "Make sure you lock the door behind me," he warned. "And use the new deadbolt too."

Before he opened the door, I seized his arm.

"You'd tell me if we were in some real danger, wouldn't you? You wouldn't hide something like that from me? From Kena?" Worry bubbled forth on every word. I'd meant to simply ask if he thought whatever threat they were concerned about was viable, not appear shaken and nervous, riddled with stress over the whole situation. If only I knew exactly what was going on; then maybe I could relax. But nothing was simple and upfront with these guys.

Codes.

Underlying messages.

Secrecy.

"We're just being cautious, Braylen. That's it."

"You promise?"

Jagger had the decency to look away for a brief moment, inadvertently telling me everything I didn't want to know. "Ryder will be here in the morning. He'll meet you outside as usual."

"If he's just being cautious, then I don't need him to continue to follow me to and from work. I think it's overkill, don't you?"

He knew what I was doing, trying to trick him into revealing that they weren't simply being vigilant. There was some sort of real danger and it could possibly involve Kena and me.

"Don't."

"Don't what?" We were both standing near the door, a battle of wills ensuing the more hush-hush he remained.

"Just let him do this for you. It puts his mind at ease. Mine too, and no doubt your sister's."

"Had to play the sister card, didn't you?"

"I do what I have to." He winked, a small smile tilting his lips. His phone rang, killing anything else he would have said. "I gotta go. Call us if you need us."

For a brief moment, I'd thought about texting Ryder and telling him I didn't need him to babysit me any longer, but I had a feeling he'd either call to argue or show up on my doorstep to convince me otherwise. The energy required for such a confrontation was my sole deterrent.

CHAPTER ELEVEN

Ryder

"SETTLE DOWN," MAREK DEMANDED, LOOKING a little worse for wear. Although the stress of the Reapers most likely being responsible for threatening some of the women, and knowing our enemy was certainly planning some kind of retaliation for the absence of their president, Psych, the Knights Corruption leader looked to be in control. For the first time in what seemed like a very long time.

After everything he and his wife, Sully, had battled, there wasn't anything he couldn't push through, knowing damn well he had a great woman waiting for him at home. And although Sully had technically been kidnapped and forced to marry the man sitting at the head of the table, their love was one for the ages.

Not that I was all sappy or anything, but everyone knew those two were meant to be together.

Placing the gavel to his right, Marek leaned back in his chair and not so patiently waited for the chatter to cease. All of the men's words soon faded as we focused on our leader.

"I'd bet my life it's a fuckin' Reaper who's rattling our women, and for that alone he'll pay with his life."

We all nodded. Even though our club had gone legit, cutting off all ties with Los Zappas Cartel and the drug trade, we still dealt with whomever we deemed a threat. There wasn't anything we wouldn't do to protect our family, both at the club and at home.

"Has anyone been able to describe the guy?" Trigger asked, fidgeting in his chair like he was uncomfortable with the topic. He had every right to be twitchy; not only was he concerned about his brothers, but his niece, Adelaide, was involved with Stone. They even had a kid together, with another on the way.

"All they could tell us was that he was about six foot, had short dark hair and tats runnin' up both arms," Tripp offered, the nomad becoming quite the permanent fixture at the oblong wooden table. He'd come to stay with our club, giving up the open road for the time being. When Indulge first opened, Marek had asked him to stick around and see that everything fell into place. It just so happened that he met his woman, Reece, there, pulling out all stops to keep her safe, which unfortunately included dealing with her crazy ex-husband. And by dealing with . . . well, I supposed it was self-explanatory.

"That could be any of 'em," Cutter replied, shaking his head in obvious disgust. Breck was sitting to the right of his ol' man, pissed off right along with him. Hell, we all had the same anger bubbling up inside, threatening to explode given the right time and opportunity.

"Yeah it could be," Stone said. "We'll just have to take out every one of those fuckers. That'll solve the problem," he grunted, leaning forward and resting his forearms on the hard surface of the table.

"No one is gonna do a damn thing until I give the go-ahead," Marek warned, looking to Stone first, then the rest of us. "Just like with every-thing else in the past, I know you all want revenge, and to put this threat to bed once and for all, but we have to be smart about this. More now than ever before. That sonofabitch Koritz is gonna be watchin', waiting for us to fuck up. And now we have to also deal with that bastard Rabid."

"Who knew *that* guy would be a threat?" Jagger asked, scratching his jaw with one hand while drumming the fingers of his other on the edge of the table.

Marek leaned closer, his blue eyes darkening in seriousness and an-ger. "I underestimated him. It won't happen again." The rasp of his tone indicated he held the majority of his temper at bay.

A bout of silence ensued, all of us processing what could potentially take place in the upcoming days, weeks and even months. We simply had no idea what to expect, except the unexpected. If history was any sort of indication.

"Do we have eyes on Rabid?" I asked, looking around the room before finally resting my attention on Marek.

"Hawke."

Without thinking, I blurted, "Is that the smartest choice?" I took a breath to continue to speak but Hawke cut me off by slamming his fist down and shooting me the dirtiest look. Hawke and I had our issues, mainly itching to always get a rise out of the other, but there was no bad blood between us.

I may've just changed that.

"What the fuck does that mean?" he shouted, rising halfway from his chair as if he was set to lunge over the table at me. His eyes were wild with ferocity and I feared if he didn't get a grip soon, we'd be goin' toe-to-toe in the next several seconds.

Tripp sat next to his younger brother. The nomad shot me a disbelieving look before placing his hand on Hawke's shoulder, doing his best to try and calm him down before things escalated out of control.

"Settle down, man. I just meant that you might be a little too close to this, more so than the rest of us." Confusion shrouded his expression. "After everything that happened with Edana, can you seriously tell us you won't do something drastic if given the opportunity?" I had my doubts he'd be able to restrain himself. Not that I'd blame him, but when it came to being strategic, we had to hold off until Marek gave the orders. Any other move and a shitstorm could blow back our way and devastate the entire club forever.

Slowly lowering himself back into his seat, he replied, "I'm not gonna fuck it up." He closed his mouth and turned toward Marek, no longer wanting to engage me in any further conversation.

"I didn't say you would."

"Yes you fuckin' did. When you questioned me." He was still facing Marek when he responded.

"All right. Calm down. Both of you," Marek shouted, then sighed. "I'm too young for this," he mumbled, pushing his chair back from the lip of the table.

"What about that fucker who's making threats to our women?" Stone threw out that question, locking eyes solely on his best friend for the answer.

"Keep watch over them." Stone's mouth dropped open. "Hey, he came up to Adelaide *and* Sully. Don't forget that. My wife is just as upset as your woman."

"I know. I know," Stone said, shaking his head in aggravation. "I just hate the thought that anyone has the balls to approach Addy and freak her out with some lame-ass threat. I'm stressed out the way it is, constantly worrying about her and Riley. And now that Addy's pregnant. . . ." Stone stopped speaking, emotion rising in his voice and threatening to crumble the man right in front of all of us.

I feared for Braylen's safety every day. I could only imagine how I'd feel if she was my fiancée, or wife, or had my kid. It would only amplify the issue until I was giving myself a daily heart attack.

"We'll get 'em. He can't hide forever. Until then, keep your eyes and ears open. If you have to deal with family stuff and need someone to replace you in the rotation at Jagger's fights, or checking in on things at Indulge and Flings, just let me know. We're all in the same boat." Grabbing the gavel, he said, "Is there anything else?"

Everyone just shook their heads.

CHAPTER
TWELVE

Braylen

LOUD VOICES OUTSIDE WOKE ME from sleep, rousing me only hours after I'd drifted off to dreamland. I couldn't make out what they were saying, but the longer I laid there, the more evident it became that the voices were familiar.

One was from the man who continued to confuse the hell out of me, twisting me all around until I didn't know which end was up, and the other was from the man who was completely head over heels for my sister.

I threw off the covers and groggily shuffled toward my window, tossing it open and leaning my head outside.

"What are you two doing?" I yelled, the night's breeze blowing strands of my blonde hair back in my face. I was sure I looked the sight, but ask me if I cared. Not a minute later, I heard my bedroom door open but didn't bother to look behind me, knowing it was Kena who had come to see what all of the commotion was about.

"He insisted I bring him here," Jagger finally answered, supporting Ryder under his left arm to help hold him upright. Ryder wasn't drunk off his ass but he was definitely feeling no pain.

"Oh yeah? Why's that?"

"'Cause I need ta see ya," Ryder slurred, shoving Jagger away from him. "Ya need ta stahhhh . . . stop ignorin' me, toots."

Kena tapped my shoulder. *Toots?* She rubbed at her eyes, smiling at me and then down at the sight on the street.

"Sorry for waking you, baby," Jagger shouted, louder than he needed to. He'd been drinking as well, but not nearly as much as his buddy next to him.

"Go home," I said, leaning back into my room. As my hands came up to pull down the window, Ryder started shouting.

"Woman! If you don't let me inside I'm gonna bust down your front door."

"No he won't," Jagger jumped in, having the decency to look somewhat embarrassed.

"I will. I'll da . . . do it."

"Why?"

"'Cause you won't get outta here," Ryder confessed, pointing to his head before taking several steps toward our front door. Within seconds the pounding started. Jagger was still under the streetlight, shaking his head and shrugging when Ryder just wouldn't let up.

"Fine, but stop banging. We do have neighbors, you know."

"I don't shit."

"I'm sure you do," Jagger razzed, laughing full-on when Ryder tried to swing at him, almost falling on his ass.

"You kn . . . know what I meant," he garbled.

Kena and I walked through the house until we reached the front door. As my fingers circled the handle, my sister tapped my arm once more.

Are you sure you want to let him in? If you really don't want to see him, I'll tell Jagger to take him away. Your choice. She stood back to give me space, gifting me with a sympathetic look. She knew I was torn up over Ryder because I'd confided as much after a few glasses of wine the other day.

"May as well get this over with." My sister nodded. I pulled open the door and was almost hit in the face. Ryder had his fist raised, ready to pound the wood when I'd suddenly appeared.

"'Bout time," he grumbled before entering our house, not a care in the world that I'd told him to go home moments prior. "You got anythin' to drink?"

"You've had enough," Jagger and I said simultaneously. Grinning, Jagger kicked the door closed behind him before grabbing Kena's hand, leading her back to her room and leaving Ryder and me alone, standing in the middle of the entryway just staring at each other.

After neither of us spoke, I flipped the deadbolt and turned around, heading toward the couch. I doubt he'd be able to make it much farther, so the sofa seemed like the best idea.

Planting myself down, I folded my arms over my chest, much like I'd done at his place right before we started arguing about him not opening up.

"What do you want? What couldn't wait until a decent hour?" My eyes raked over him as he leaned against the wall, no doubt needing the structure's support to hold him up. His dark eyes were glazed over and droopy but he was still coherent. He looked scrumptious, even while inebriated. His dark hair was sticking up on top, the result of him tugging at it I was sure. His teeth captured his bottom lip while he contemplated his answer. "Well?" I prompted.

"I wanna see ya."

"Why? You made it perfectly clear you don't wanna let me in. That we're nothin' more than just fuck buddies, so why the scene? Why all the dramatics?"

He pushed off the wall and slowly put one foot in front of the other. The look in his eyes was definitely predatory. Drunk or not, Ryder had a way of making me feel all hot and bothered with a simple glance.

Damn him, and damn my overactive hormones.

"Stop right there," I warned. "We're not doin' anything. You can sleep on the couch, but then you have to leave in the morning. I'm not staying out here with you, and you sure as hell aren't coming to my bedroom." I made a move to stand, but he was on me before I could get my feet underneath me.

His hands wrapped around my waist and as he crashed down on the couch, he spun me around and hoisted me on top of him. It happened so fast I had no time to fight him. The only thing I could do was plant my hands on his hard chest to ensure I didn't fall over. I straddled his lap, and he wasted no time leaning in and trying to kiss me, but I dodged his advances before his mouth could connect with mine. While I wanted nothing more than to give myself to him, he'd only hurt me. One way or another.

"Stop it, Ryder. I mean it. You can't just wake me up in the middle of the night, barge into my house and have sex with me. It doesn't work that way." I struggled to get off him, but his hold was fierce. Not painful but definitely strong.

"I can't."

"You can't what?" He didn't answer me right away, so I tilted my head and repeated, "You can't what?"

"I can't get you out of my head." He leaned forward, his warm breath lapping over my collarbone. The smell of beer would've been overpowering had his other scents not filled my nose as well. One of leather, the outdoors and his natural male scent.

"So you said."

"I'm not foolin' 'round here, baby." He raised his head and his mouth was millimeters from mine, his tongue wetting his bottom lip and turning me on like he normally did. I hated my body's reaction, and the last thing I wanted to do was give in to this type of behavior, but I feared my heart and hormones were going to win the battle against my brain.

"Really? 'Cause I thought that's all we were doing." I arched my brow, leaning back so our faces weren't so close.

"I didn't mean it," he confessed. "You just got me all twisted up inside." He threw his head back against the top of the couch, his hold on my waist still ironclad. "I can't stop thinkin' about you. All I do is worry."

"What do you mean 'worry'?" I knew the answer as soon as I asked, but thankfully he didn't remind me of the supposed threat.

Again I tried to move and again he held me to him, my thighs on the outside of his muscular ones. If I sat in the same position for too long, I'd start to cramp up, and then he'd have to let me up. Unfortunately I was probably close to ten minutes from that situation.

And a lot could happen in ten minutes.

Bodies could become one in ten minutes. Then again, hearts could be crushed in ten minutes as well.

"Can't you forgive me?" he asked, that time looking directly into my eyes. I studied every facet of his face, like I'd done many times before, only this time there was a sadness and vulnerability laced behind his stunning browns that I hadn't seen before. Maybe he really was all twisted up inside like he'd said.

"You never apologized," I reminded him. "Not once did you say you were sorry."

His hands moved from my waist and traveled up my body, finding their place on my cheeks. He pulled me close, his mouth practically touching mine when he said, "I'm sorry, baby. Please forgive me."

My answer was to seal my lips to his, my tongue searching for his warmth as he writhed beneath me. His hardened excitement elicited a primal need inside me, one I was powerless to control, let alone stop. The heat from him fueled my own, the need to crawl inside him such an odd feeling, yet it made perfect sense to me. As he dominated me with his kiss and while his hands cupped and squeezed my breasts, pinching my nipples through my thin camisole, I couldn't help but think that if we had sex right then, nothing would change.

Ryder would continue to keep me at bay, throwing me tiny scraps of affection and wilted promises whenever the mood, or alcohol, struck him. If I had any hope of recovering from the already brutal attack he'd had on my heart, then I needed to stop giving in to him.

One more second.

Okay, two more seconds. Then I'll pull away.

Oh hell, I had to slowly count to twenty before I ended the kiss, pushing off his large frame and stumbling to my feet. He reached for me, the frown painting his face enticing me to jump right back into his arms.

This man is dangerous.

"I need to go back to bed now." I backed up a few steps, keeping a close eye on him for any sudden movements.

"I'll come with you," he offered, trying to push off the couch, a feat which failed miserably as he simply couldn't find his footing. Our sofa was worn in and super comfy, the cushions molding to the body like a second skin. Add in a large, muscular man, whose reflexes were compromised from drinking, and there was no way he was getting off the couch without some help. And I knew if I approached him, he'd just yank me back down on top of him.

Ryder quickly gave up, his eyes starting to close as his body leaned to the side. Eventually he ended up lying on his back, his right foot resting on the floor while his left one was stretched out in front of him. Reaching behind me, I grabbed a blanket from the recliner and draped it over him. Pulling off his boots, I tossed them to the side and tucked the edges of the blanket underneath him. I watched as his breathing evened out, a peace drifting over him as if nothing in the world bothered him. Too bad I knew it was only a façade. Ryder was plagued by things he deemed too dark to ever confess.

When I turned and quietly walked across the room, about to turn the corner, I heard him say, "I saw him kill my mom. How do I ever get over something like that?"

I stopped dead in my tracks, every muscle on lockdown while I waited for another confession, but no other words filled the air.

CHAPTER
THIRTEEN

Ryder

THE BLARE OF A CAR alarm jolted me awake, my hands instantly clutching my head to try and stop the pounding. Normally, I didn't suffer from hangovers; I must've drank an awful lot of shitty beer last night.

I hadn't been so out of it that I didn't remember what happened, however. I knew damn well I'd threatened Jagger to drive me to Braylen's house, the need to see her greater than I'd ever felt before in my life. With minimal reluctance, he'd finally agreed, not so much to help me out but because I was sure he wanted to spend time with Kena. Either way, mission accomplished.

I remembered pulling Braylen on top of me as I fell onto the couch, then apologizing and spewing something about not being able to get her out of my head. Then kissing her sweet lips. Then trying to get off the couch but failing, my body finally giving in to exhaustion, the alcohol flowing through my veins thickening and rendering me useless.

As I struggled to sit up, I suddenly remembered the worst thing of all. My hands came up to cradle my face, a groan of disbelief barreling from my mouth as I tried like hell to wish it away. I'd said out loud that I saw my mother killed in front of me.

Did she hear me? Had she left the room by the time the words escaped? If she did hear me, will she ask me about it? So many questions, none of which I would find the answer to unless I brought it up.

Reaching inside my jeans, I pulled my phone out to check the time—5:00 a.m. A sudden feeling of nerves took hold, so I scrambled off the couch, almost fell the fuck over, righted myself and went in search of Jagger. I needed the keys to his truck. I had to get out of there before Braylen woke up, before she decided to *shrink* me into telling her all about my sordid past.

———— ◆ ————

AFTER BRIEFLY RETURNING HOME, I showered, changed and headed toward the club, remnants of my drunken haze still lingering. Being alone with my thoughts was the last thing I wanted to do. I needed a distraction, and who better to gift me with such a thing than my brothers. While it was still relatively early—six thirty, to be exact—I was sure someone would be there. And if not, then I'd set up at the bar and start *forgetting* right away.

Forgetting I'd made a fool of myself by showing up at Braylen's house, drunk and insistent she see me.

Forgetting I'd basically passed out on her couch after having a taste of her sweetness.

Forgetting I'd mentioned my mother.

Forgetting Jagger was gonna be pissed that I'd taken his truck without his knowledge.

Forgetting I even cared.

I was close to ten minutes away from my destination when a vehicle unexpectedly cut in front of me, crossing lanes without any sort of warning. Besides being pissed, something screamed at me to pay attention, more so than I normally would have. An Oldsmobile Cutlass with faded and peeling blue paint, along with a bumper that was held on by duct tape, careened into the opposing lane before righting the wheel, slowing down and then speeding up. I kept my distance when normally I would have sped up and passed him off. At first glance it appeared as if a drunk driver was behind the wheel, but I quickly realized that wasn't the case.

The Cutlass pulled closer to the side of the road but never stopped completely. I let up on the gas, slowing the truck even more. The next thing I knew something was tossed from the passenger side window, and as soon as the object cleared the car's interior, the driver gunned it and took off like a shot. I was honestly shocked the ol' girl had so much gumption left in her.

Several moments later, I pulled over to where the Cutlass had slowed, my tires kicking up gravel until I eventually came to a stop. I had no idea what had been discarded, but I knew I couldn't leave without checking what it was. It could've been a bag of trash, the bastard too lazy to dispose of it properly, although my gut was telling me otherwise.

Throwing the truck in Park, I exited and walked around the back until I came to the side of the road closest to the small embankment. And that was when I saw a white garbage bag with black handles. Upon closer inspection, I saw the bag was moving ever so slightly. When I was a few feet away, I finally heard a noise, a whimpering sound trapped inside the confinement.

What the fuck? I proceeded with caution. For all I knew the guy could've tossed out a raccoon he'd caught, or a skunk, or any other kind of rodent. The closer I got the more I knew the animal inside wasn't any of those things. Crouching down, I cautiously untied the knotted black plastic handles, pulling apart the ends of the garbage bag until I could peer inside.

Looking back up at me were a tiny pair of pale blue eyes, a face so bewildered it tugged at my heart. It was a puppy. I'd always been an animal lover, even had a dog I loved with all my heart when I was young, so when I saw what that bastard threw out of his window, fury pounded through me. My skin was hot, my heart thumping wildly inside my chest.

I had a choice. I could hop back in my truck and take off after him, or I could tend to the defenseless puppy. Without much deliberation at all, I chose the puppy.

Tearing the rest of the bag away, I inspected the tiny creature. It didn't take long to discover that the puppy only had three legs—two front ones and the back right. From what I could tell, it looked like the missing limb was a birth defect and not the result of some sort of accident or mistreatment. Checking underneath, I saw the puppy was male, his tiny tail tucked under when I scooped him up.

He looked to only be around six weeks old, yet there was an old soul to this dog as I stared into his eyes. It was the oddest moment, but I swore to Christ I bonded with the little bastard, right there on the side of the road. While I wasn't sure exactly what breed of dog he was, his coloring was quite unique: gray and white fur covered his body, with a black patch circling his left eye.

Walking back to the truck, the little guy tucked close to me, I grabbed a blanket Jagger had in the back and threw it over the passenger seat before climbing back behind the wheel. Turning over the ignition, I gently placed the puppy on the blanket.

He started to shiver, so I put my hand over him. Surprisingly he stopped, licking his little lips before closing his eyes, as if he knew I wouldn't harm him.

I drove the rest of the way to the club with a discarded, three-legged animal next to me and an odd feeling of affection in my heart.

CHAPTER FOURTEEN

Ryder

STRIDING THROUGH THE DOORS OF the club, I hid the puppy underneath my cut. The morning air was crisp and the poor guy had been through enough; the least I could do was try and keep him warm.

No one was out in the common room, and the door to Chambers was wide open. There was a strong possibility some of the guys were sleeping in one of the rooms in the back. There were plenty of designated spaces for us to crash if we needed to. A night of overindulgence or a fight with an ol' lady—whatever the reason, all the men had a place to stay if the occasion called for it.

Disappearing into the kitchen, I rooted around for something edible I could feed the pup. What the hell did I even give him? We certainly didn't have any puppy chow on hand. Opening the refrigerator, I saw some leftover fried chicken, so still holding tightly to the dog, I wrangled the plate from the shelf, kicked the door closed and set up on the counter.

A whimper escaped the little creature when I removed the saran wrap from the dish, my own stomach rumbling from the smell. It was then I realized I hadn't eaten since early the day before, choosing to drown myself in alcohol instead of food.

"I know, little buddy. Just give me a minute." Deeming I needed the use of both hands, I found a dishtowel near the sink, folded it to create a little cushion and placed the puppy on top, far enough back on the counter that he wouldn't fall if he decided to become a bit lively.

"Talkin' to your dick again, are ya?" a gravelly voice sounded behind me, shuffling feet approaching before I had a chance to recognize the voice.

Hawke.

He sidled up next to me and peered over my shoulder. "Well if I was, what's your excuse for trying to sneak a peek?"

"You wish." He took a step back and leaned his hip against the counter. Wearing an old KISS T-shirt and boxer shorts, Hawke looked a little worse for wear, his dark hair sticking out all over the place and a pillow line running down the entire length of his cheek.

"Rough night?" I teased, my hands busy tearing the chicken from the bone and putting aside small pieces for the pup.

"You could say that?" he gruffed, narrowing his eyes at me while he watched me destroy the food. "What are you doing? Isn't it a little early for leftovers?" Running his hand through his hair and making it worse, he pushed off the counter and grabbed some orange juice from the fridge. Chugging back a few gulps straight from the carton, he wiped his mouth afterward before putting the drink back in the fridge.

Hawke still hadn't seen the surprise visitor sitting patiently on the counter next to me. Not until he heard him whimper.

"What was that?" His confusion was comical. Looking all around the room first, he glanced up at the ceiling as if something was gonna drop down on top of us.

The puppy whimpered again. Before Hawke started shouting for me to tell him what was making the noise, scaring the dog in the process, I moved out of the way so he could see the little guy.

"Some asshole threw him out of his car while driving in front of me." I didn't have to say any more before Hawke approached the puppy with his hand out so the dog could smell him, a goofy smile appearing as he gently pet the puppy's head.

"I can't believe someone would do that. That's seriously fucked up."

"You're tellin' me."

"What are you gonna do with it?" he asked, picking him up so he could get a better look. It was then he noticed the puppy was missing one of his back legs. "What the hell?" he shouted, startling the little guy. "Did they cut it off?" He turned the creature from side to side, lifting him up to the light to see him better.

"I think he was born that way," I offered, finishing my hack job on the chicken. "Here, gimme him."

Hawke passed him to me, continuing to pet him as I fed him small pieces of chicken. He was hungry enough, biting my fingers in his eagerness to eat, his little teeth like razors. That bastard probably starved him as well, although he didn't look too gangly from what I could see.

"Are ya gonna keep him?"

"What am I gonna do with a puppy?" The thought had briefly crossed my mind on the way to the clubhouse, but then I decided against it. Puppies were a lot of work, let alone one with a disability. No, it was better if I did what I could, then passed him off to one of the no-kill shelters in the area so they could find him a permanent home with people who had the time to care for him.

"You need somethin' to go home to, man."

Ignoring his observant comment, I asked, "Speaking of, why didn't you go home last night?" I knew things had been rough between him and Edana. Ever since she'd been attacked, she'd been having some nasty nightmares, pulling away from Hawke which in turn strained their already tumultuous relationship.

"I can't help her. She doesn't wanna talk about it, and every time I even try to touch her she freaks out and starts cryin'." He ran his hands over his face. "I don't know what to do. She wants to go stay with her sister in Florida."

"Maybe it's the best thing right now," I suggested. Even as the words left my lips I knew I would've never followed my own advice if I were in his shoes. I'd be fighting to keep my woman close.

"Well, apparently I don't get a say. She's already packed a fuckin' bag." He plopped down in a nearby chair and hung his head. "I just don't know what to do," he mumbled.

I'd never seen Hawke so despondent. Normally, he was taunting the guys, crossing lines to where they'd retaliate and put him in his place. Or at least try to if Tripp wasn't there to interject.

After a few minutes of him wallowing and me feeding the rest of the scraps to the puppy, we both acknowledged our conversation was over with a simple nod, then proceeded to walk out into the common room.

Sitting on the sofa with a beer in hand and the puppy next to me, I welcomed the sweet arms of numbness. I needed one last ride to oblivion before I had to man up and deal with my shit with Braylen. I had to decide if I wanted to let her all the way in or let her go. It wasn't fair to string her along and I knew it. We'd both be worse in the end if I didn't make a decision once and for all.

CHAPTER FIFTEEN

Braylen

I SAW HIM KILL MY mom. How do I ever get over something like that? Those words kept me awake for an hour after I'd left Ryder on the couch. Who did he see? How did his mother die? What happened to the man who did it? How old was he?

I wanted so desperately to push him to tell me more, but I knew in his state he'd either refuse or ignore me completely. Much like he'd do if he was sober. The only difference between him being intoxicated or lucid, however, was that in his oblivion, he'd let something personal slip through. I wasn't even sure if he knew he'd said anything out loud.

His statement explained a lot, like the nightmares. Hell, even when he'd unknowingly attacked me in his sleep. In his dreams, was he trying to protect his mother? Had he tried when it happened for real? I was riddled with questions, but I knew enough about Ryder that no amount of persuasion would make him open up. Irritatingly, he had to come to that step all on his own; the more I pushed him, the more he'd shut down and distance himself.

———◆———

RYDER WAS GONE WHEN I woke up. I tried his cell to make sure he was okay but it went straight to voice mail. Apparently, he'd stolen Jagger's keys while he was sleeping and took off at God knew what hour of the morning. I prayed he had at least sobered up before he left.

Kena was off from work, so I gave Jagger a ride home before heading to work. He asked me to wait until one of the guys could pick him up so they could follow me to the salon, but I insisted I was fine. It was the middle of the day; what could possibly happen? He tried Ryder on his cell, and he also got his voice mail. After some reluctance, Jagger agreed to let me leave.

How gracious.

It was noon when I finally arrived, and since my first client of the day was waiting for me, I wasted no time diving right in. I could certainly use the much-needed distraction from all things Ryder.

——————◆——————

"I'M SORRY IF I CAUSED any kind of tension between you and your boyfriend," George said, flashing me an apologetic smile while I worked on his hair later that afternoon.

"He's not my boyfriend," I blurted, slamming my mouth closed as soon as I'd spoken. It was the truth, but George didn't need to know anything more about my personal business.

"Oh, I thought—"

"It's complicated." I kept my eyes down, pretending I was focusing on what I was doing, but the truth was I didn't want to talk about Ryder with him. Or anyone for that matter. The topic only served to upset me.

"If you ever want to uncomplicate things, just let me know. I'll be the first in line to take you out." He chuckled, trying his best to lighten the mood. Too bad for him mine was already soured.

Five minutes later I was done. He came in so often it didn't take long to shape up his hair. "All finished," I announced, unsnapping the cape from behind his neck. "Did you want to make an appointment for next time or just call?"

"Just book me in two weeks."

I should've known.

"Sure thing." After he paid and left me a large tip as usual, Sia strolled out from the office, looking exhausted and a little unwell.

"Are you feeling okay?" She'd changed her hair from pink to light purple, and I swore she was one of the few women who could pull off the look.

"My stomach's a little upset. I think I may be coming down with something. Do you mind closing up for me?"

"Not at all. Tammy and Michelle left already, and I don't have any more clients. Do you mind if I finish what I'm doing, then close up early?" *Please say yes.* The last thing I wanted to do was wait around for another hour just in case someone decided to pop in.

"Of course," Sia agreed. She slung her purse over her shoulder, gave me a weakened smile and walked out to her car.

Music was what I needed in order to make the mundane task of sweeping not so bad, so I flicked the switch for the sound system and got to work. Both Tammy and Michelle were great stylists, but when they were done for the day, they were done. Which meant that sometimes they didn't sweep up their stations or put their used towels in the back room to be washed. And since I told my friend I would close up, I wanted to ensure the salon looked its best when opened the following day.

Ten minutes into my task, I heard the bell over the door ring, alerting me that someone had walked in. "I'm sorry but we're closing early for the evening," I called out over my shoulder.

No answer.

Silence.

And the door's bell didn't ring again, indicating the person had left.

Maybe they didn't hear me over the music, although I'd kept it a reasonable level. Resting the broom against one of the stations, I slowly turned around, goose bumps prickling my skin with the oddest sensation of unease. I wasn't even fully facing the person before his hands were around my throat, my eyes popping wide in fear as he backed me against the nearest wall.

Looking into the face of a complete stranger, one who was intent on doing me harm, was the scariest thing I'd ever encountered.

Terror raced through every cell.

My lungs seized.

My heart raced.

My vision tunneled.

My body went on lockdown, all of my senses heightened in fear.

I had no idea who the man was or what he wanted. Well, I could guess what he wanted, but I hoped he was just there to rob the place. Maybe he was a drug addict looking for his next fix. Or maybe he was looking to do something a bit more sinister.

He was tall and lanky, but there was no doubt he was strong, his grip on my throat rendering me powerless. My fingers scratched at his hands but it only served to anger him more than he already was, so I dropped them to my sides, hoping and praying he'd let me go soon.

Looking at him was painful, and would no doubt give me nightmares for years to come, but I wanted to be able to describe him in case I made it out of there alive. Eyes the color of coal peered back at me while I struggled to breathe. His shoulder-length hair was light brown, but there were streaks of gray running through it. Scars riddled his face, one in particular standing out amongst the others—a long-since healed, jagged mutilation ran from the corner of his mouth all the way up to his hairline.

"You sure are a pretty one, aren't ya?" he asked, leaning closer and inhaling the air around me. His breath smelled like garlic and smoke, one whiff of it enough to make me wanna pass out. "I think maybe I'll take ya for a test drive as well." I wanted to shout, 'As well as what?' but obviously I couldn't.

Cocking his head ever so slightly, a menacing grin spread across his mouth, warning me something bad was about to happen. When his free hand shot out and seized my breast, I found my strength to struggle once more. If he was going to rape me, then I'd give him the fight of his life. Tightening his grip around my neck, he kicked my legs apart before lowering his hand to cup me between my thighs.

"You're gonna like what I do to you, bitch. So much you're gonna go runnin' back to your boyfriend to tell him what a real man feels like inside your cunt." Spittle hit my cheek as he tried to unbutton my jeans. I rocked my hips from side to side to try and escape his touch, but he was just too strong. "After I've had my fill of you, I'm gonna sample your little sister. Don't think that fighter is gonna stop me," he blurted, laughing when he saw the pure horror light up my face.

All of a sudden I didn't care what he did to me, as long as he didn't touch Kena. How did he even know about her, or me for that matter?

As he unzipped my jeans, the bell over the door sounded once more. It was then I mentally berated myself for not calling Ryder to see if he was going to meet me there to follow me home. I'd been so stubborn about him being my shadow that I'd inadvertently put myself in danger.

"We have to go," another stranger shouted. I couldn't see who it was because the man throttling me blocked my view of the front door.

"We have time," my attacker said, pulling the waistband away from my jeans, his fingers fumbling with the material of my panties. I closed my eyes and tried to imagine I was somewhere else, but it didn't work. I felt every callus on his fingers, smelled his breath as it hit my face and heard his breathing increase as he scraped his rough hand over my shivered skin.

"No we don't," the other guy warned, a touch of panic in his voice as he stood guard, openly allowing his friend to assault me. "We gotta get outta here before he shows up. You know he's coming."

Is he talking about Ryder?

Pulling his hand free from my jeans, thankfully not touching my most private of areas, he smirked before releasing me. My hands instantly shielded my neck, flinching at the already forming bruises.

Taking a step back, he spat, "Fuckin' Knights. They took out our prez, and now we'll stop at nothing until we wipe out every last one of 'em."

Without another word, the evil bastard spun around and walked out of the salon as calm as could be. His partner in crime had already disappeared before I could get a good look at him, but I figured none of it mattered. All that was important was making sure that Kena was safe.

After my initial shock finally wore off, I grabbed my phone from the counter and texted my sister. No response. I sent her another message. Then another, and another. Still nothing. Before leaving the salon, I made sure the coast was clear, locking up before racing toward my car. I dialed Jagger's number, but it only went to voice mail after a few rings. Leaving him a rushed message to call me back right away, I hung up and tried to call Ryder, but he wasn't answering either.

What the hell?

Why isn't anyone answering their phones?

Thankfully we lived close, but that didn't stop me from speeding home so fast I swore I broke every traffic law. I barely put the car in Park and shut off the engine before I was racing toward the front of our house, keys in hand and fumbling with the lock before practically kicking open the door.

"Kena!" I shouted, running from room to room searching for her. But she wasn't home. I tried texting her again, but again she didn't respond. I called Jagger but still nothing.

Frustration fueled my emotions, switching from shock and fear for what I'd been through to an unbearable need to protect my sister from the man who'd attacked me.

Barreling out of the house, I jumped back in my car and took off toward Ryder's, trying him again as well. When my calls continued to go unanswered, I tossed my cell on the passenger seat and concentrated on getting to Ryder's as fast as possible.

As it turned out, he wasn't home either. Slumping down on his front porch steps, I cradled my head in my hands and finally allowed myself to release what I'd been feeling as soon as that bastard had left the salon. Tears rushed down my cheeks, the adrenaline of trying to find Kena finally wearing off. My body trembled until I expelled every last bit of anxiety swirling inside me. Minutes later, I gathered myself, wiped away the rest of my tears and headed back toward my car.

There was only one other place I could check. I just hoped I remembered how to get there.

CHAPTER
SIXTEEN

Ryder

STONE AND HIS WOMAN STOPPED by to talk to Marek before heading out to shop for more baby stuff. Adelaide was just over four months pregnant, and the bigger she got, the more Stone had a permanent look of worry imprinted on his face. The last time she found out she was pregnant, she also found out she had ovarian cancer, and while she was now in remission, the fear was there that the disease could always return.

The club's VP cradled his daughter, Riley, close to his chest when they'd approached and saw that there was a ball of fur on my lap, resting peacefully from a very trying and dramatic day. I'd told them both all about what had happened, and that was when Adelaide recommended Dr. Rubin. Of course, she fussed over the little guy, petting him and then stealing him from me, showing him to Riley before finally handing him back a few minutes later.

Luckily, the vet's office was able to take me on short notice, especially after I gave them a rundown of what had happened. The doctor confirmed the puppy was in good health, and a purebred to boot. A border collie. He also placed him at around six weeks, exactly what I'd guessed.

I had just been coming back from the bathroom, Hawke watching over the dog in my absence, when I heard a commotion outside. Before any of us could find out what it was, the door burst open and in ran Braylen, her blonde hair wild and matching the look in her eyes.

Terror.

Rushing forward, I reached her in no time, my eyes landing on her neck, the skin discolored from forming bruises.

"What happened?" I yelled, gently touching her throat. She flinched, which only served to infuriate me. Not at her but at whoever dared to put their hands on her. Every passing second restricted my breathing, a fierceness racing through my veins the likes of which I hadn't felt in a very long time. "Who did this?"

"I don't know," she confessed. Braylen looked around the room before giving me her attention. "Where's Kena?"

"I have no idea. She's probably with Jagger."

"Where is he?" She was frantic.

I shook my head, looking to Stone before turning toward Marek, who'd been hanging out in the doorway of Chambers.

"Anyone know where the hell Jagger's at?" I asked.

"I'll call him," Marek offered, reaching for his phone and dialing Jagger's number right away. After the third try, he'd finally gotten through. "Where you at?" Seconds of silence. "Is Kena with you? Then get to the clubhouse ASAP." Another second of silence. "Now, and make sure to keep an eye out on the way here." Our prez tossed his phone on the table next to him and said, "They're on their way."

I saw Braylen relax a little, but she was still freaked out, and I couldn't blame her. "Tell me exactly what happened," I coaxed, guiding her to the couch to take a seat. I kicked Hawke's leg for him to move and he got up, walking over to the bar without complaint. Crouching in front of her, I hooked my fingers under her chin and raised her head. She flinched but then steadied herself as soon as she looked at me.

"Sorry," she whispered, a lone tear coating her cheek. Wiping it away, she began telling me, and everyone standing around us, what happened to her. "I was closing up early at the salon when a guy came in. I didn't see him at first because my back was to him, and by the time I turned around, it was too late."

I couldn't help it. My anger bubbled forth before I could halt it. "Why were you there by yourself, and why didn't you lock the door?"

"Ryder," Adelaide warned, frowning at my brief snap of interrogation. "Stop." Her voice was softer on her last command.

Taking a breath, I nodded at Braylen, silently asking her to continue.

"He wrapped his hands around my throat and pushed me against the
wall. And then when he tried to take off my jeans . . . I really thought. . . ."
Her gaze drifted away as if lost to the horrific ordeal all over again.

"Fuck," I growled, my hands instantly curling into tight fists. My
outburst threw her back into the moment. She fiddled with the bottom
of her shirt, not quite knowing what to do with herself. When another
tear appeared, I placed my hands over hers and tried to soothe her, letting
her know I was there and no one was gonna hurt her.

"What did he look like?" Stone asked, approaching from the side.
"Did he say anything specific?"

"Back up," I warned, throwing him a threatening look before hoisting myself off my haunches and taking the seat directly next to Braylen.

"We need to know, Ryder," Stone rasped, taking a step back when
he saw I was about to lose my shit. Adelaide placed her hand on Stone's
arm and gently shook her head as if to tell him to wait.

Braylen started speaking, answering Stone's questions before I could
ask her anything of my own. "He was tall and skinny, shoulder-length
gray-brown hair with facial scars. One long nasty one from here to here,"
she said, running her finger from her mouth to her forehead. She took a
moment before continuing, glancing from each person present to the next
before opening her mouth again. "He said something about you taking
out their president, so now they're gonna wipe out every last one of you."

Shivers racked her body, but when I slung my arm over her, offering
her comfort and protection, she leaned into me. I was wrought with guilt
from not protecting her from that asshole, but I sure as hell wouldn't make
that mistake again. "Oh, and there was another guy with him, standing
by the door." Turning to face me, she uttered, "They know all about me
and you . . . and Kena. How do they about my sister?" Her voice became
panicked, and streams of tears began to fall again.

I pulled her close and kissed her temple over and over. "It's okay. No
one is gonna hurt you or your sister. I promise." I heard some of the guys

mumbling something to each other, but I wasn't about to leave Braylen's side to find out what. Not right then.

Ten minutes later, Jagger and Kena finally arrived at the club, rushing through the door because they knew Marek had meant business when he called.

"What's going on," Jagger asked, looking all around and waiting for someone to fill him in.

"Braylen was attacked," Adelaide blurted, looking at Kena specifically when she said it.

Right away, Kena raced forward and sat on the other side of her sister. *Are you okay? What happened?* She didn't even wait for Braylen to answer before she was hugging her so tightly I thought they'd never separate. But they finally did.

"I'm fine now. I'm just worried about you," she confessed, pulling Kena in for another hug. When they finally broke apart for the second time, Braylen looked up at Jagger. "Please make sure you don't let anything happen to her. Stay glued to her side if you have to. Please, Jagger," she begged, more tears welling in her eyes as she pleaded with him to keep her little sister safe.

"You have my word. Nothing will ever happen to her."

In reality, none of us could keep our women safe, not 100 percent, no matter how much we wanted. Not unless we had a . . .

"We need to go on lockdown, Prez," I yelled, standing and walking toward him with purpose. "Enough is enough. We need to find out who the fuck keeps threatening us."

"We know who keeps doing it," Hawke said, walking right up to us. "And the bastard Braylen described sounds exactly like one of the guys who attacked Edana." His posture went rigid, the look in his eyes one of determination. "Do you know how lucky your woman is, Ryder?"

I did, but I wanted to be sure Braylen wasn't leaving anything out, no matter how difficult it was to tell me. Spinning around, I was back next to her in three long strides. "Did anything else happen? Did he . . . ?" She knew what I meant and shook her head. "You can tell me." Even as I said the words, I had no idea what I'd do if I found out she'd suffered the same fate as Edana.

"No, nothing like that."

I thought someone was gonna put up a fight about my demand for a lockdown, but all of my brothers simply nodded.

"Okay," Marek agreed. "We go on lockdown till we can find 'em."

I should've been relieved. I should've been happy that Braylen would be at the clubhouse safe and sound, but I wasn't. Not entirely. Yes, she would be safe under our constant watch, but because we had to go in search of the bastards threatening our club, and our families, we were sure to get bloody.

CHAPTER
SEVENTEEN

Braylen

RYDER EXPLAINED WHAT A LOCKDOWN meant, and while my initial reaction would've been to reject such a thing, I was only too happy to stay at the club until they sorted everything out. "Eliminated the threat," as Jagger so casually stated. I wasn't sure what that meant exactly, and I didn't think I wanted to.

The guys had taken Kena and me back to our place to pack a bag, enough for a week's stay. They said it shouldn't take any longer than that. Once back at the club, Ryder showed me to his room, placing my bag on the chair and pulling me in for a hug. I knew he was upset about what happened to me, but the one good thing that came out of it was that he seemed to be showing more of an affectionate side. A more tender side, to be more precise. Maybe it took an incident so drastic to finally make him realize that his feelings toward me might be more than what he wanted to let on.

No matter how tired I was, I just couldn't fall asleep. Ryder told me that he had to leave for a bit but would be back as soon as he could. He wouldn't tell me where he was going, other than that it was club business, but he assured me he wouldn't be in any danger. I wasn't so sure I believed him.

After another half hour of restlessness, I gave up, pushed off the covers and left his room, walking toward the front part of the club where a few of the members were still gathered, straddling the barstools and throwing back shot after shot.

It was close to eleven at night, and I had a feeling these guys were just starting their evening. Kena and Jagger weren't present, so I assumed they were in his room. My anxiety had started to come back, thinking about my sister being in danger, when Sully came striding out from the kitchen. I hadn't seen her in some time, and she was certainly welcome company.

"Hey, Braylen," she greeted. "How are you holding up?" Ryder had told me a few things about Sully's past, and I thought she was the bravest woman I knew. Surely the club's lockdown was nothing compared to what she'd been through.

"I'm all right, I suppose. Just worried, ya know?"

She gestured toward the couch, and I followed, sitting next to her and smiling at her genuine kindness.

"Try not to fret too much. The men will handle it." She sounded so sure. "They'll die before they let anything happen to us."

"That's what I'm afraid of," I whispered.

"Sorry, I probably shouldn't have put it like that." Sully shot me an apologetic smile, patting my hand before leaning back against the sofa. Her dark eyes roamed over the space of the common area, smiling while watching the mundane task of men drinking and talking. Looking back toward me, she said, "You probably think I'm crazy for smiling, but I'm still getting used to this life."

"But I thought you've been with them for quite some time now."

"I have, and while it was a little bumpy in the beginning between Cole and me, the entire club has always treated me well. I constantly waited for the other shoe to drop, but it never did. Not with them." Her smile was infectious, and I soon find myself mirroring her expression. "So tell me, how are things with you and Ryder?"

"Bumpy." We both chuckled at my word choice, but it fit perfectly. I caught glimpses of another side of Ryder, but just when I thought he'd show me more, he'd throw those walls back up. It was frustrating, to say the least.

"Give him time. He cares about you. A lot. He tries to hide it but I see it, and so does everyone else." Her words gave me comfort, something I very much needed after the day I'd had. Twisting her black hair up into a messy bun on top of her head, she threw her arms over her head and stretched, a yawn coming out of nowhere. "Oh my God, I'm so sorry. It's not you, I promise." She chuckled. "It's just that I haven't been getting much sleep lately.

"Because of everything with the club?"

"No. Sadly I'm used to that. It's because of Kaden."

"Who?" I didn't remember Ryder mentioning anyone named Kaden.

"The little boy Cole and I have been caring for. Tripp's ex dropped him off out of the blue, claiming he was his when in fact he wasn't. When she didn't get what she wanted from Tripp—although who knows what that even was—she took off and left her baby here. He hasn't been able to locate her as of yet." A mixed look of hope and sorrow took over Sully's expression, and I couldn't help but feel bad for her.

"So he's been keeping you up late?" I wanted to take her mind off whatever plagued her, and the mere mention of the baby had her smiling once again.

"Yes, but I'm not complaining. I've always wanted children. I know he's not really mine, but I can't help feeling an attachment to him. It's one of the reasons Cole was hesitant to take him while Tripp searched for his ex. He knew how hard it would be for me to give him back when he finds her." She let out a hefty sigh. "But I can't think of that right now, can I?" Her question was rhetorical. A brief moment of silence lingered between us before she asked, "Do you want kids someday?"

"Do I want kids?" I repeated. "Well, it's not like I've never thought about it, but I guess I just never settled on an answer. I guess . . . I don't know. With the right guy, I suppose I'd be open to the idea."

She bumped my shoulder with hers. "Could that be Ryder?" She wiggled her brows and I laughed.

"I'm not sure." *Better to be neutral, right?*

"I wonder if he wants any more. Then again, I doubted Cole would come around to the idea of Kaden, but when I see him with the little boy now, my heart swells. He's fallen in love with him as much as I have."

I stopped listening after she uttered the first sentence.

"Wait. Go back. What did you mean by 'any *more*'? Does Ryder have kids?" My voice rose higher than intended, drawing the attention of Hawke, who was busy drinking at the bar.

Sully's eyes widened before she mumbled, "Shit." Turning fully toward me, she continued with, "Sorry, Braylen. I thought you knew. He has a daughter. I think she's around ten."

Tears of anger flooded my vision, but I refused to cry. Pulling in a deep breath, I exhaled before speaking again. "No. I didn't know. I guess he didn't want to share that with me." What did that say about his feelings toward me, that he wouldn't tell me he had a child? Just when I thought he might be coming around to the idea of us being more than a casual thing—in his eyes, at least—he abolished all of those crazy notions with his secret. One of many, apparently.

"I'm so sorry. Truly. Maybe he just wanted to make sure you were it for him before he told you?" I knew Sully was only trying to help, but she was inadvertently making it worse.

I rose from the couch while trying to keep my composure, and it was at that exact moment that Ryder walked through the door, amused at something Stone had said.

His eyes instantly found mine. He muttered something to the club's VP before advancing toward me, but when he saw the irate and hurt look on my face, he stopped midstride.

"Braylen?"

"Don't come near me," I shouted. I hadn't meant to cause a scene, but my temper escaped before I could rein it in. I clamped my mouth shut before hurrying off toward the back of the club, heading straight for his room. I prayed there was a lock on the door; otherwise, I couldn't be held accountable for my actions if he came after me.

I heard Sully apologizing to him as I slammed the bedroom door with such ferocity I swore it shook the entire clubhouse.

CHAPTER
EIGHTEEN

Ryder

"GODDAMNIT, SULLY. WHAT WERE YOU thinking?" I paced back and forth. "This is why I keep my shit private," I gritted, flashing everyone a pissed-off look even though I knew none of them deserved it. This was all on me.

"You better watch how you're talkin' to my wife," Marek growled, appearing out of nowhere. "It's not her fault you didn't tell Braylen about your kid."

Not acknowledging him or his truthful spewing, I hauled off toward the back of the club, knowing damn well I was the last person Braylen wanted to see. I had to deal with the issue before it escalated. Part of me wanted to leave it alone and get drunk, but the other part, the one that had developed feelings for the feisty woman, wanted to apologize and see if I could make things right between us. We'd been at odds for weeks, and I wanted the stress to stop. I had enough on my mind with the threat against the club; I needed to check her forgiveness off the ever-growing list.

Without knocking, I flung open the door to my assigned room and found her. She was sitting on the edge of the bed, the bag she'd packed resting on her lap.

"Where do you think you're going?" I hadn't meant to sound so gruff, but there was no way in hell she was leaving. Not until we'd eliminated the threat, which could take days.

"I'm not staying here."

"You're not leaving."

She raised her head and glared at me. Clutching her bag tightly, she said, "You can't keep me here against my will. That's called kidnapping, Ryder. Look it up."

"Well, then I'll kidnap you if I have to. You're not going anywhere." She parted her lips to respond, but I took a step closer and cut her off. "I know you're aware of the threat against us, and unfortunately that threat extends to you and your sister." Underhanded move, but I had to use it. Her breath hitched. "So until we can take care of it, no one is allowed to leave."

"You can leave." It wasn't a question.

"I have to help keep us safe, so yeah, I do get to leave."

"That's not fair," she mumbled, fidgeting with her bag again before standing and walking across the room, farther away from me. I didn't know if she thought by releasing the bag she was surrendering to her fate for the next few days, but she refused to let it go. "I want to be alone. You need to leave."

"No." I braced myself for impact. She'd been through a lot; surely all of her fear, anger, and uncertainty was gonna come bursting from her in the next few seconds.

"No?" she yelled, her mouth agape in astonishment. I wasn't goin' anywhere, not until I convinced her she was safe with us at the club. Not until I gained her forgiveness for not telling her about my daughter. Not until . . . fuck! I didn't know what else I wanted from Braylen, but it sure as hell wasn't for her to be standing so far away from me, looking at me like she didn't know who the fuck I was. Admittedly, I had a lot of demons, personal and shared with the other men of the Knights, but I was just me. A man fumbling through life trying to find some goddamn meaning.

Braylen was the sliver of light in an otherwise dark and lonely world. I'd always had an inferno burning inside me my entire life, and the woman standing in front of me was the first person to ever calm me. I couldn't explain it—I just knew she was it for me. I just had to convince her that

I wanted her once and for all.

No more mixed signals.

No more thoughtless words.

No more secrets.

"Braylen," I said softly, relaxing my tensed muscles before erasing some of the distance between us. "I need you to listen to me."

"Listen to you? Why? Because you wanna lie some more?" Before I saw it coming, she launched her bag at me, hitting me in the chest and knocking me back a step. "Oh, sorry," she spat sarcastically. "Not lie. Just omit everything!" Her voice rose a few octaves. If I didn't calm her down, and fast, I knew our business was gonna be made public for the entire club to hear.

"Calm down."

"No, I won't calm down. You won't share any of yourself with me. You refused to tell me why you attacked me in your sleep, and then you kept something as huge as having a child from me." She backed up a step. "Do you know how that makes me feel? I know I may appear strong and brave, but I'm hurt." Her bottom lip quivered, and it almost gutted me. "You hurt me," she said softly. "You've basically told me that I mean nothing to you. That I'm just someone to pass the time with when you're bored. Someone to have sex with when you're horny." A lone tear fell and she wiped it away with an irritated swipe of her finger.

"You know that's not true."

"No, I don't."

"Yes, you do." I took a tentative step closer.

"Don't" was all she said before lowering her head, breaking eye contact with me and essentially giving up.

"Braylen."

Nothing. Not a single muscle moved in her body. I swore she held her breath as well.

"Braylen," I said with more authority, hoping she'd hear something in my tone that would make her look at me.

Still nothing.

"Goddamnit, Braylen! Fuckin' look at me." Apparently when I shouted it worked.

She finally picked her head up, her stare cutting into me like a thousand knives. More tears streaked her cheeks, and I couldn't stop myself. I rushed forward and pulled her into me before she could stop me, wrapping my arms around her so tightly I feared I'd bruise her ribs.

"Just let me go," she cried, feebly trying to push me away, but I refused.

"I can't." She trembled in my arms. "I'll tell you anything you want to know," I promised, kissing the top of her head, continuing to crush her distraught body to mine. "No more secrets."

It was in that moment that I fully let go, relieved I could finally share myself completely with someone. A ton of bricks dropped from me as I felt her nod against my chest.

Here goes nothin'.

CHAPTER NINETEEN

Braylen

I SAT ON THE EDGE of the bed while Ryder pulled up a chair so he could sit in front of me. Hesitancy stroked the air around him but he pushed on, taking a deep breath before he started to talk.

"You heard what I said back at your place, didn't you?" His brown eyes bored into mine, searching for something I was unclear of in that moment. "Before you left me on the couch?"

I wanted him to be truthful with me, so I made sure to return the favor. "Yes." Short and simple, yet it was anything but. Even though I had an idea he knew what my answer would be, he still looked a little shocked. He quickly regained his composure, wasting no more time before he told me what happened to his mother.

"Richard came into our lives when I was just five. From what I could remember he seemed okay, bringing me a toy whenever he visited, but it wasn't long after they met that he moved in with us. And that's when things changed. Most of my memories of him after that point are of him being drunk, and when he'd been drinking, he'd whale on my mother. When I tried to help her, I got it too."

I reached forward and captured his hands, offering him support while he worked up to the worst part. Even though I was still hurt, and angry with him, I knew I had to put all of my emotions aside and allow Ryder to tell me his story.

Breathless moments passed where the both of us remained silent, him working up the courage to tell me the reason he seemed so closed off and secretive, and me silently contemplating if I had the energy to forge ahead with a relationship with the very intense and complicated man sitting in front of me.

He loosened his hands from mine and pulled back, running them down his thighs in uncertainty. "One night it got really bad. I woke up to her screaming, and when I ran downstairs, I saw her on the ground, bleeding and clutching her stomach. I tried to save her, but I couldn't. She begged me to go back to my room and I did." He rose from the chair so fast it skidded behind him. "Fuck!" His fingers gripped his hair and I watched him slowly losing it. "If only I hadn't gone down there that night, maybe she'd still be alive."

"What do you mean? You just said he was beating her."

"He was, but when I tried to help her, he came after me. Came up to my room and tried to—" He suddenly stopped talking, and I knew reliving his past tore him up inside. So I waited, giving him the time he needed before finishing. "Looking back, I think he was gonna rape me, and when my mother saw his pants unzipped, pinning me facedown, she screamed for him to leave me alone. That's when he wrapped his belt around her neck and strangled her to death."

A shocked gasp escaped me. I couldn't stop it. Ryder muttering "I saw him kill my mom" when he was drunk did nothing to prepare me for the full story. I couldn't even imagine what he went through, watching his mother's life extinguished right in front of him.

"You were only trying to protect her. It's not your fault. The only one to blame is him. Only him," I repeated, hoping my words would break his irrational thought. I stood and tentatively approached him, his back to me as I walked up behind him. Resting my hand on the middle of his back, he flinched but then quickly relaxed.

Turning to face me, he looked emotionally beaten down. I knew it had been difficult, but I was thankful he'd finally told me, even after everything that'd happened between us.

"I wasn't sure I wanted you in my life," he announced. "Not permanently. After my mother's death, I closed myself off from everyone, only giving people the bare minimum. I think that's why I kept putting off telling you about my daughter."

His confession hurt, but at least now I understood him a little more. "And now?"

He seized my hands and placed them on his chest. "Now I can't imagine my life without you. I can't explain the pull you have over me, but I know I don't want to lose you. Ever." He circled his arm around my waist and drew me forward. "Please forgive me for not telling you sooner."

I looked deep into his eyes, drew his undivided attention because I needed him to really hear me. "I need some time to think about . . . us."

His arm fell to his side and he took a step back, my hand sliding off his chest. Ryder looked distraught, but for as much as I wanted to wipe away his sadness, I needed to make sure forging ahead with him was what I truly wanted.

I completely understood what he meant by the pull that existed between us because I felt it as well. Attraction, chemistry and raw passion certainly weren't an issue either. But could I trust him? Not only to continue to share himself with me, but with my heart?

I was in love with Ryder, but was it enough?

"Okay. Fair enough." He strode toward the door, but I didn't want him to leave just yet. So I decided to change the subject.

"Was there a puppy out there?" My question told him I was open to talking about something other than us, that I wanted to engage him while still taking the time I needed to process everything.

"Yeah," he answered over his shoulder, his hand gripping the door handle. "Come on, let's go see him."

———————•———————

"WHAT ARE YOU GONNA NAME him?" I asked, accepting all of the puppy's kisses and trying not to smother him because he was so damn cute. Ryder told me how he found him, and while my heart broke for the little guy, I wanted to find the asshole who discarded him so carelessly and beat the hell out of him myself.

"I'm not."

"Why?"

"'Cause I'm not keepin' him." I looked at him like he was nuts, to which he said, "Bray, I can't have a puppy. You know how much work they are?"

"And? What's your point?" I passed the dog to Ryder, and without an ounce of hesitation, he took him, clutching him close to his chest. "You've already formed a bond with him. Don't give him away."

He didn't answer because he knew what I said was true.

"I'll take him," Hawke yelled from across the room. "He's a cute little fucker." He laughed when Ryder turned around and gave him a threatening glance.

"See. You don't wanna give him to anyone."

"No, I just don't want to give him to that jackass."

"I heard that," Hawke shouted before finishing off his drink.

"Good," Ryder replied, a small smirk appearing on his gorgeous face. Looking back at me, he shrugged. "You're right. Even though it's only been a day, I'm already attached to him, but I don't think I'm up for the commitment."

"What if I help you?" I offered, surprised the words came out so freely. *So much for needing time to think about us.*

"I thought you said you needed time to think about whether or not you wanted to be with me." His voice lowered as he spoke, and I knew it was because he wanted to keep our conversation as private as possible.

"We still have a lot to work through. Namely you telling me all about your daughter—the full story—but I'm not going anywhere, Ryder." I smiled and snatched the puppy from him, kissing his furry little head before walking toward the exit to take him outside. Ryder jogged until he caught up with me, smacking me on the ass as he ushered me forward.

CHAPTER TWENTY

Ryder

SIX DAYS THE LOCKDOWN LASTED.

Six days of knowing Braylen was safe.

Six days of not knowing if or when we'd ever catch the break we needed to finally move forward and put a plan in place to end the war between us and the Reapers once and for all.

"We got a hit," Marek shouted as soon as he walked into the clubhouse. "Chambers. Now." He strode into our meeting room and everyone present followed after him. The only ones missing were Stone and Breck. I knew our VP was in his room with Adelaide, and while I didn't have to guess what they were doing, it was gonna have to be cut short because we had an impromptu meeting.

After making sure Braylen was still asleep in my room, I rapped on Stone's door.

"Go away," he barked, grunting incoherently while I continued to bang on the door. I really didn't need to hear them goin' at it, but I had no other choice. His presence was needed, and I wouldn't walk away until he answered.

"Stone. Let's go."

"What the fuck?" I heard his heavy footsteps right before he yanked open the door, looking at me like he wanted to kill me. I could see Adelaide in the background, lying on the bed with tousled hair and the bedsheet pulled up to her neck. She was laughing, which only served to make me smile. "You better have a good reason, brother."

"Marek wants everyone in Chambers. Now. Then you can go back to trying to satisfy your woman." I moved back as he swung at me, practically tripping because he was using the door to shield his dick from view. "Let's go, lover boy," I shouted over my shoulder as I disappeared down the hallway.

Walking into Chambers, I could feel the tension and worry pouring off every member. We probably all had the same question popping around inside our heads: *When the hell will all this end?* Unfortunately, there was gonna be more bloodshed before it was all said and done.

Once Stone joined us, throwing me another annoyed look to which I just smiled, Marek grabbed everyone's attention when he started to speak.

"I just got a call that a guy fitting the description of the one who attacked Braylen was spotted going into the Overbrook. He's not alone, though. Two other guys are with him." The Overbrook was a low-class stripper joint close to forty minutes away, a place we knew most of the Savage Reapers visited.

"Who called you?" Jagger asked, looking around the room and seeing everyone present except one man. "Breck?"

"Yeah," Marek affirmed.

"So what now?" Cutter asked, his stare darkening and looking none too pleased that his son was close to the enemy without any backup. "Are we goin' to get 'em? Just give me five minutes and they'll spill their guts, literally and figuratively."

Cutter wasn't shy about torturing when the situation called for it, but I'd have to intercede on this one, for at least one of the Reapers. The fucker who dared to put his hands on Braylen was gonna die a slow and painful death, whether or not he gave us pertinent information on his club. His fate would be sealed as soon as we captured him.

"I know our club has been through a lot over the past year or so, and normally I'd tell ya to be patient. That the time to react should be planned out." Marek slapped the table. "But fuck that!"

A few of the guys shouted, "Yeah!" while the rest of us just nodded. Of course, we'd follow whatever our prez said, but we couldn't hide our excitement that we'd be able to do something about our predicament sooner rather than later.

Marek doled out instructions like he always did, forever the leader. "Jagger, Tripp, and Cutter, you're goin' to meet Breck. Call him to find out exactly where he is. You know enough to stay in the background, showing yourselves only when necessary." He withdrew a plastic baggie from inside his cut, tossing the package on the table and sliding it toward where they sat. Trackers. "Put these on any of their bikes you see." The devices were small, would be virtually undetectable by the human eye, but for as high tech as they would undoubtedly be, they would only last two weeks. Three, tops.

The Reapers thought they were safe visiting the Overbrook, no doubt meeting whoever for deals as well as harassing the strippers. We'd never stepped foot there before, but we were always aware of their comings and goings throughout the years. We were just waiting for the perfect opportunity.

Looks like it's here.

"I want in on this one, Prez," I said, leaning forward and placing my hands on the table.

"And you will be. At the safe house, when they bring those bastards there. Take Hawke with you."

"What do you want me to do?" Trigger asked, intent on receiving his orders.

"You're gonna stay back with Stone and me."

Trigger gave a curt nod, the relief on his face that he'd be able to stay behind to watch over his pregnant niece more comforting to him than retaliating against our enemy. I couldn't say I blamed him. If I weren't so focused on making the scarred Reaper pay for what he did to Braylen, I'd be completely okay with staying back at the clubhouse with her.

"Anything else?" Marek looked to each man, giving us the opportunity to say whatever was on our minds. We only shared in the taste for revenge, so there was nothing but silence and anticipation swirling all around us, thick and heavy.

The gavel struck the wood with a thunderous sound, vibrating through the air and amping us up for what was gonna happen soon enough.

CHAPTER
TWENTY-ONE

Braylen

I WOKE TO THE MATTRESS dipping beside me. Brief panic enveloped me until I realized it was Ryder. I felt safe whenever he was close, which was quite the conundrum since it was because of him that I'd been attacked and was now involved in his club's lockdown, essentially trapping me inside their clubhouse until they deemed otherwise.

"Sorry, babe. Didn't mean to scare you." I loved when he used terms of endearment. I knew it was corny, but they made me feel like he was truly mine.

"It's okay. Are you coming to bed?" I turned to face him, conscious of the puppy lying close to me, one eye open to see what all the noise was about.

"Not yet. I have to leave, but I'll be back. I promise." Even though he tried to mask it, I heard the worry in his voice. Ryder was a tough-looking man, had the personality to match, but there were times, like right then, when he was simply a human being. A flawed, unsure, slightly nervous person. It was his flaws that kept me interested in knowing the whole man. If that made any sense, because it sure as hell didn't to me most days.

"Where are you going? I thought the club was on lockdown." I was confused, and from the look on his face, I soon became alarmed. More for him than myself.

"Marek, Stone, and Trigger will be here to watch over you all. The rest of us are leaving. We have business to take care of. When it's done, we'll be back."

"But I don't want you to go." Sitting up, I moved the puppy to the other side of the bed so I could be closer to Ryder, wrapping my arms around his neck and pulling him to me. "Please don't go," I pleaded, having a bad feeling something was going to go terribly wrong. Having no idea where they were even headed off to, I still knew in my gut it wasn't a good thing.

"If I could stay here with you, I would, but I can't." Tension laced his words, but rather than argue with him, which was what I would have done before, I gave him what he needed—my acceptance of the situation. Besides, there wasn't anything I could do to change his mind. I knew when it came to his club, he would do what he needed to, come hell or high water.

He gave me a quick kiss, unhooked my hands clasped behind his neck and stood up. "Make sure to take care of Brutus."

"Who?"

"Brutus," he repeated, pointing toward the bundle of fur drifting in and out of sleep next to me.

"I thought you weren't gonna name him. Does this mean you're definitely keeping him?" With everything going on, I still couldn't hide my smile. I considered it a small win.

"Yeah, so make sure you watch over him." Ryder grabbed a few things from the dresser and tucked something into the waistband of his jeans before stopping by the door. Without looking at me, he said, "We'll talk more when I get back."

———◆———

THE MINUTES TURNED TO HOURS and still I heard nothing from Ryder, and neither had anyone else. At least I didn't think so. I doubted Marek or Stone were going to give me a play-by-play regarding their club's business.

Adelaide and Reece carefully sat down next to me, Adelaide rubbing her belly and grimacing. "I swore I wasn't gonna let that man come near me again after I gave birth to Riley." She smiled big when Stone's eyes caught hers. "But I just can't resist his charms."

"I don't think it's his charms that got you pregnant," Reece countered. I laughed, but it felt empty.

Seeing the worry on my face, Adelaide soothed, "It's better you know this now rather than years in. The club does stuff that won't make you happy. Ryder won't be able to tell you things, and it's frustrating, but he'll do it for your own good. For your safety." She continued to rub her stomach. "Stone's always telling me that there's an end in sight, that the danger toward the Knights won't always exist, but then shit like this happens."

"What exactly *is* going on?"

"Hell if I know. Just because I'm engaged to the VP doesn't mean I'm privy to information."

"How do you deal with not knowing, always wondering if he'll come back unharmed? Or at all?" I squirmed in my seat while looking at both of them, hesitant to hear the answer.

"When he goes away and can't tell me why, I remind him why he has to come back to me. That we have a family, and that if he stupidly puts himself in danger, I'll marry Tripp."

Reece chuckled at that one, her blue-gray eyes lighting up at the mention of her man. She was aware of the special bond Adelaide and Tripp shared, and she apparently had no issue with it.

"In all seriousness, there's nothing I *can* do but wait and pray he stays safe."

"That's it?"

"I'm afraid so." She gave me a grin before getting to her feet, Stone watching her and rushing right over. I thought it was adorable how much he fussed over her.

"Damnit, woman, you need to go lie down."

"Wanna come with me? Finish where we left off before?" Marek overheard their conversation and lifted his chin toward his VP. "We have your friend's approval. Now help me back to your room."

Stone just shook his head as he picked up his fiancée, carrying her down the hallway instead of allowing her to walk.

After briefly chatting about her own pregnancy, Reece and I soon followed suit and went back to our respective rooms.

The more I slept, the sooner Ryder would come back to me.

CHAPTER
TWENTY-TWO

Ryder

MY MIND RACED WITH EVERYTHING I still wanted to tell Braylen, but I knew I had to focus on what was going to happen as soon as Breck, Jagger, Tripp and Cutter arrived. I had no doubt they'd snag the Reapers and bring them to us to be dealt with.

Hawke and I were in the basement of our club's safe house, which was only an hour away from our compound. It was located in an average-looking residential area—hiding in plain sight, so to speak.

The room was soundproof, which made it perfect to do what we needed to and remain inconspicuous with our neighbors. I was sure they often wondered about who lived there, but they never saw any of us long enough to inquire. We visited mostly at night, pulling directly into the garage and sealing out the rest of the world until our job was finished.

That night would be no different.

"I can't take this much longer," Hawke complained, pacing while driving the both of us crazy.

"If you don't stay still, I'm gonna put you on your ass, brother," I threatened, his anxiety increasing my own.

"Fuck you."

"No, thanks. I got a woman for that."

"Yeah, a woman those fuckers attacked."

He just had to go and throw that back at me, didn't he? I advanced on him, shoving him against the nearest wall, my hands clutching his cut and barely keeping him still.

"I know exactly what they did to her, one bastard in particular. Don't forget that shit." I drew my hands back but stayed planted in his personal space. "I know you want revenge for what they did to your woman. I only have a sliver of an idea of the rage flowing through your veins, but you need to rein it in. And do it before they get here. Otherwise you could do something that'll blow back on all of us."

Hawke's expression was blank, his eyes glazing over before becoming glassy. If I didn't know any better, I would've thought he was about to cry, and I knew it would have nothing to do with him being scared or sad or any of that crap. I knew it was because the fury ricocheting through him was almost too much, and his body needed some sort of release.

After several minutes of the both of us standing toe-to-toe, the silence both our friend and enemy, he gathered himself and nodded, the glassiness of his eyes disappearing as if it never existed.

My phone dinged a half hour later with a text message. Looking to Hawke, I said, "They're coming down the street now."

———— ◆ ————

I SHOULD'VE BEEN USED TO blood-curdling screams from these bastards, but I wasn't. It took me a few minutes after Cutter started in on one of the two Reapers they'd ambushed at the Overbrook to regain my steel composure. The smell of blood, piss, and vomit filled my nostrils and turned my stomach.

Breck had been keeping watch in the dark across the street from the strip joint when a man fitting the description of the one who attacked Braylen pulled up on his bike, two more of his buddies flanking him on his right side. More of them had arrived after his initial call to Marek. I was sure if anyone saw Breck, they would've thought he was some sort of creeper, hiding in the cage—aka van—with a large pair of binoculars attached to his face.

Once backup had arrived in the form of his father, Jagger and Tripp hid in the back until Breck told them their opportunity had arrived. Two stumbling Reapers appeared outside and briefly argued, their scene enough of a distraction to allow our men to swoop in and snatch them. Jagger had explained it had been easy—a few punches and both of the enemy's men had been rendered unconscious.

Now they were both strapped to chairs, their hands and feet bound so they had no chance of escape. They'd die in this basement, their bodies never to be discovered. Their disappearance from the Overbook would be speculated over, but no one would be able to prove what happened to them. Much like their president, Psych. They all figured we had something to do with him vanishing, but they had no proof.

And they never would.

The guys had put trackers on all of the Reapers' bikes sitting outside the joint. We knew their club would recover their rides and take them back to their relocated compound. The night Psych had Zip killed, kidnapping Adelaide and Kena, we'd called in reinforcements from our Laredo chapter, wiping out the Reapers' clubhouse, killing as many as we could during the battle and setting their compound ablaze.

Circling the two men, reveling in their distress, I cracked my neck from side to side, thinking about exactly what I wanted to do to them. The one with the jagged scar more than the other fucker.

"I'll tell you whatever you want to know," one of them cried. "Please just stop." Cutter had detached a few of his fingers and was preparing to take off his right thumb when he pleaded with us to cease the torture.

"Man the fuck up," Breck yelled. "You knew what you were getting into when you joined that cesspool of a club." He landed a harrowing punch straight to the guy's nose and blood spurted everywhere. "We don't need to hear anything you wanna tell us."

"The time for talkin' is over," Hawke mumbled loud enough for the two men to hear.

The crunch of bone had the man screaming once again, the look on Cutter's face stoic . . . and a bit unnerving. Once his thumb had been severed, the man passed out. It was the only time Cutter smirked.

Knowing he was up next, the man who'd attacked Braylen smiled, although there was a fleeting look of fear that passed over him as his eyes flitted to each of us. He completely ignored his buddy, instead choosing to try and intimidate us with his lack of fear. Little did he know that Hawke and I had something special planned for him.

I'd snapped pics of both of them and sent them to Marek, asking him to show them to Braylen, Adelaide, and Sully. I was still waiting for a response when Jagger spoke up.

"Listen, as much as I'd love to hang out and see these two take their last breath, I wanna get back. Do you need me for anything?"

"I think we're good," I said. "Take my bike. We're definitely gonna need the cage to get rid of 'em."

"I'm gonna go too," Tripp announced. "I need to make sure this whole thing isn't stressing Reece out too much. Don't want anything to happen to her or the baby."

"You can take my bike," Hawke said to his brother. "But if you do anything to it, I'm gonna kick your ass."

"You'd like to think you can," the nomad responded, snatching Hawke's keys midair before giving him the finger. Jagger and Tripp ascended the basement steps, leaving Cutter, Breck, Hawke and me to take care of the two Reapers. The guy who'd passed out was slowly coming to, and as soon as his eyes finally focused, his body started trembling.

"Oh for fuck's sake," Breck barked. "I can't take this guy anymore." Before any of us could stop him, he pulled his gun from his waistband, pointed it at the guy's chest and pulled the trigger. Perfect aim. Right to his heart. The man slumped over as blood coated his shirt, his cut hanging open so we could all see the fatal damage Breck had caused.

My hands flew to my ears. "Goddamnit! You could've warned us," I roared. "My fuckin' ears are ringin'" To say I was pissed was an understatement, but it wasn't me who shoved Breck. It was his father.

"What were you thinkin'?" Cutter asked.

"What's the big deal? The room is soundproof."

"Yeah, but it's not idiot-proof," Hawke retorted, wiggling his finger in his ear while throwing Breck a nasty look.

"I don't wanna be here all night," Breck continued. "We snatched these two, now let's just kill 'em. Get it over with." Tossing his gun on the metal tray in the corner, he stared at his father, then looked to Hawke and me. "What?" He threw his hands up in frustration.

"Cutter, maybe you and Breck should go. We'll take care of these two," I said, knowing damn well it was gonna come down to Hawke and me finally ending the lone Reaper's life.

A hesitant look flashed across Cutter's face.

"Are you sure?" He reached for a rag and wiped some of the blood from his hands.

"Yeah, we got it," I replied, glancing to Hawke before turning back to father and son.

"Okay. We'll see ya back at the clubhouse."

Cutter had driven his truck to meet Breck at the Overbrook, so that was what they took back with them. As soon as we heard the squeak of the garage door, Hawke and I stood in front of the Reaper, feet spread wide and our hands resting in front of us.

"Then there was one," Hawke uttered, rolling his shoulders and fisting his hands. "You know we're gonna fuck you up, don't ya?" Hawke asked, landing a punch to the Reaper's ribs, knocking the breath from him before taking a step back.

It was then my phone dinged, and I hoped and feared it was the answer I'd been waiting for. Opening the screen, I saw the reply from Marek. He said that while Adelaide and Sully didn't recognize him, Braylen did. Closing my eyes and desperately trying to gain some sort of control, I took a deep breath, but it was useless.

No words were spoken as I landed a few quick jabs to his face before turning to face Hawke. "It's him," I confirmed. "Braylen identified him from the pic I sent Marek." I knew in my gut he was also the one who'd raped Edana, the description on point from what Hawke had told me.

The next few minutes were a blur of Hawke and me going at him, one after the other, until he was covered in blood and air barely filled his lungs. Only when we took a quick reprieve did he attempt to goad us.

"B . . . big tough guys," he gasped. "Un . . . untie me. Then we . . . we'll see." The enemy bargained for freedom but he wasn't gonna get it. It wasn't about beating on a man who was tied up, his hands and feet restrained so he couldn't fight back. Under other circumstances, we would've gladly released him, given him the chance to defend himself. But he lost that privilege when he raped Edana and attacked Braylen. They were defenseless. Helpless. But that didn't stop *him*.

"If we released you, it'd be over too soon," I taunted. "And we wanna have our fun."

Blood spilled from his mouth when he coughed, the grimace on his face indicating we'd broken some of his ribs. However, his injuries didn't stop him from further sealing his fate.

"The kind of fun I had with your wo . . . woman?" His head lolled but he kept eye contact with me briefly before glaring at Hawke. "But I gotta say . . . I prefer the sweet taste of redheads." The evil smirk that appeared on his ugly-ass face sparked the simmering rage rattling around inside Hawke.

He lost it.

His eyes darkened.

His movements became meticulous.

Swift.

Deadly.

Before I could stop him, Hawke snatched the hatchet from the metal rolling tray beside him and buried it in the top of the Reaper's skull.

CHAPTER
TWENTY-THREE

Ryder

IT WAS CLOSE TO NOON when we finally pulled into the clubhouse lot. Tired, dirty and sore, I flung open the driver door and stumbled from the cage, catching my footing before I fell on my face. Hawke didn't say a word as he exited the other side of the vehicle, trudging across the open space until he disappeared inside the main building.

After he'd abruptly snatched the life of our enemy, we drove an hour out to the secluded area we'd used to get rid of countless other bastards, disposing of the Reapers without so much as another thought.

We never knew their names. Didn't matter. The only thing that was important was that we were able to exact revenge on the man who'd attacked Edana and Braylen, and rid the world of two more of their kind.

I didn't make it ten feet from the truck before Braylen came sprinting out of the clubhouse, Brutus doing his best to keep up with her, his missing leg not much of an obstacle. She ran straight for me, throwing her arms around my neck and jumping on me. She wrapped her legs around my waist and pressed her lips to mine as I held on to her for dear life.

Never in a million years would I have pictured that exact scene unfolding in front of me. Braylen was stubborn and mouthy, with a fiery temper to match. To see her fear and elation mixed together—for me, of all people—kicked me in the ass while making my heart thump a little faster.

"Miss me?" I chuckled, welcoming the breath of fresh air that was this woman. Especially after everything I'd just dealt with.

She hugged me tighter, essentially answering my question. But for as hurriedly as she welcomed me, she held no punches either. Unhooking her legs from around my waist, she lowered to the ground and steadied herself before smacking my chest. Hard.

"You're an ass," she chided, stepping back and planting her hands on her hips, her expression angry.

There she is.

"Man, you go from one extreme to the next. You on the rag?" I knew my mistake as soon as I said it. Never, ever say that to a woman. It only intensified her mood, as I soon witnessed.

"Shut up. No, I don't have my period." She narrowed her eyes and silently cursed me. "I was worried about you. You couldn't call? Text? Nothing?"

"Bray—"

"No, you don't get to give me some stupid excuse that you can't contact me when you're dealing with 'club business.'" She used air quotes when she said it, like that was not what I was really doing. "Not after everything you've already put me through. Understand?"

Her brown eyes darkened, the fire behind them turning me on like never before. Here was this petite, feisty woman, throwing orders at me as if she held the reins in our relationship. Like she was in charge. For as much as it annoyed me, it made me want to hike up her skirt and fuck her right there in the open. Her pouty mouth and adorable scowl only added fuel to my overactive horniness.

Bending over and picking up Brutus, who was busy sniffing my boots, I cradled him under one arm and snatched Braylen's hand with my free one. I dragged her behind me and made it to the clubhouse door in no time. Luckily, Reece was on her way out, Tripp following swiftly behind her, so I was able to snag the door with my foot since my hands were full. For the quick glance I'd given them, it looked like they'd been involved in some sort of heated conversation. I didn't have the time or energy to ask if he was okay, and the annoyed look he'd shot me was enough of a warning to keep my questions and comments to myself. Besides, I had someone of my own I had to deal with, and I couldn't waste any more time.

"Slow down," Braylen shouted, tugging on my hand to free hers, but her attempts were laughable.

As soon as I entered the space, I saw Adelaide standing near the kitchen talking to Kena and Sully. Walking toward them, I untucked Brutus from under my arm and passed him to Braylen.

I finally released her hand. "You stay here. Talk to them," I said, gesturing toward the other women. "I'm gonna take a quick shower." She took a step closer, as if she wanted to come with me. "No." I walked off before she could argue, hurrying toward my room to wash off the remnants of the past two days.

After the quickest shower of my life, I strode out into the common room, a towel slung around my waist and water droplets running down my chest. Braylen was still in the same place I'd left her, engaged in conversation, when I walked up behind her. Without warning, I swung her around and she let out a surprised shriek. I tossed her over my shoulder before she realized what was happening and practically ran back to my room. I heard everyone's laughter follow us but I didn't care.

As soon as we entered my room, I slammed the door behind me and locked it.

"Let me down, you Neanderthal," she shouted, pounding on my back as if she could convince me to do so with her tiny fists. "What is wrong with you?" Walking toward the bed, I flung her down onto the mattress, straddling her before she could attempt to get up. "Seriously, what's wrong with y—"

I cut her off by crashing my mouth to hers, nipping her bottom lip before thrusting my tongue inside.

Braylen moaned, the vibration and sound making my dick harder than I ever thought possible. When the shock of what I'd done finally wore off, she gave herself over to me completely, sucking on my tongue and even biting me back. "I can't stand you sometimes, you know that."

"You love me," I goaded, realizing what I'd said right after the words left my mouth. I thought for sure she would deny it, but she said nothing, just stared at me before pressing her lips to mine once more.

Swinging my leg over so I was kneeling next to her, I whipped off my towel before hastily taking off her clothes.

"No foreplay?" she asked, smiling as she asked the question.

"Not today. Now spread your legs for me. Let me see you."

She inhaled a ragged breath, desire filling her eyes as she did as she was told. Her arousal was staring me in the face, and I thought she'd never looked so damn delicious. I restrained myself, albeit briefly.

I raked my eyes over her, from her gorgeous face to her toned legs. The woman was perfection, and yet she had no idea. When I couldn't take one more second of not being inside her, I moved closer and positioned her legs so they draped over my shoulders. And for the next hour, I made her scream my name, over and over again, until her voice finally fell silent.

———◆———

LOUNGING FLAT ON MY BACK with my arms tucked behind my head, I turned my head toward her, the hesitancy on her face telling me that she wanted to talk about something. So I did something I would've never done before—I encouraged her. "Go ahead. Ask me what you want to."

She didn't refute or deny, instead parting her lips and saying, "Tell me about your daughter." Without thinking, I groaned. I hadn't meant to, really I didn't. It was just a reflex. "Ryder, you have to tell me eventually."

"I know, and I'm fine answering anything you want. Old habits, ya know?" I flashed her a smile before starting. "Zoe is gonna be eleven in a few months."

"Zoe? That's a pretty name."

"It fits her. I didn't pick it, though. Her mother did."

"What's the story there? With the two of you?" Braylen flipped onto her side, and I did the same, running my fingers up and down her arm, then resting my hand on her side, pulling her closer so I could kiss her.

What the hell is happening to me?

"Rose and I met in high school, believe it or not. We weren't high school sweethearts or anything like that, but we did date on and off. Well, when I say date, I mean. . . ."

"Yeah, I get it." She shook her head and smiled, placing her hand on my chest and drawing circles. I didn't even think she knew she was doing it, but the motion soothed me. And I certainly needed it after what I'd recently dealt with.

"Anyway, we hooked up again a few years later and decided to give it a go. Thing was, she got pregnant a month into the relationship, and even though I didn't see it working out in the long run, I stuck with her. You know, for Zoe. But it crumbled, just like I thought it would. She left and moved to Illinois. She had family there still."

Braylen rose up on her forearm. "She took Zoe with her? Didn't you have a problem with that?"

"Yes and no. While I missed my daughter, I knew it was for the best. Our club wasn't the safest then, so I was okay with them both being away from me. After they moved, I went to see Zoe twice a year or so, calling her often."

"I can't wait to meet her." There was a brief silence before she spoke again. "Do you get along with Rose?"

"Yeah, for the most part." I rolled her on her back and pinned her to the mattress. "Are you done with your questions?"

"For now." She laughed, wriggling beneath me to try and escape, but the only thing she was doing was sealing her fate.

For the next half hour, at least.

CHAPTER TWENTY-FOUR

Ryder

BRAYLEN LOOKED SO PEACEFUL WHILE she slept, her hair fanned out on the pillow, lips slightly parted. She'd been staying at my place, taking the bed while I slept on the couch. We'd argued about the separation, but I couldn't take the risk of attacking her again while I slept.

Sure, I'd let her in, more than I ever had for anyone else, but I still had walls thrown up. And for them to start to crumble, I had to put the final piece of my past to rest before I could move forward.

Clutching a piece of paper in my hand, I quietly exited my bedroom, gently closing the door behind me so as not to wake her. I'd left her a note telling her I had club business to take care of and that I wouldn't be back until the following day. I'd also told her that Hawke would be stopping by to follow her to and from work, and for her to not try and ditch him because I'd be royally pissed off. I could picture her rolling her eyes and mumbling to herself after she'd read it, and the image made me smile.

I knew damn well if I'd told Braylen in person that I had to leave, she would've seen the look of indecision on my face and known I was lying. She would've questioned me until I'd either revealed the truth, something I wanted to shield her from, or we would've started to argue. And that was the last thing I needed to deal with, especially since we were in a pretty good place. We'd finally turned a corner.

It'd taken me a while to get there, of course. I'd been a dick and had made her believe that she meant nothing more to me than someone to just hang out with, a chick I hooked up with when the mood struck me. She had every right to pull away, and at the time I even welcomed the distance; it meant she was less likely to be pulled into my club's shit. But then I'd been proved wrong.

When that fuckin' bastard paid her a visit, I knew the only way she would be safe would be if she was by my side. Once and for all. But in order for her to forgive me, I knew I needed to finally let her in. Tell her things about my past I'd kept secret from even my brothers. It was difficult but necessary. In my gut, I knew Braylen was the woman for me; I just had to get out of my own goddamn way and see her for the blessing she was.

Straddling my bike, I kicked over the engine and took off down the long and narrow dirt road, heading toward the highway. I welcomed the solace of the early California breeze, allowing my thoughts to drift from the woman I'd left sleeping in my bed, to the threat against my club, to what I was about to do. My mind fired off in all three directions, flitting back and forth and driving me crazy.

Being on the open road was normally therapeutic. The freedom it provided usually helped to sooth my anxiousness—put everything back into perspective. But this trip wasn't like any other.

For more reasons than not, it paid to know people in law enforcement. The Knights had certainly taken advantage of the information we'd obtained, giving us the edge we needed, whether it was locations for drops or addresses for people we needed to pay a visit to. Granted, we didn't bother with such leads anymore, not since the club cut ties with the cartel, getting out of the drug trade a while back. But I'd called in a favor, and it was because of that favor that I was on my way to Roseburg, Oregon.

I'd had the information for two months but only now decided to act on it. The first night I received the news, I had my first nightmare. How convenient, right?

The mind was a strange thing. No matter how much I tried to suppress the memories, they still bled out, finding a way to terrorize me all over again as soon as I closed my eyes.

—————◆·—————

CLOSE TO EIGHT HOURS LATER, I was finally creeping up to my destination, the address scribbled on the piece of paper held in the palm of my hand as I pulled off to the side of the road. The house in question was two blocks away, and since I needed the element of surprise, I made sure to hide my bike between two large SUVs.

I wasted no time advancing with purpose, darkness settling in, the low dim of the streetlights barely illuminating the sidewalks. The area was residential, and while the homes had seen better days, it certainly wasn't the worst place I'd seen.

The building in question had faded green siding with dingy white shutters. A few cracked steps led to a small porch. Normally I was heavy-footed, especially with the shit-kickin' boots I had on, but I tried to tread lightly. The creaky floorboards weren't so forgiving, however.

I heard the click of a recliner's footrest going back into place. I waited several seconds while the footsteps trudged across the floor. Blowing out a rushed breath, I widened my stance and opened the screen door.

"Is someone there?" I heard a man croak out, walking the final steps until the large wooden door slowly opened. "Can I help you?" He opened the door wider, leaning forward so he could see me better.

Standing on his doorstep with the intention of finally ridding myself of the guilt and fear that had stolen my peace my entire life, I was surprised when a pair of dark brown eyes looked back at me. This wasn't the man I remembered. Not at all. The man standing before me was old, possibly in his early seventies. Feeble. Gone was his intimidating presence, the power he had wielded over me years before. His hair was closely cropped to his head and stark white. Deep lines etched his face, the evidence of a hard life of abuses.

The years had certainly not been a friend to him, weakening his muscles and aging his body faster than I thought possible. But then again, it had been decades—although for me it felt like months, days even.

It was him, though. There was no doubt about that.

I wasn't sure how I was gonna feel as soon as I saw him again. In truth, fear was a strong assumption, but then I had to remind myself that I wasn't scared or weak any longer.

Instead, anger and hatred mixed together to form the perfect cocktail as soon as my eyes landed on my mark.

"What do you want?" The longer I stood there in silence, the more uncomfortable he seemed to become. I couldn't blame him, though. He wasn't blind. He knew I meant him harm, as was evident when he took a quick step back and tried to slam the door in my face.

"I don't think so," I finally said, pushing until he stumbled back and almost fell over. Entering his house, I kicked the door shut behind me, making sure to lock it so we wouldn't be interrupted.

"I don't have any money." He held his hands up in front of him as if he was surrendering. Little did he know he'd be doing that for real very soon.

"I don't want your money."

"What do you want, then?" He looked petrified, and I reveled in his fear, the adrenaline coursing through me thick and hot.

"Your life."

CHAPTER TWENTY-FIVE

Ryder

TIME SLOWED.

My eyes bored into his, waiting for the moment when he realized the only thing I wanted to rob from him was the beat of his heart.

"Oh my God," he gasped. "Roman."

The evilest grin spread across my face before I gripped his throat and shoved him backward. To say I was surprised he'd recognized me was an understatement; the last time he saw me I was only seven years old. But maybe since he knew exactly who I was, he'd realize that I would be the last person he saw before he drew his final breath.

Clawing at my hand, he struggled to walk while trying to dislodge my hold. I slammed him against the wall, tightening my grip until his eyes started to pop out of his head. His hands finally fell to his sides and he was seconds from passing out when I withdrew and put some distance between us.

"Please" was all he said while his body revolted against the air rushing into his body. He rubbed at his throat, glancing at me every few seconds as if he was planning some sort of defense in case I made any sudden movements.

Still choosing to remain silent, an unnerving tactic I'd learned a long time ago, I pulled my gun from my waistband and placed it on the arm of the chair. I removed my cut and set it next to my weapon.

"What are you gonna do?" he asked, slowly moving to the side because I had him caged in. "Listen, I'm sorry. I wasn't in my right mind back then. The booze . . . the drugs . . . made me . . . different."

With one stride forward we were chest to chest again, his frail body racked with fear while I stood tall and fierce. The roles were certainly reversed, and I was gonna take full advantage.

I shut my mind off, blocking the memories until he started talking again.

"I'm not the same man I was. I swear."

Balling my fist, I hit him as hard as I could, the cracking of his rib signifying success. He fell to the floor and clutched his side, his breathing quite painful from the look on his aged face. "I paid . . . my . . . debt."

I wanted to remain silent, stoic and deadly, but after he spewed that shit, I snapped. No longer was I a man who held any sort of restraint. I was barely sane when I bent down and snatched him up, pulling his limp body closer.

"Paid your debt?" I roared. "Paid your motherfuckin' *debt*? You killed my mother! Right in front of me!" Hauling my arm back, I focused all of my strength as I let loose and punched him harder than I ever had anyone before. I didn't care that he was more than twice my age, frail and unable to defend himself. He deserved everything I had to give.

"Listen. Please. I'm . . . sorry," he gasped, blood flowing from his nose, dripping down his chin and onto the dingy carpet beneath him. "If I could . . . take it back—" He coughed, holding his side before finishing with, "I would. I didn't know . . . what I was doin' . . . when I . . . I. . . ."

"Fuckin' say it," I demanded, hauling him off his feet and throwing him back against the wall. He stumbled but didn't fall down. "Say it!"

"I wasn't in my right mind when I . . . killed your mother." His breathing was labored, and all of the color had drained from his face. "I'm sorry," he repeated, actually looking somewhat sincere. But it was all an act. It had to be. No way this man wasn't the same guy who murdered my mother. Sure, he was older and weaker, but evil still lurked within him.

Only . . . I hadn't seen the glimmer of darkness when I stared into his eyes. Shaking my head to rid myself of some fucked-up internal debate, I reached behind me and seized my gun from the couch. His eyes followed my movements.

"What do you think I should do to you?" I asked, the cool steel resting at my side. With every fiber of my being, I wanted to eviscerate him from existence.

"What?" Blood continued to drip down his face.

"What do you think I should do with you?" I repeated, enunciating every syllable. "It's not a hard question."

"Let me live," he finally muttered, his breathing continuing to worsen.

"Why?" The gun twitched in my palm.

His eyes flicked to my hand before looking me in the eye once more. "Because I made a mistake, and I've paid for it. For twenty-seven years."

"So I should just turn around and walk back out that door?" My anger pulsated in my veins, the audacity of the bastard in front me making me so desperately want to force my gun in his mouth and pull the trigger. *Why are you hesitating?* "Did you think you'd just come home and live out the rest of your days without consequence?"

"I just wanna . . . live in peace."

"Peace?" I laughed, the eerily dark sound foreign to my ears. "You think I should leave you in peace?" I took a step forward.

"Please . . . Roman."

"Stop saying my name!" The more he talked, the more the past and present swirled together. There were brief moments when I'd first laid eyes on him, where I'd been transported back to that seven-year-old kid. Frightened of the man who beat my mom and me. Terrified of the man who stole my mom's life. Then I'd switch to the man I'd become, someone people didn't fuck with because they knew I'd make them pay, sometimes with their life.

I was strong and fearless, so why was I allowing Richard to confuse me, to draw on some part of me that second-guessed ending him right where he cowered?

For the next ten minutes, I found myself at a crossroads, somewhere I thought I'd never be. I knew, or at least I thought I did, that I was coming to his house to kill him. No question. But something was stopping me, and I had no idea what.

Richard deserved to die, yet I still found myself hesitating. And it was during one of those weaker moments that he decided to plead for his life once more.

"Please," he appealed, trying to stand tall, but due to his injuries, it was a half-assed attempt. "I'm begging you not to kill me. I'll do anything. Anything you want. Just let me live."

I hated that I was even considering it. It showed weakness. Doubt. It went against every notion I'd ever had about seeking justice for my mother.

Then I had an idea. Along with the information about where he'd lived, I'd also been told he had a daughter, Ann. She lived somewhere nearby, and while I had no idea whether or not they were close, especially after he'd been away for almost three decades, I decided to test him. To see if he was indeed a changed man.

"I'll tell ya what. I'll let you live, but first you have to decide."

The prospective of him not having a bullet in his brain made him perk up a bit.

"Decide what?"

"You have to choose. Your life . . . or Ann's."

His mouth hung open in surprise, his thin lips trembling while he tried to form words. I could see the proverbial wheels spinning in his head. Was he contemplating giving up his daughter, or was he trying to somehow negotiate for them both to live?

"Five seconds."

A tear fell down his cheek, the sight definitely unexpected. "I don't need five seconds. Kill me. Don't hurt my daughter."

CHAPTER
TWENTY-SIX

Braylen

I AWOKE TO A NOTE from Ryder, telling me he had club business to deal with and that he'd be back the following day. He also left instructions for me to wait for Hawke so that he could follow me to work. Rolling my eyes, picturing the look on Ryder's face as I did so, I knew better than to not follow his wish. Besides, I was still very much shaken up over the attack.

I had to admit, I never thought Ryder and I would ever get to the point in our relationship where he'd finally open up to me. Yes, the road to get there had been riddled with obstacles, frustrating and even hurtful at times, but we finally made it. That wasn't to say it'd be easy from here on out, of course; if I knew anything about that man, the word "easy" should never be used.

But it was a start for sure.

Everyone was allowed to leave the clubhouse the same day Hawke and Ryder returned. After hours of glorious sex, Ryder took me back to his house, insisting I stay with him for the next week, just to be safe. I told him I couldn't, that I was worried about Kena, but he assured me that Jagger was going to stay with her at our place. Once I'd confirmed with my sister, I gave Ryder my acceptance.

There was only one simple rule, and that was that I was to sleep in his room while he took the couch. Afraid he'd hurt me again while he slept, he said it was the only way until he could figure something else out.

———— ◆ ————

HOW ARE THINGS WITH RYDER going? Kena asked, looking from me to the stage where our friend Kevin was performing. He was the lead guitarist for the local band Breakers. They'd built up quite the following, so much that he'd quit working at our family's restaurant to pursue his music full time. We had no doubt he'd make it, he was that good.

Kevin had casually chased my sister but she'd never accepted, not wanting to deal with groupies. She'd come to find that she still had to deal with brazen women throwing themselves at her man, although the situation wasn't as bad with Jagger. Especially since he never paid attention to any woman at his fights other than Kena.

"Better than before. He still drives me nuts, giving me crap about flirting with my male clients, but he's calmed down some. I think now that he's comfortable enough to let me in, he's more relaxed." I took a sip of my drink. "With life in general, you know?"

Yeah, I do, she signed.

Ryder was supposed to have been back earlier that day, but since I hadn't yet spoken to him, Hawke giving me some excuse about him being out of range or some crap, I'd decided to take Kena up on her offer to get together. We hadn't been able to spend much time hanging out recently. If we weren't working, we were both spending time with our guys; there simply wasn't much time left over for anything else. That was why, when she insisted we go out, just the two of us, I jumped all over the invitation.

I really thought Jagger would've shown up at some point during the evening, if not to check on her to make sure she was okay, then to make sure Kevin didn't try to move in on his woman. What Jagger failed to remember sometimes was that he was it for my sister. Whatever interest she'd held toward Kevin was but a speck of what she felt toward Jagger. No comparison whatsoever.

"I'm having a lot of fun tonight, sis." I raised my glass and she clinked hers to mine. "We need to do this more often for sure."

She smiled and nodded, both of us taking a drink before chitchatting about the latest fashion trends and movies we both wanted to see. We settled in afterward to fully enjoy the band's set, which lasted for another hour.

On my way back from the bathroom, I stopped off at the bar to grab another soda since I was the designated driver. When I turned around, I saw Kena frantically waving to me from our booth. She looked worried, so I hurried over as fast as I could.

"What's the matter?" I asked, looking all around to try and figure out if there was some sort of danger present. I unfortunately had some sort of idea what that would actually look like now.

Your phone keeps ringing. She'd just finished signing when my phone lit up again. "Unknown" flashed across my screen. I didn't pick it up because I had no idea who was calling. While I was in the middle of my internal reasoning for ignoring the calls, my cell flashed again. Whoever was calling wasn't gonna give up. Not until I answered.

Swiping the screen, I answered, "Hello."

"Jesus Christ, Braylen. What the hell?" It was Jagger.

"What's the matter?" His tone unnerved me, put me on alert, yet I had no idea why. "Are you looking for Kena? Why didn't you just text her?"

"I have. A million times. She's not answering."

Holding the phone away from my mouth, I said, "It's Jagger. He said he's been texting you, but you're not responding."

Kena picked up her phone but she couldn't turn it on. The battery had died.

What does he want?

Positioning the phone back to my mouth, I asked, "What's so important that you're blowing up my phone?"

I chuckled but stopped as soon as he said, "You need to get over here. Ryder is flipping the fuck out."

"So you're not calling for Ke—"

"No! You need to get over here. *Now!*" he shouted. I heard people screaming in the background, and one of those voices was Ryder's. From what I could decipher over the phone, his speech sounded slurred.

"What's goin' on?"

"We don't know. All we can tell is that he got his hands on some hard liquor and now he's out of his damn mind." Jagger must've pulled the phone away as he shouted to someone as I couldn't make it out.

"What can *I* do?" I was clueless as to what good he thought I'd be to an out-of-control Ryder. If anything he'd probably scare me. I thought it best to let them handle him, calm him down until he eventually passed out. "Jagger, I don't think—"

"Listen, Braylen. Hear me now. I don't care what you think. I don't care if you're arguing or whatever. You need to put all that aside and get your ass to the club. Right. Now."

"We're not arguing."

He cursed into the phone before hanging up on me. I understood he was concerned about the welfare of his friend, but that didn't give him an excuse to yell at me and then hang up.

"Your boyfriend is a bit of a dick." I reached for my purse and flung it over my shoulder.

He can be. She smiled but stopped when she saw I wasn't joking. *What's going on?*

"I don't know, but I guess we're gonna go find out."

CHAPTER
TWENTY-SEVEN

Braylen

AS SOON AS KENA AND I walked in, fear made my heart slam against my chest, and I still had no idea what was going on. A few of the guys were surrounding someone, shouting for him to let go of something or else he was going to be taken down. It wasn't until we took a few more steps forward that Jagger saw us and came running over.

"Oh thank God you're here. You need to try and talk some sense into him." He grabbed my hand and dragged me across the room. I tried to break away from him but the guy was too damn strong.

"Jagger, I don't know what you want me to do. What's wrong with him?"

"He got into that shit. That's the problem." He released me, flicking back the strand of hair that had fallen over his eye. He had a darkening bruise forming high on his cheekbone.

"What happened to your face? Was that from your last fight?"

"No, your boyfriend clocked me."

"What? Why would he hit you?"

"Because Ryder is a goddamn psychotic motherfucker when he drinks like this. He hit at least three other guys, and the only way to make him stop is for us to beat the hell out of him. All of us at once. I don't know why, but when that stuff is flowing through his blood, he has the strength of a goddamn gorilla."

That was an awful lot of information for Jagger to vomit at me all at one time. Trying my hardest to wrap my head around everything, I made a move toward Ryder. Tripp turned around and saw me, hesitation flickering across his face before he looked to Jagger.

"I really think she can calm him."

"I don't know. I think it was a bad move calling her here," Marek added, taking a step forward to shield my presence. He blocked my view, and when I tried to walk away from him, he grabbed my upper arm and pulled me back. He didn't hurt me, but his hold was strong. "I think you should leave, Braylen. We got this."

Choosing to ignore him, I asked, "What happened? Why is Ryder freaking out?"

"We don't know," Tripp answered, switching his attention back and forth from me to Ryder and back again. "He yelled something about not being able to do it. That he's weak and pathetic. He's not making any sense." Tripp looked back toward Ryder once more. "He's got blood on his clothes and his knuckles are split. We didn't do that to him." He ran a frustrated hand over his head. "I probably cracked his rib, but that's it."

"Cracked his rib? Why would you do that?"

"Because he came at me." He said it like it was a normal occurrence, like he had no regrets about hurting his friend when he was in an obvious altered state.

"Get away from me!" Ryder roared, throwing a bottle he'd been holding at the crowd of men caging him in.

"Calm the fuck down, man," someone shouted.

"At least he got rid of his drink," Marek said, finally releasing my arm. "But I still think you need to leave."

As if finally sensing I was near, Ryder pushed through the crowd of men and came straight for me. I wasn't gonna lie—he scared me. I'd never seen him like that before, and the fact that he seemed to be a bit out of his mind was unsettling to say the least.

His dark hair was disheveled. His face was cut and bruised, his gray shirt ripped in several places and spattered with blood. His hands were swollen, his knuckles cracked and covered in the red stuff as well.

"Bra . . . Braylen," he slurred, "What are you doin' here?" Before I could answer, he yelled, "Go! You need to go."

Marek and Tripp tried to hold him back, but he pushed them, causing them to lose their footing. Jagger was right, Ryder seemed to have the strength of ten men. Okay, maybe not ten, but definitely superhuman strength.

"What's wrong, baby," I soothed, reaching out to touch him, to try and offer him some sort of solace in his crazed state of mind.

"You can . . . can't be here. You ca . . . can't see me like this." He erased the remaining distance between us and all of the men froze, waiting to see what he'd do. When I looked into his eyes, they were blank, a void shadowing his essence. I'd never seen anything like it, not in all my life.

"Ryder, please tell me how I can help you. Do you want to go somewhere? Just you and me?"

It was like he never heard me, schooling his expression before grabbing me and pulling me impossibly close. The smell of the whiskey on his breath made my eyes water.

"Let her go!" Jagger shouted, trying to pry Ryder's hands off me, but to no avail. My upper arms started to ache, but I needed to make him see that I was right there with him. For him.

"Tell me what happened," I pleaded.

A tear fell from the corner of his eye but he made no move to wipe it away, allowing the trickle of emotion to show his distress. I'd never seen him look so broken before and it tore at my soul. Something had devastated him. Destroyed him.

"I couldn't do it," he whispered, another tear falling as his shoulders started to shake. He was having some sort of breakdown.

I had to try and be strong enough for the both of us. I had to push aside my fear and attempt to reach him, make him tell me what happened.

"You couldn't do what?"

"He stole every . . . everything from me," he slurred, "and I couldn't fu . . . fuckin' do it." His breathing turned labored. "My mom," he garbled, but I'd heard him.

"Who did?" I tried to keep him on point, but he was drifting all over the place.

"I gave him a ch . . . choice and he didn't pick her."

At that point, I had absolutely no idea what he was talking about. Had he really split from reality? Were his nightmares filtering into his consciousness, making it difficult to decipher what was real and what wasn't?

As if finally realizing he was holding me, a look drifted over his face before he shoved me away from him, stronger than I believed he meant to. I lost my footing and fell on my ass, hurting my wrist on the way to the ground because I was trying to break my fall.

"Goddamnit!" Stone yelled, rushing forward with Jagger and Tripp. They tackled him, but not before Ryder threw out a few punches on his way down.

Kena rushed toward me and helped me to my feet, pulling me back toward the other side of the room. Other than my wrist, I wasn't hurt.

Scared.

Shook up.

But physically intact.

"Don't hurt him," I cried, but my pleas fell on deaf ears. It took all three men just to hold him down. "Please, let him go." I cradled my head in my hands. I just couldn't bear to watch them hurt him any longer.

"Hold him still," someone shouted. "I need to get this in his arm before he hurts someone else. Or himself."

Several moments passed before the shouts subsided. I was afraid to look, so I kept my head down until someone tapped my shoulder. When I didn't budge, they smacked my arm. My head shot up.

Kena.

He's out cold. I think they injected him with something. Tears drifted down her face, she was so shaken up. I hated that she'd witnessed Ryder shove me, but I was fine. I had to convince her of that. Besides, the man who pushed me wasn't Ryder at all. That was someone else inhabiting his body. There was a reason, a dark reason he went off the rails, and I needed to find out what it was.

Jagger finally came over to see me. "Are you okay, Braylen? Are you hurt?"

"I'm fine."

"Shit. I'm sorry. I really thought you being here would've calmed him down. Instead I think I made it worse." Jagger looked so distraught. I felt bad for the guy.

"I'm fine," I repeated. "Really. Don't worry about me." I tried to see if Ryder was still in the room with us, but I couldn't find him anywhere. "Where did they take him?"

"They dragged him to his room and cuffed him to the bed."

"They can't do that. Oh my God." I tried to shove past Jagger, but he caught me midstride, pulling me back toward him. "Let go. Please. I need to see him."

"Uh-uh. No way, Braylen. Not a chance in hell. I learned my lesson the first time. You're not going near him until he sobers up. And even then. . . ."

My body tensed as I asked, "Even then what? Finish what you were gonna say."

"When he sobers up, if he remembers you being here and that you hurt yourself because of him, he won't forgive himself."

"It's only my wrist," I said, gingerly holding my arm. "I'll show him I'm okay. That he didn't really hurt me." I pleaded with him to release me so I could at least check on Ryder, but he held firm, ushering me toward the exit.

"Kena, I need you to take your sister home. Now." Looking at me, he said, "For your own good . . . you're not allowed back here to see him. Do you understand me?"

I remained silent because there were no words sufficient to convey my distress.

"Do you understand me?"

Finally I nodded, Kena helping to hold me upright while guiding me outside.

CHAPTER
TWENTY-EIGHT

Ryder

THE CLINK OF STEEL RATTLED and drew me out of my haziness. I moved my limb and the noise sounded again, the soreness creeping down my extended arm causing me to flinch. In truth, I felt like I'd been run over by a goddamn Mack truck. Everything pained me, from my temple to my jaw, to my ribs and arms. Hell, even my tailbone hurt, although I couldn't fathom why.

"Fuck," I grunted, not quite sure what the hell was goin' on. Only half opening my eyes, partly because I was beyond exhausted and partly because my head was gonna explode as soon as the light spearing in through the window hit my pupils, I glanced warily around the room. It was mine, at the clubhouse.

Why am I here?

Craning my neck, I looked toward the iron headboard and saw my left wrist cuffed to one of the rungs, my flesh reddened from the pressure of its grip.

"Hey!" I shouted as loud as my lungs would allow, which wasn't much. The effort instantly made my head hurt, thumping so badly I could feel the bile rise in my throat. Still dressed from the night before, I scooted over toward the edge of the bed and placed my foot on the ground, and I stomped with my heavy boot. When minutes passed and still no one came, I searched my immediate area to see if there was something I could use instead. I couldn't find anything, so I clumsily removed one of the boots I'd been wearing, and with as much strength as I could muster I flung it at the door. It thumped against the hollow wood, and within seconds I heard someone walking down the hallway.

"You better be back to normal," a gruff voice said, the door slowly opening. Jagger's face appeared, and when he gave me a quick once-over, deciding I wasn't any kind of threat, he strolled forward. How much of a threat could I be restrained to a bed?

He looked tired, like he'd been through the ringer. When he pushed his hair away from his face, I saw a pretty nasty bruise near his eye. "Did you have a fight last night?"

"Yeah," he scoffed. "With your ragin' ass."

At first I thought he was joking, but then I realized that he was tellin' the truth. Otherwise, why would I have been handcuffed? I could only recall bits and pieces, not enough for me to fully understand what went down.

Shaking his head, and with a pained expression of disappointment, he removed a key from the front pocket of his jeans. "I can't believe you did this again, man." He leaned over me and unlocked the restraint, letting it dangle around the bottom of the bar once I'd freed myself. "You promised us all last time that it was, well, the last time."

"Cut me some slack," I argued, not entirely sure what made me break my promise to my brothers never to get as out of control as I had the last time. "I don't even remember what happened."

"You never do," he retorted.

I'd been good for years, but obviously something had pushed me over the edge. Rubbing my temples, I asked, "What did I do? Where did I get the whiskey from?" I'd always given the guys slack for not allowing me to drink the hard shit when we were together, threatening to sneak some behind their backs. Hell, I could've stopped by the liquor store at any time and bought some, but I'd made a promise. To them and myself.

Whenever I had mentioned needing something stronger than beer, they'd shout for Trigger to keep an eye on me, or tell Carla to make sure to serve me only beer whenever we swung by Indulge to check things out. To be honest, I loved that they looked out for me, as I would for any one of them.

"You're askin' me?"

His humorless laugh irritated me, but not because I was pissed at him. I was upset with myself. Disappointed even, that I allowed something to affect me so greatly that I threw all caution to the wind and said goodbye to any restraint I'd been holding onto.

"How did I get here?"

"You just showed up, already annihilated as you stumbled through the door."

"Did I say anything?" Stretching my neck, careful not to jostle my head too much for fear the pounding in my brain would increase, I prayed Jagger could give me some kind of answer.

"You were shouting something about not being able to do it. That someone stole something from you and that he made the wrong choice. . . ." Jagger's voice drifted off, his words jumbling together as I desperately tried to recall just what the hell he was talking about.

Then a splintered memory rushed in, an image of an older man lying on the ground with blood running down on his face. Who was he? Clutching strands of my hair, I closed my eyes and willed more images to come forth, but there was nothing. Not until a flash of Braylen popped up, the look of worry and helplessness laced in her eyes . . . for me.

"Braylen." I opened my eyes and found Jagger sitting on the edge of the bed. "Was she here last night?" My body tensed with the thought that she'd witnessed me at my lowest. My worst.

"Yeah," he whispered, knowing his answer would send me back into a tailspin. Not nearly of the same caliber as the prior night, but enough to break me further.

"No, no, no," I repeated, pacing while trying to calm myself. I knew in my gut that whatever had caused me to freak out was bad, and for Braylen to see me like that, after all she's already been through, was unforgivable.

"It gets worse," he confessed, standing before tentatively approaching.

My lungs refused to work. My legs locked into place and I braced myself for what he was gonna say next.

"You shoved her."

"Who?" I knew who he was referring to, but I asked the question anyway.

"Braylen. You grabbed her when she was trying to help you. Then you pushed her away from you and she fell. I think she hurt her wrist even though she said she was fine. She begged me to see you after we carted you off, but for obvious reasons I told her no."

Shaking my head, ignoring the pain radiating behind my eyes, all I could do was stand there in disbelief. Not only had my outburst brought chaos to the club, but I'd injured my woman in the process. She had to know that wasn't me. I would never hurt her. Not even if my life depended on it.

Right before I stormed out of the room to go look for Braylen, every muscle in my body still tender and aching, I stalked toward Jagger. His eyes averted from mine briefly before reconnecting.

"Why was Braylen even here last night?" I had my suspicions; I just needed him to confirm them.

"Uh . . . 'cause I called her."

I didn't even let him continue before I was on him, shoving him against the wall, my forearm pinning him in place. Under normal circumstances, Jagger could give me a run for my money, probably even best me given the right opportunity. The guy was twelve years my junior and was a champion fighter. But right then he knew not to move a fuckin' muscle. He knew he was wrong for calling Braylen to the club while I was out of my mind.

"Why would you do that? Why would you let her see me like that?" I was more hurt than I was embarrassed.

"Because," he scowled, "you were the worst I've ever see you. Whatever happened seemed to have sucked the life out of you, and I needed to do something."

I pulled him forward a few inches before slamming him against the wall again.

"So you put her in danger?" I was livid. *How stupid can he be?*

"I thought she could help you. I really did," he said when I glared at him in disbelief. "I see the way you are when you're around her. You're . . . calmer. I can't explain it, but I see it."

I knew exactly what he was talking about because it was the truth. Braylen soothed me in ways I myself couldn't explain.

"You still shouldn't've called her."

"I know that now," he admitted.

I stepped back but remained close.

"Is there a problem here?" Stone asked, waltzing into my room and frowning at Jagger and me.

I didn't answer right away because I wasn't sure which emotion to claim. I was angry Jagger had called Braylen to come and see me, thinking she could help in some way. Even though I knew his intentions were driven from concern for me, she ended up getting hurt.

"Is there a problem?" our VP repeated. "Because I can get in on this too." Stone glared at me, completely ignoring Jagger because he knew the issue resided with me.

"No," I finally answered, taking a few more steps away from Jagger. Looking more closely at Stone, I pointed at his face and asked, "Did I do that?" His bottom lip was split, and there was a small bruise on his jaw.

"Yeah, ya bastard. You're lucky I didn't feel it, or I would've fucked you up." His smirk told me he'd already forgiven me. "But it gets me some extra lovin' from Addy, so I'm not really complaining."

Stone had a condition called congenital insensitivity to pain. *Lucky bastard.* And I knew Adelaide. Any mark on her man and she was driven to care for him, make him feel better even though she knew he wasn't affected by it. I figured it was the nurse in her.

"So what now?" I asked, plopping down on the edge of my bed.

"You take a shower 'cause you still smell like a brewery, grab something to eat and go make sure your woman is okay," Jagger said so matter-of-factly, as if I would've argued with him.

"Sounds good to me." Normally, before Braylen had come into my life, I would've escaped to my house for the better part of a week, ignoring everyone because of the guilt of my freak-out. But everything was different now. Not only did I have to make sure she was okay, I had to make sure she continued to be safe. It was my job, and for once in a very long time I had a purpose, other than my part in the club.

As I washed away the prior evening, all I could think about was how

I hoped Braylen had some sort of insight as to what I'd been rambling about. My gut told me she'd be able to clue me in, but maybe that was simply desperation talking.

CHAPTER
TWENTY-NINE

Braylen

TOSSING AND TURNING BECAUSE I'D hardly gotten any sleep, I was startled when Kena threw open my bedroom door and barged in. Her long dark hair was piled high on top of her head, sticking out in all different directions and making her look like a crazy person.

"My God, woman. You scared me," I cried out, clutching my chest while being careful of my sore wrist. With everything that'd happened, I knew it could've been worse. Never having seen Ryder in such a way truly scared me, but I'd been more worried than frightened. I'd witnessed him drunk before but never violent. His eyes had never been vacant, and I'd never seen him so . . . lost.

Someone is here to see you. He looks pretty desperate, so go easy on him. Kena knew I would shoot first, then ask questions later, so she was right to give me her warning. What she didn't realize was that I wasn't angry with Ryder. All of my thoughts were consumed by what had happened to him. Jagger mentioned the guys cuffing him to his bed. Had he fought against the restraint and hurt himself?

My whirlwind thoughts flipped from being worried about the man to realizing that he softened me, so to speak. My temper still existed, my protective side over those I loved still fueling my mouth when need be, but

I knew I was changing. Whether or not I embraced it was another story.

Flinging off the covers, I didn't even have my feet planted on the carpet before Ryder strode into my room. The sight of him made me feel helpless all over again, his flesh torn apart in places and bruised from fighting with his friends, and from whatever happened that had driven him to lose himself to the evils of the amber liquid he poured down his throat.

"What are you doing here?" Surprised he was even standing in front of me, especially after Jagger had indicated that Ryder would probably not want to see me anytime soon due to guilt, I leaned back on the bed, as if the small amount of distance would save me from a plethora of questions and emotions.

He didn't utter a word as he stalked toward me, reaching me with a few long strides. His hand shot out and wrapped around my waist, hoisting me off the bed and into his arms before I could say anything else. Kena closed the door behind her as she left to give us some privacy.

"Jagger told me what happened to you. I'm so sorry, Bray. Please forgive me."

The warmth from his body relaxed me, the all-too-familiar scent of him enveloping me until all I wanted to do was exist in his embrace. But I knew we had to have a serious talk, so I prepared myself to be strong enough to accept whatever he chose to reveal.

Pulling back so he could see my face, he said, "I would never intentionally hurt you, you know that, right?" He feared I viewed him as a violent man. In some aspects I knew he was, but never with me. I knew in my heart that he would never physically hurt me.

Emotionally . . . that was yet to be determined. He was a man, after all, and men were stupid when it came to affairs of the heart, especially one who'd never truly given himself to anyone before.

One thing at a time, though.

"I know," I answered, leaning back into him to try and soothe the both of us. "I know," I repeated.

A shiver shot through his body, his shoulders twitching before he kissed the top of my head. We stood locked together for countless moments, remaining silent, reveling in the comfort of the other.

The tall, muscular, tough and conflicted man holding me close had so many dimensions, some of which I'd borne witness to and some he guarded with his life, too afraid to let others see. But we were making progress. I believed Ryder was almost ready to let me all the way in, his being there with me a sign he truly cared.

Finally separating, he guided me back to the edge of the bed, sitting beside me and reaching for my hands. I winced when he touched my right wrist.

"Let me see."

I pulled my arm back because I didn't want him to focus on the fact that I'd hurt myself, not badly, but he'd see it as a failure on his part, as if he was completely to blame for what happened to me.

He was and he wasn't. I chose to approach him while I knew he wasn't in his right mind. I thought I could get through to him, but he'd been too far gone to truly see me. Besides, it wasn't like he ran at me and knocked me on my ass. I knew it was an accident. I just had to make sure he never allowed himself to get into such a state ever again.

"I'm fine."

"Again with that word." A half smile graced his mouth before his expression fell back into a serious one. "I wanna see your wrist." He held out his palm and patiently waited for me to place my hand in his. Finally, I gave in. The sooner he inspected me, the sooner we could move on.

Gently handling me, he turned my wrist from side to side, feeling all around by gingerly pressing the pads of his fingers along the area. "There's some minor swelling, but I don't think you broke anything. You really should have this wrapped. Do you have any bandages?"

"In the cupboard, under the sink in the bathroom," I replied, pointing toward the hallway. He rose from the bed, and right before he left, he turned back to look at me. He opened his mouth to speak but no words came out. Thinking better of whatever he was going to say, he clamped his lips shut before disappearing, only to reenter my room two minutes later.

"You have a lot of crap under the sink." The mattress dipped as he sat back down next to me.

"That's not all mine. Some of it is Kena's." A mundane topic, but just the kind of normality I needed in order to soak up my nervousness. Not from Ryder bandaging my wrist but from discovering what was going to happen in the next several minutes. Heck, hours, even weeks.

I watched as he carefully wrapped my wrist, cautious not to tighten the cloth too much for fear of hurting me, applying just the right amount of pressure for the bandage to effectively do its job.

His focus was laser sharp, and in any other situation, I would've found it rather comical. The narrowing of his brows. The way the tip of his tongue peeked out from behind his full lips. The twitch in his jaw when I flinched ever so slightly. Gone was the brooding, sometimes arrogant and infuriating man, replaced with someone who was concerned about the smallest injury, his carefulness not to injure me further mixed with regret and worry that I'd distance myself from him because of what happened. He never spoke those exact words, but he didn't have to. He had very expressive eyes, and I hadn't seen his tell until right then.

As he finished up, placing a piece of tape around the end of the bandage, he inspected his work before resting my hand back on my lap.

"There. That should hold for a bit. Just try not to use it too much." His eyes found mine. "I'm really sorry."

"Stop apologizing. I told you I'm okay."

"I thought you said you were *fine*."

"I'm that too." I smiled. I reached for his hand, lacing the fingers of my good hand with his before scooting closer. Our thighs touched and, although we were fully clothed—him more than me—an electric current coursed through my body. Without realizing, a moan escaped from me as I leaned into him, his mouth mere inches from my own when he interrupted the moment.

"I don't think we should."

"Why?" I hadn't meant to come across as insensitive, knowing he was still dealing with a lot.

"Because my head is still all fucked up. I'm gonna go crazy if I don't start remembering something soon." He held my hand a bit tighter before hanging his head, inhaling deeply while a hush surrounded us.

I wanted to offer him some sort of escape by offering myself to him, but clearly he needed something else.

To remember.

And I'd do my best to help him.

Lifting his head, he slowly brought his eyes to mine, his stare locking me firmly in place. The fear behind his browns gutted me. "Did I say anything to you, ya know, before. . . ." He glanced down at my wrapped wrist.

"You were mumbling a lot of things. Something about how you couldn't do it, and that someone stole everything from you." I wasn't making any sense, but then initially neither had he. Suddenly, I remembered something else. "You mentioned your mom."

He frowned and I could see the wheels turning in his head, urgently trying to connect the dots. Before I knew it, it appeared as if a lightbulb went off. He pulled his hand from mine and shot off the bed, rushing halfway across the room before stopping.

"I remember standing over an old man. He was bleeding and pleading with me not to kill him."

I couldn't help it. I gasped, holding my hand in front of my mouth, which only added to Ryder's anxiousness. I knew something bad had happened, and I knew there was a possibility he'd hurt someone, but I think I refused to believe he could've killed someone. Denial and ignorance worked in most cases, but apparently not when that shit slapped you in the face. But I couldn't focus on that. I had to be there for him so he could try and remember and hopefully move past it. If at all possible. I'd worry about how I felt afterward.

Thankfully he ignored my reaction, raking his fingers through his hair, shaking his head before saying, "I told him to choose. I'd either kill him or his daughter." Ryder still looked like he was piecing together a scattered puzzle. "He begged me not to touch her. He told me to kill him." His expression froze, as if he'd finally remembered. "It was Richard. He was the man I went to see."

"Richard? The man who . . . ?" I couldn't even finish my question.

"Yeah, the man who killed my mother," he finished, sadness and anger twirling together to create a whole other kind of emotion.

"Did you . . . ?" Again, I was at a loss for completion.

He was silent for a few moments, locking eyes with me but looking right through me. I knew he needed to work up to telling me the truth, probably running through all the different reactions I'd surely have if his response was what I thought it might be. Finally, he whispered his answer.

"No."

My lungs deflated as a rush of relieved air pushed from my lips. I believed I would've understood if his answer had been *yes*, but I was thankful it wasn't. Without allowing one more second to pass, I deleted the small space between us and wrapped my arms around his waist, resting my head on his chest.

"No," he repeated, holding on to me as if he feared I'd disappear. "I couldn't do it. I hate myself for allowing him to live, but I just couldn't do it." Ryder was in pure confession mode, and I allowed him to unburden his soul by continuing to remain silent. "He said he was sorry, that he was a different man back then. That he hadn't been in his right mind. I didn't believe him, not until he chose his daughter over himself."

His arms fell from me and he retreated until his back hit the wall with a small thud. Shoving his hands in his pockets, he looked down at the floor.

"Ryder."

No response.

"Ryder," I called out again, that time with more force in my voice. "Look at me." I drew near while still giving him the space he needed. "Please."

"Don't," he finally responded. "I should've snatched his life without a second thought. I should've made him pay for what he did." He shrugged in defeat. "But I didn't. I'm pathetic. I'm weak," he muttered.

"No, you're not. You made a choice. The right one." When we stood toe-to-toe, my bare feet touching the tips of his boots, I placed my hand on his chest. I could feel his heart ramming against his ribcage. "I think you recognized a difference between the man he was and the man he'd become. He chose his daughter, Ryder. He chose her life over his. He was clearly willing to die to protect someone he loved."

I couldn't even begin to understand what he'd gone through, coming face-to-face with the person who stole his mother's life, and right in front of him when he was just seven years of age. But I was with him now, and I wanted to help him. To do whatever I could to make him see that he wasn't weak and pathetic. That he was the exact opposite.

He was strong.

He was brave.

He was complicated.

He was unlike any man I'd ever met.

CHAPTER THIRTY

Ryder

EVERYTHING CAME RUSHING BACK TO me as soon as Braylen told me that I'd mentioned my mother while in the midst of my delirium. Images of holding Richard's address in my hand for hours as I drove to Oregon. Memories of pushing past his front door before beating him flooded my brain, only to end with the recollection that I'd left him cowering in his house as I walked away, my gun resting in the waistband of my jeans, never having been fired.

I heard her words, but I still couldn't shake the feeling that I'd been weak in my decision to allow that bastard to live.

Who am I turning into? What is happening to me?

In my heart I knew what Braylen had said was true, and I believed the reason I didn't shoot Richard in the head *was* because he'd chosen his daughter over himself, but it didn't take away the remorse that I hadn't been able to exact revenge for my mother.

"I need to forget," I said, tugging Braylen closer. "Help me do it."

Without warning, I captured her lips, breathing in her warmth like it was the only thing that kept me grounded. Kept me sane. I lifted her up my body, and she wrapped her legs around me, kissing me back with such need that I knew she was exactly who I needed to lose myself in.

"Are you sure?" she asked, pulling back long enough to look deep into my eyes. "I'm here for you, no matter what, but if you're not up to this, we can just lie together."

"And what? Cuddle?"

"Whatever you need."

"I just need you. Naked and spread for me."

Her hands interlocked behind my neck, but when she tightened her hold, she winced.

"Watch your hand," I instructed. "I feel bad enough, I don't want you to make it any worse."

"I'll be—"

"Fine?"

"Smartass." She laughed before giving me a quick kiss. "Now put me down and do with me what you will." She unhooked her legs from around my waist and slid down my body, every bit of her rubbing against me until she found her footing.

Braylen was wearing a pair of white cotton panties, half of her left ass cheek exposed because I'd had my hands all over her just moments before. A matching cami rode halfway up her belly, exposing her delectable skin. My eyes feasted on her, my hunger increasing the more she looked like she wanted me to devour her.

Jerking my head toward the mattress, she shuffled backward until the backs of her legs hit the edge. Without breaking eye contact, she shimmied her top up and off, tossing the material to the floor. Then she proceeded to lower her panties, the expanse of her creamy flesh driving me insane with the need to claim her. Only when she was completely naked did she lower herself onto the bed, reaching out to pull me close.

Removing my clothes faster than I ever had before, even with all my injuries, I finally covered her body with mine. The heat from our skin mashing together created a fire I prayed would never burn out.

"I need you so much right now," I proclaimed, nipping her throat while spreading her legs with my hand. "I don't know if I'll ever get over what happened, but for now, I wanna forget." My desperation was apparent, but instead of pushing Braylen away, it only drew her closer. The look in her eyes wasn't one of pity but of love.

We hadn't told each other how we felt, and I didn't think I was ready to do it right then, but this woman meant everything to me.

"Then use me however you want. However you need." She squirmed beneath me, her hands coming up to tangle in the thick of my hair.

"Raise your arms above your head and don't move them." Not only did I want to dominate Braylen, I wanted to make sure she wasn't putting any strain on her wrist. Every time I glanced at the bandage, which was every other second, a pang of guilt ate at me. I knew it wasn't a serious injury, but it cut me just the same.

"So bossy," she teased, licking her lips in anticipation of what I would do. A flush spread from her neck to her cheeks, making her look so god-damn sexy. She wanted me, and I wasn't gonna keep either of us waiting much longer.

"You have no idea." Completely pushing aside any thoughts other than the woman lying beneath me, I claimed her mouth while my fingers trailed over her skin. First over her collarbone, then down to her nipple, pinching the erect bud and making her moan. When I moved over her ribcage to her hipbone, her back arched off the bed, knowing where my fingers were headed next.

I lightly tapped her pussy, the air in her lungs catching midbreath before I stroked between her folds. She was drenched, her body trembling when my thumb finally circled her clit. Her moans drove me crazy, the way her body went limp seconds before tensing again, then relaxing once more. Back and forth I played with her, teasing and tormenting her just how I knew she loved.

Inserting two fingers inside her while continuing to play with her clit, I slowly pumped them in and out, the rhythm bringing her closer to release. Before she tipped over, though, I removed my hand.

"What are you doing?" she groaned, annoyed that I'd stolen her pleasure.

"I wanna taste you." Bringing my fingers to my mouth, I deliberately sucked on each one, making sure to keep my eyes on her to see her reaction. "You always taste so sweet." Her eyes widened and her lips parted, but she said nothing. Instead, her breaths came out short and choppy, the flush painting her skin deepening. "Do you want me to lick your pussy now?"

"Please," she begged, keeping her arms above her head while thrusting her hips toward me. I wanted to take my time, draw out her pleasure, but I was anxious to bury myself inside her. The quicker she came on my tongue, the sooner I could fuck her, so I spread her legs farther apart and trailed my finger down the inside of her thigh. Goose bumps covered her skin the closer my mouth moved toward her pussy. Kissing beneath her navel, I moved lower still, blowing over her wetness before licking her juices. "So fuckin' wet," I murmured.

"Please," she repeated, her body rocking against my mouth as I lapped up her sweetness like a starving man.

"I think I'm addicted to you," I confessed, pressing on her clit with my thumb while I fucked her with my tongue.

"Don't stop. Oh . . . I'm so close already," she whimpered. "Oh my God, yeah, keep doin' that."

Within moments, Braylen found her rhythm, crying out as she hovered on the verge. I'd come to know her body almost as well as I knew my own, knew just what she needed to finally come undone.

Flattening my tongue, I licked the length of her, pinching her clit before wrapping my lips around the overly sensitive bud. I pumped two fingers inside her, hitting her sweet spot until she cried out my name over and over again.

With my face still buried between her legs, I waited until her breathing evened out. Giving her one final kiss on the inside of each of her thighs, I moved up the bed and almost lost it when I came face-to-face with the woman who was slowly changing me.

As cliché as it sounded, she made me wanna be a better man. She called me out on my shit, showing me boundaries when I'd never paid attention to such things before. Even though I continued to struggle with my decision not to end Richard, Braylen made me feel somewhat okay with it—as okay as any man could feel with not killing his mother's murderer, anyway. The entire situation was fucked up beyond belief, but at least I had someone by my side to help me through it. I knew I wasn't an easy man to love, but I truly believed she was destined to be mine.

She better learn to love my ornery ways, or else I'll strap her to my bed until she changes her mind.

The thought of restraining Braylen made my dick twitch. I fisted myself and rubbed back and forth between her velvet lips. "Is this what you want?"

A simple nod from her was all it took for me to bury myself to the hilt. It was like coming home.

———◆———

I RAVAGED HER FOR HOURS, my stamina even impressing me. I'd flipped her into various positions, always careful of her wrist. I thought for sure after round three I would've slowed down, but I needed to lose myself for as long as possible. And she wasn't complaining.

When we were finally sated—or I should say when I had finally exhausted myself—I fell onto my back beside her. She snuggled close, resting her head on my chest. Careful of the bruises coating parts of my torso, she drew countless circles on my skin. The action was so soothing I'd almost drifted off to sleep, but I knew she wanted to ask me something.

"Ask me what you want," I blurted, waiting for her to deny that she had anything to inquire about. Instead, she surprised me by apologizing, for what I wasn't sure.

"Sorry."

"No need to apologize. Trust me, I've done it enough for the both of us. Just ask me what you want." My breathing remained even, hopefully letting her know I was becoming more comfortable with opening up.

"What was in the needle they shoved in your arm?"

"A mild sedative."

"They just happen to have that stuff lying around?"

"Yeah, for various reasons."

"Like what?"

I should've known she'd push for more.

"Like for whatever reasons they need it for." My last response was a hint for her to move on. I wasn't about to divulge any club business, no matter how much she pestered me. Some topics were just off-limits.

I'd been resting my arm across my chest, a slight welt marking my skin, along with two small tears where the metal had cut into me, no doubt struggling against the cuffs as soon as they'd restrained me.

Braylen gently ran her fingers over my wrist. "Did they really cuff you to your bed?"

"Sure did," I said, almost proudly. "And they had every right to."

"Does it hurt?"

"Not anymore. But don't worry, when I use the handcuffs on you, I'll make sure they're the fur ones."

And just like that, I turned the tables on her, making her squirm with thoughts of more sex.

CHAPTER
THIRTY-ONE

Braylen

I HEARD SHOUTING COMING FROM the living room, and although I was extremely tired and wanted nothing more than to fall asleep, I had to find out what was causing Ryder to argue so loudly.

For the past several weeks, his mood would switch on a dime. Stress from the club or thoughts of Richard would do it easily enough. Oh, and I couldn't forget jealousy whenever he stopped by the salon to see me and witnessed me working on some of my male clients—George being his least favorite, of course.

"Yeah? Well I'm tellin' you. . . ." Silence "No, I'm not signing off on that. I don't care. Absolutely not."

I shuffled my bare feet along the hardwood floor until I came to the entrance of the living room. Clenching the sheet tightly around my naked body, I leaned against the wall and waited for him to see me. Some would say I was eavesdropping, but I chose to think I was giving him time to finish his conversation before having to deal with my intrusion.

"I don't care how many assurances you give me, Rose. Zoe's my daughter too, and I'm not comfortable with it." Turning around, he finally spotted me standing there. "I'll call you back. No, I'll call you back," he said through clenched teeth. Ending the call, he threw his phone on the couch. "Ask me again if I get along with Rose?" He snagged his half-full bottle of beer off the counter and chugged down the rest of the contents.

"What happened? Why are you so upset?" I trudged forward and sat on the arm of the sofa. "Do you mind me asking?"

"No, I don't mind." He grabbed another beer from the fridge and drank half of it before answering. "She wants to let Zoe go to Ireland with a group of kids from her school."

"Like a field trip or something?"

"Yeah, somethin' like that."

"And why don't you want her to go?" I knew I was treading a fine line, but I was curious why he was so upset.

"Why?" he shouted, furrowing his brows at me like I was some kind of alien. "Because it's a foreign fuckin' country and neither of her parents will be with her." Okay, that kinda made some sense. "She's a beautiful girl. Someone's gonna snatch her up and sell her. The sex trade is alive and booming all over the world." He paced, trying to regain some semblance of control.

I didn't know what to say. I'd watched enough shows and read enough books to understand where he was coming from.

"Did you tell Rose those things?"

"She wouldn't let me get a word in edgewise. Ramblin' and arguin'," he mumbled.

I wanted to comfort him, to offer him advice, but what did I know about raising kids and what was best for them? What was safe?

Before I knew it, Ryder was standing directly in front of me, his hands resting on my shoulders, his fingers stroking back and forth over my naked skin. "Why don't you lose the sheet?" I knew what he was doing, distracting himself with the prospect of sex.

"Why don't you deal with the issue with Zoe before it escalates and causes you to have a stroke?" I arched a brow, enticing him to disagree, but he remained silent. The only indication he was considering it was the slight tick of his jaw.

"I'd rather deal with you." He tried to tug the sheet from me, but I moved back, falling onto the couch before I could right myself. Ryder laughed, which was a welcome sound indeed, plopped down on the cushion beside me and positioned me on top of him.

Before we started anything, me still shielded and straddling Ryder's lap, Brutus waddled up next to us and sat at Ryder's feet. He was still too little to jump onto the couch, although he definitely tried enough times. The only thing the little pup would accomplish was falling on his butt, only to try again. I had to give it to him—he was persistent, much like his owner.

Brutus was one lucky dog, thriving in his new home, his missing limb never slowing him down. I hated thinking what would've happened to him had Ryder not followed his gut instinct and trailed the bastard who so carelessly tossed the three-legged puppy from a moving vehicle.

"What's up, buddy?" Ryder asked, moving me slightly to the side so he could lean over and see him. "Tell Mommy she needs to give me some lovin'."

"Mommy? Since when am I Mommy?" To say I was shocked was putting it mildly.

"Well . . . I've been meaning to talk to you about something." He hesitated, and I had no idea what he was gonna bring up. Was him calling me Mommy his subtle way of telling me he wanted to have a baby? Because I was nowhere ready for something like that. Besides, we were still working on our relationship, and some days it was really hard. I tried to move off his lap but he held me in place.

"Stop freakin' out, babe. You have no idea what I want, so stop over-thinking it." The bastard smiled as I continued to try and stand up. But it was useless. He was too strong and if he didn't want me going anywhere, I simply wasn't moving.

"What did you want to talk about?" *If he says "baby" I'm gonna throw myself backward and hope Brutus moves out of the way in time.*

"I think you should move in with me. You're here all the time anyway." He shrugged. "It just makes sense."

The words came out of my mouth before I could stop them. "Oh, so you don't want a baby?" Closing my eyes briefly, I could've kicked myself.

"What?" He laughed, making the entire scene much more humiliating. "What made you think I wanted a kid?" He continued to chuckle while loosening his grip on me, so I seized the opportunity and swung my leg over his so I could finally plant my feet on the ground. "Hey," he rumbled, "where do you think you're goin'? We're not done talkin'."

"Then stop laughing at me," I snapped, unexpectedly irritated with the turn of our conversation. Brutus barked behind me, sticking his nose into our business, and I found myself outnumbered all of a sudden.

I had no time to escape before Ryder hopped off the couch and grabbed my hand. "I'm not laughing at you," he snickered.

"You still are," I pointed out.

He finally composed himself. "Let's try this again. What made you think I wanted a kid?"

"Because you called me Mommy." Even saying the word made me feel somewhat awkward.

"I said that in reference to Brutus. I wasn't even thinkin' about it when I said it." He crowded my personal space. "It just fit. Besides, I think he likes you better than me." He looked down at the puppy and feigned annoyance.

"No, he doesn't." The words weren't even fully out of my mouth before Brutus grabbed hold of the bottom of the sheet and tugged. I hadn't been expecting it, and before I could gather the material to my body, he ran off with it, leaving me completely naked.

"You're right. He just might like me better after all."

CHAPTER
THIRTY-TWO

Braylen

SITTING ON MY COUCH, I became antsy waiting for Kena to come home. Flipping through the channels, I couldn't settle on any one show. Reality, comedy, drama . . . nothing. Even a *Law & Order* episode did nothing to hold my attention because my mind was elsewhere.

Looking down at my phone, I saw I didn't have any new messages. I'd texted my sister earlier and told her I had something I wanted to discuss, and I wanted to do it sooner rather than later. After convincing her that it wasn't anything terrible, she agreed to stop by the house and talk to me before she met up with Jagger. He had a fight later that evening, but I wasn't going. Between late nights with Ryder and working crazy hours at the salon, I was utterly exhausted. And being boxed in at an overly crowded, loud and smelly room was the last place I wanted to spend my evening. Thankfully the next day was Sunday and I didn't have work, so I could rest as much as I needed to.

Finally, at half past six in the evening, Kena strolled through the door, but Jagger and Ryder were hot on her heels.

They showed up outside, she signed. *I can kick them out if you want.* She smiled, but I knew she was serious. Kena would have no reservations about telling the guys to step back outside until we finished our conversation.

My sister looked tired, much how I felt, although she still had a rosy glow to her. Her dark hair was styled in a loose ponytail, and she was wearing her typical work attire, jeans and a T-shirt. Kena always looked nice, even wearing something so simple. Then again, there was no need for her to get all dressed up, because her job was taking care of the finances at our family's restaurant. Her office was in the back of the building, so it wasn't like she socialized a lot, not unless my parents were desperate for her to fill in for the waitstaff due to call offs.

Most of the customers were regulars so they were aware of her challenge, as we liked to refer to it. Disability or handicap didn't fit, because nothing held my sister back from living a full life. Not since Jagger, anyway.

I was happy she had someone, and although he was a bit questionable in the beginning and hadn't always earned my approval, he turned out to be a great guy. Loyal, fierce and protective.

Not that my disapproval would change Kena's mind—she was head over heels for him, and he returned her love tenfold—but having her sister on board just made it easier.

"Why you gonna kick me out?" Jagger teased, pulling his woman in for a kiss as if they were the only ones in the room. "I didn't do anything wrong." He gave her two more pecks before releasing her, his eyes following her every movement. Then he finally looked my way and gave me a wink. "Are you kicking me out?"

"Who's getting kicked out?" Ryder asked, moving to stand next to me.

"No one's getting kicked out," I rebuffed, my voice lower than normal. It appeared my energy was draining with each passing second.

"Are you okay? You look tired." Ryder focused all his attention on me and completely forgot about the possibility of being asked to leave.

"I'm fine."

"Uh-huh," he grunted.

Deciding to ignore his grunted response because I had other pressing matters to attend to, I said, "You guys stay here while Kena and I talk."

They took a seat on the couch and flipped through the channels while they waited.

As soon as we sat on the edge of my bed, side by side, I turned to Kena and blurted, "Ryder wants me to move in with him." No point in beating around the bush. I waited for her reaction. Worry. Sadness. Confusion. These were some of the examples of emotions I'd expected, but I certainly didn't anticipate that she'd be smiling. "What's so funny?"

I thought you were going to tell me you're pregnant.

"Oh my God! No!" I gasped, yelling louder than I meant to. "Don't even say that." I couldn't even imagine if that was true. Instead of bringing bad karma my way, I redirected the conversation back to my original statement, but it took me several seconds to relax my face from a horrified expression.

"So how do you feel about me moving out?" I braced myself to deal with whatever happened. If she didn't want me to leave, I wouldn't.

Well, now that you brought it up, Jagger wants to move in here. We were waiting to tell you until we found the right time, but it looks like you found it for us.

"Oh, well, yeah. It looks like it'll all work out for the best, then." Why, after finding out that our situations were perfectly synced up, did I start crying?

Kena hugged me tightly before asking, *Why are you upset?*

There was no hesitation before I started rambling uncontrollably. "Because we won't be living together anymore. Because we won't be able to just hang out in our pajamas, stuff our faces with junk food and watch corny horror movies. Because—" I sniffed. "—I won't have anywhere to go when Ryder drives me nuts." We both laughed at my last reason, and although Kena never made a sound, the grin on her beautiful face was huge and her chest shook in amusement.

Then we'll kick the men out when one of us has an argument and we'll hang out. Sisters before misters. Kena often found ways to make me feel better, even though that was rightly my job because I was her big sis. Regardless, we hashed out a few minor details, like when the moving was all going to take place, what furniture would be staying and which pieces would be moved. Kena had to make room for Jagger's things just like Ryder did for mine.

After about a half hour, we joined the men. They were in the same exact position, leaning back on the sofa with their legs spread. The typical way men sit.

As soon as Ryder saw me approach, his expression changed.

Apparently, I looked drained. "Wait here," he instructed, pushing me to sit down. Moments later he had my overnight bag in his hand.

"You stayin' here?" he asked Jagger.

"Yeah, man."

"Okay, we're going home, then."

Home. What a strange but wonderful thought that Ryder had not only accepted me in his life but that we were going to be living together. Apparently starting right away.

After throwing my bag on the back of his bike, he handed me a helmet. "I don't think I can ride on that tonight." I must've really been out of it since I'd never even heard him pull up. Normally I'd heard the roar of his engine a mile away.

"Yeah, what was I thinkin'? You look like hell."

"Gee, thanks," I said sarcastically. "You sure know how to kick a woman when she's down." I didn't even possess enough energy to be angry at him.

"Sorry, that's not what I meant at all. I just meant. . . ."

"Go get Jagger's keys," I instructed, halfheartedly pointing toward the house.

He jogged off, returning soon after and helping me into Jagger's truck. A half hour later he was practically carrying me into his house, shooing Brutus out of the way so he didn't trip over him.

As soon as Ryder undressed me and tucked me into bed, I closed my eyes, but before he could leave the room, I asked him to stay. "Please lie with me."

A brief silence ensued before he asked, "What if I fall asleep?" At some point we had to try and sleep in the same bed again.

"Please stay."

The bed dipped beside me as I drifted off to sleep.

CHAPTER
THIRTY-THREE

Ryder

I HAD AN IDEA WHY Marek had called the impromptu meeting, but I wouldn't be 100 percent sure until he started talking. I glanced around the room and saw every man present looked tense, ready to blow if we had to continue to wait and exact our revenge on the rest of the Reapers.

Two less Reapers in the world, the ones we'd most recently dealt with, helped to ease my mind, a sentiment shared by every single member sitting around our wooden meeting table, but the annihilation of the entire club would feel much better.

"Tell us we're not gonna wait one second longer," Hawke barked, leaning forward and staring at Marek. "Because that'll be bullshit. We need to do something, Prez."

I'd watched Hawke transform from someone who used to fuck about, not really caring about much else other than the club and his woman, to a man who'd become harder, not so quick with the jokes.

He'd remained faithful to Edana, trying to help her through the aftermath of the attack, but nothing seemed to work. She'd packed up and left to stay with her sister, so all he had now was his laser focus on taking out as many Reapers as he could.

"And we're gonna." Marek turned to look at Stone. "We still got a signal on the trackers?"

"Yeah," our VP answered. "Last I checked they're all in the same place."

"Then we move out tonight."

"Isn't that kind of a sloppy move?" I asked, hearing my words only after they'd left my mouth. I had essentially told the leader of the Knights Corruption that he wasn't thinking clearly. Quickly backpedaling, especially seeing the angry look on Marek's face, I added, "What I meant to say was, don't you find it odd that all the trackers are still live? After all these weeks? And that they're all in the same place? Together? Call me crazy but I think we might be walking into a trap."

A few of the men contemplated what I'd said and some of them nodded. Marek surveyed the room, leaned over and whispered something to Stone. I had the utmost faith that Marek would take my questions into consideration before he made another move. It was why he was so effective in leading the club. He accepted ideas and suggestions, valuing each member's insight. Maybe he didn't take kindly to anyone blurting out shit like "Isn't that kind of a sloppy move," but he'd allow people to redeem themselves instead of being pissed and writing them off.

"Okay." He looked directly at me when he said, "We act like it's a trap."

"Why now?" Tripp asked. "Not that I'm complaining."

"Because I had to put a few things into play before we went after them." Elaborating, he added, "Salzar and the rest of the men are gonna watch over the women and children for a few days. They just got back and are ready to go."

Salzar was the head of our Laredo chapter. He was a good man, and I had no doubt he'd take good care of our families while we were gone.

Marek reclined in his seat, already knowing our ol' ladies were gonna give us a hard time. For as difficult as Braylen was gonna be, at least she'd have her sister with her. I could only imagine the fight Adelaide was gonna give Stone. Not only would she not want to stay with a bunch of strangers, but she wouldn't want their daughter around them either. I knew Stone didn't want to do it just as much as I didn't, but we had no other choice. If it was indeed a trap, the Reapers would have a game plan in place to come after everyone close to us.

No, we couldn't risk it.

Question was, how the hell did I break the news to Braylen?

———— ◆ ————

"I'M NOT GOING," SHE HUFFED, crossing her arms over her chest and givin' me her most defiant stance. Normally, I'd challenge her until she gave in, but I knew damn well this scenario was entirely different. I was askin' her to go somewhere I didn't completely want to send her. Not because I didn't trust my brothers in Laredo, but because they had a few new members I didn't know, and shoving Braylen under their noses for God knew how long was certainly gonna fuck with me.

"You have to."

"I don't have to do anything I don't want to. That's the beauty of it."

I moved toward her but she backed away, sure to keep her voice low so no one could hear us. I'd surprised her at her job, knowing if I tried to break the news to her at home, she'd rain holy hell on me. I was dealin' with enough; I didn't need to add anything else to my list.

"Bray," I warned, "don't argue with me about this. You have to go."

"Why? Why can't I just stay home? We have a top-of-the-line security system. Besides, Brutus will be with me."

"Really?" I had to laugh at that one. "Brutus is no guard dog, sweetheart. Besides, he's still a puppy. What is he gonna do? Maul someone's ankles? Nice try, though." Speaking of which, I had to find someone to take the little guy while everyone was away. Maybe Braylen's parents could watch him for us. They'd fallen for him almost as fast as I had, so I knew he'd be in good hands.

"Then Kena and I will stay with our parents."

I didn't want to get into too much detail, informing her that her parents would also be in danger if she went that route.

"No."

"Yes," she argued.

I couldn't help it. My voice rose. "I said no!" Her eyes widened before she tried to shove past me, but I caught her by the arm. "Uh-uh, you're not goin' anywhere but out the door with me. So don't make a scene. Or do, I don't care." I dragged her out of the breakroom and past the front desk, her friend slash boss staring at us as I approached the door. "Braylen needs the next week off," I shouted over my shoulder right before I hauled her outside.

"I can't believe you just did that. You had no right." She stood next to my bike, staring at me, stunned I'd done what I had.

Wanting to shield her from the actual reason I needed her to comply, I shook my head and closed my eyes for a brief moment. Taking a few deep breaths, I opened my eyes, reached for her and pulled her to me.

"Look." She parted her lips to interrupt me so I slapped my hand over her mouth to keep her quiet. *God, this woman.* "You're in danger. We all are. We have to take care of something, and when it's all over with, I'll bring you home. Safe and sound. But until then, be quiet and do as I say. Got it?" I didn't want to come off as mean and uncaring, but I was trying to shield her from our enemy. Trying to keep her safe. But all she wanted to do was give me a hard time.

Only able to see her nose and up because my hand was covering half of her face, she shot me a death glare, but I ignored her. Finally, after a solid minute, when I thought she had calmed down some, I removed my hand. She instantly started mumbling. Something about me being an asshole, and I'd pay for this shit and a few other things I couldn't understand.

But the important thing was she hopped on the back of my bike and wrapped her arms around my waist. She could say whatever she wanted as long as she didn't fight me on leaving.

CHAPTER
THIRTY-FOUR

Braylen

ANGRILY THROWING CLOTHES INTO MY suitcase, I stomped around the bedroom like a child having a tantrum. But I couldn't help it. I was pissed off. Ryder showed up at my job and told me I had to stay with their charter in Texas. He'd given me no warning whatsoever, spewing some bullshit about the decision being last minute. Maybe if he'd fully explained just what the problem was, I would find myself more on board with the sudden plans, but all he would tell me was that it was club business. Oh wait, he did tell me I was in danger. That was more than he usually gave me.

"We gotta leave soon," he announced, popping into the bedroom and leaning against the doorframe. He watched me for a few minutes before speaking again. "You can be as mad at me as you want, but this is happening."

"You see me packing, don't you?" He smirked, which only served to infuriate me even more. "You can go back to waiting in the living room."

He threw up his hands in mock surrender, turned around and left without another word.

The entire ride to the clubhouse was in silence. I wasn't happy about my life being uprooted over something Ryder wouldn't even fill me in on; I sure as hell wasn't about to make idle chitchat just to pass the time.

There was more than one reason why I was so upset, though. Not only was he shipping me off to Texas, but I knew in my gut that Ryder was putting himself in harm's way, only he wouldn't tell me why. *Club business.* If I heard those two words one more time, I was gonna scream bloody murder.

We eventually pulled into the clubhouse lot and parked. I saw a group of women gathered together and a separate group of men off to the side, reminding me of recess during elementary school. Only this wasn't a break from school—it was more like a break from our everyday lives. And not the good kind.

Slamming the truck's door behind me, I headed toward my sister and the other women she was speaking with. "Hi," I greeted, hugging Kena before smiling at Adelaide, Sully, and Reece. If I thought I'd been upset about having to leave, I could only imagine how Adelaide and Reece felt. Both of them were pregnant, and Adelaide had an infant on her hip as well. Kaden, the baby Sully and Marek had been caring for, was in Sully's arms, tugging on a strand of her long black hair. Knowing these women had more to worry about than I did, I calmed my anger to a simmering boil.

"Don't be too worried," Reece comforted me, placing her hand on my forearm. Seeing my obvious displeasure, she said, "I know I'm pretty new to all this, but I have every faith the men are doing this as a last resort. I know Tripp's torn up about it." She flashed me a sympathetic smile, making me realize everyone standing around me was affected. I needed to get on board and lose the crappy attitude.

We chatted for close to twenty minutes, trying to keep the topics off the next few days and on lighter subjects like children.

Eventually, Ryder came to stand behind me, cautiously putting his hand on the small of my back. My white tank top was split in the back, just above my skirt's waistband, so when he touched me, he stroked his thumb over my bare skin. When I didn't yell at him or pull away, he leaned down and kissed my temple.

"You ladies ready to go?" Jagger asked, pulling Kena in for a kiss. She seemed to be handling the situation much better than I was, and I had no idea why.

On our brief walk toward one of the two black SUVs that were taking us to Texas, I stopped her. "Aren't you upset?"

I'm more scared than upset. Not for us, but for the guys. But my emotions will do nothing except distract Jagger, and I need him focused. For whatever they have to do.

Damnit! I hadn't even thought of it like that, thinking that my mood might inadvertently be a distraction for Ryder. And if he was worried about dealing with my surly ass, then maybe he might get hurt. I couldn't have that on my conscience.

"Thanks, sis." I hugged her again before taking off to search for Ryder. It didn't take me long to find him, seeing as how he was helping to load the suitcases into the back of one of the vehicles.

"I don't wanna argue," he said as I approached. "I can't deal with that right now."

"I know. I'm sorry. I should have been more sensitive to what you're going through. Sorry for acting like such a brat."

He stopped midthrow and turned to look at me.

"Is this some sort of trick?" He was serious, which made me feel even worse.

"No, it's not." I moved toward him until I could wrap my arms around his neck. Pulling him down, I covered his mouth with mine. When I tried to break away, he grabbed the back of my head and deepened the kiss, swirling his tongue with mine until I completely lost myself to him.

"Get a room," Tripp teased, moving in front of Ryder to help finish the job he'd started. We finally parted and Ryder ushered me toward the side of the truck, where we had some privacy from everyone else standing around.

"I'm sorry we have to do this, but it's necessary. I don't know what I'd do if something happened to you."

"But what if something happens to you? What will I do?" The question rattled me because I knew there was a possibility Ryder could be harmed. In what way and by whom I had no clue, but it didn't matter. The simple fact that he could be scared me.

"Nothin' is gonna happen to me." He wrapped his arm around my waist and stroked the exposed skin on my lower back once more. "But somethin' is gonna happen to someone if they even look at you the wrong way."

I smiled because it was his way of telling me we were all good. And that was the thing with Ryder. He didn't hold grudges.

I could certainly learn a thing or two from him.

———— ◆ ————

LAREDO WAS APPROXIMATELY A TWENTY-FIVE-HOUR trip, and because we couldn't afford to waste any time, the guys took turns driving. We stopped every six hours so we could stretch our legs, grab something to eat, use the restroom and top off the gas tanks.

Both SUVs made the same stops. Ryder, Jagger, and Tripp were "in charge," as they called it, of our vehicle, while Marek, Stone, Sully, Kaden, Addy and Riley rode in the other one. Thank goodness both trucks had third-row seating or we'd all be sitting on each other's laps.

When we weren't talking to our men, Kena, Reece and I chatted about the latest Hollywood gossip, doing our best to pass the long stints on the road. A few times I'd drifted off to sleep, then woke up only to find out that a measly twenty minutes had passed.

"Why didn't we fly?" I asked fifteen hours into the drive, growing more agitated with each passing mile.

Jagger was driving, taking his turn at the wheel while Kena sat beside him in the passenger seat. Every time we got back in the vehicle after stopping, we were sitting next to someone new. Right then Ryder sat next to me, stroking my bare knee with his middle finger.

"Because we don't want anyone knowing," Tripp answered from behind me. He sat next to a sleeping Reece in the third row. I had no idea what he meant and I knew if I asked, one of them would only give me a vaguer answer. It simply wasn't worth getting aggravated over. I was annoyed enough as it was. Tired and miserable, to be more precise.

"You know," Ryder said, leaning close to whisper in my ear, "I would love to fingerfuck you right now." His comment completely came out of left field, but I should've expected something, especially this long into the trip. Besides, he'd been rubbing my knee for the past fifteen minutes. "What do ya think?"

"Are you serious?" I whispered back, keeping my eyes forward so as not to draw attention from any of the other passengers.

"Why not?" His gripped my knee and tried to pull my legs apart. "I'll make you come. Take your mind off being miserable."

"I'm not—"

"Yeah you are, and I don't blame ya." He kissed my neck. "Let me do this for you," he tempted, his fingers moving up the inside of my thigh. I clamped my legs closed before he reached the edge of my panties.

"Remove. Your. Hand." I turned to face him and gave him a tight smile. "You're not shoving your fingers inside me with Tripp and Jagger right next to us. Never mind that my sister is right there," I said, pointing toward the passenger seat.

"Are you sure?" He smirked, but when my expression didn't change, he removed his hand. "Fine, but I'm gonna fuck you so hard when we get to the club." He didn't say the last part quietly, both of his friends laughing out loud when they heard it, Kena turning around and smiling.

"Oh my God, Ryder!" I exclaimed. "How embarrassing."

"Don't worry about it, Braylen. I plan on putting one on your sister as well."

"Ewwww."

Kena at least had the decency to slap his arm, even though she kept the smile on her face.

"Yeah, Reece isn't gonna be able to walk for a few days after I get done with her." Tripp laughed, clasping Ryder's shoulder in amusement. Good thing his woman was asleep; otherwise, she would've joined me in being mortified.

"Oh, please stop talking. All of you. Especially you, Jagger. Just . . . no."

All three of them laughed harder. At least my humiliation helped to ease the rest of the trip for them.

CHAPTER THIRTY-FIVE

Ryder

WE PULLED INTO THE SECLUDED clubhouse compound of our Laredo chapter, closing in on nine in the evening. After spending time with our women, we gathered with our brothers, everyone present and accounted for.

"So if any of you want to come back with us, we'd sure appreciate it," Marek announced, sitting next to Salzar at the head of their meeting table. Jagger, Tripp, and Stone leaned against the nearest wall, next to me.

Salzar was one of the original members of this charter, a full head of white hair and a clean-shaven face making him look innocent. But anyone who knew the man knew the opposite was true. He was loyal as hell but as mean as they come, when driven to be so. He kind of reminded me of Cutter.

"I'll go," a man named Etch said, his long shaggy hair tied back into a low ponytail. He was older, probably mid-fifties. I'd known the guy for many years, and while he may be close to twenty years my senior, his reflexes were on point, especially with a blade.

"Count me in," another said.

"Me too, Marek. Whatever you need."

The last two were new to the charter, at least newer than two years, but I had no doubt Salzar wouldn't have patched them in if they weren't good men.

"I'm in as well," Salzar offered, nodding toward Marek. "We've dealt with the Reapers here too, although this charter has nothing on Psych's.

"Well, it's a good thing we ain't gotta deal with Psych anymore, isn't it?" Stone asked, cocking his head to the side while a ghost of a smile lifted the corners of his mouth.

Marek grinned. It'd been a sweet victory for our president to finally end the life of the man who'd put his wife through hell her entire life. Every once in a while, when he'd mention a nightmare that Sully had—which weren't as frequent anymore—or him not being able to completely push down his rage when he saw the scars that littered her skin, he said he wished that Psych was still tied up in our safe house's basement so he could torture him all over again.

I was thankful the evil fucker was dead, though. Marek was being dragged down a dark path, and we all feared he was gonna lose it once and for all. The small splinter of sanity remaining would have surely unraveled if he hadn't seen his way out of that hell.

"I'm gonna have to ask that you stay here and look after our families," Marek said, turning toward Salzar. "I know you won't let anything happen to them. They'll be safe with you here, and I'll be on my game not having to worry about them."

"Whatever you want is good with me, brother." Salzar was fierce, but the look he shared with Marek was laced with understanding, compassion and something else I couldn't quite decipher.

When the room grew quiet, I felt as if I had to make a declaration, some new faces forcing me to speak my mind. I cleared my throat. "I just wanna throw out there that if one hair is touched on any one of our ol' ladies' heads, you'll deal with us." I waved my hand toward Marek, Stone, Jagger and Tripp. "And it won't be pretty." I looked at every man around the room but focused more on the unfamiliar guys.

Salzar chuckled, easing some of the building tension. "Don't worry, Ryder. No one is gonna touch your women. Look at them? Now that's a different story, my friend." I whipped my head to glare at him. "Calm down." He laughed harder. "I'm just fuckin' with you. We'll treat them like family. You have my word."

A quick nod from me and the conversation was over. I trusted Salzar, and I had every faith he'd keep everyone in line . . . and our women, Riley, and Kaden safe.

————◆————

AFTER A FEW BEERS, I said my goodbyes and staggered back toward the room they'd given us. My exhaustion mixed with the alcohol flowing through me was enough to make me wanna pass out, but as soon as I opened the door and saw Braylen lying on top of the covers, naked and exposed, I quickly had other ideas. But I didn't want to wake her. She'd been through a lot the past couple days—hell, since the day she'd met me—so if I could give her a few more hours of peace, I would do just that.

Adjusting my dick, trying to lessen the hard-on that had popped up as soon as my eyes landed on her, I proceeded to undress before pulling back the covers and climbing underneath.

Braylen didn't budge, her breathing so slow I knew she wasn't gonna wake up anytime soon. So I lay there, thinking about everything that had happened in my life since the day I met her strong-willed ass in the park, giving Jagger a hard time for something that didn't even involve her.

I found out that day that Braylen Prescott was fierce, loyal and had a mouth I wanted to sometimes silence with my cock. She drew me in all while making me throw up stone walls to protect myself.

She pushed.

I pulled.

She gave me shit.

I demanded things from her.

But when we came together, figuratively and literally, it was out of this world. I wasn't saying our relationship was easy—it definitely wasn't—but I knew I wanted to spend my life with her. I could only hope she reciprocated those feelings.

While Braylen was a challenge to deal with sometimes, I was even more difficult. I was man enough to admit it. I was severely protective, possessive of her time and jealous. It was exactly why I needed her to push when all I wanted was to pull her under. She showed me the error of my ways, and if I didn't acknowledge them, she gave me the cold shoulder. Some days I welcomed the silence, but other days the quiet drove me borderline insane.

Braylen brought light into my world, and after everything I just described, I knew that made me sound crazy, but it sure as hell made perfect sense to me.

It wasn't until she relentlessly pushed me to tell her that I finally divulged everything that happened to my mother. And I swore afterward, even though I was still a little angry that she made me talk about it, I felt lighter. Like I could finally relinquish the past and look forward to the future. Something a lot of the men in the club never did, mainly because we didn't know if we'd be alive long enough to make any long-term plans.

Marek had taken care of those concerns a while back, though, first by breaking with Los Zappas cartel, then steering the club legit. Funny thing was, even though the Knights straddled the right side of the law, our hands were certainly not clean.

Sure, we didn't deal in drugs any longer, but snatching people's lives just happened to still be a necessary evil.

Braylen stirred, lazily rolling over on her side and throwing her arm and leg over me. The warmth from her skin had my dick coming back for a full salute in seconds. Moments passed in stillness, and then her hand slowly slid down my body until she cupped me. I was completely naked, the clubhouse on the warmer side, so when she realized she was touching my cock, she gripped me tighter before releasing a moan. She moved closer and rested her head in the crook of my neck, working her fingers up and down my hardened shaft, all without saying a word.

I'd planned on letting her sleep, but clearly she had a different idea. And who was I to deny her what she wanted? I wasn't selfish, after all.

Shifting her so she was flat on her back, her hand slipping away from me, I spread her legs and thrust inside her. Her sleepy moans thickened my blood, the need to spill myself inside her more potent than ever before.

Because I had no idea what was gonna happen once we returned home, I reveled in the feel of her, imprinting the memory so I'd never forget.

Positioning her leg over my hip opened her up, and I took full advantage, driving home how much I'd miss her with every stroke of my body.

"Look at me," I demanded, slowing my rhythm until she opened her beautiful brown eyes. Once her attention was on me, I took a deep breath, counted to five, and then released the air. "I love you."

I wasn't sure what I expected, but tears and her trying to push me off her were not it.

"Get off me," she cried out, pushing against my hips to dislodge my body from hers.

"Stop it, Bray. What's the matter?" I remained inside her, refusing to budge until she told me why my telling her I loved her made her so angry.

"You just told me you loved me," she blubbered, tears falling down her cheeks while she desperately tried to catch her breath.

"So." I'd never been so confused.

"Why would you tell me that now?"

"What do you mean? It's how I feel."

"But why now?" she repeated, whispering her question as if she didn't fully understand her reaction either. Her fingers continued to dig into my hips, which was more annoying than anything. Leaning back on my haunches and pulling her with me, still careful not to slip from her body, I grabbed her hands in mine and pinned them to the bed.

"Tell me right now what's wrong?" She stared at me, continued to cry, but didn't say a damn word. "So help me God, woman," I threatened. "If you don't tell me why you're so upset, I'm gonna. . . ." My words trailed off because I had no idea *what* the hell I was gonna do. I was stunned by her reaction, and as that feeling waned, I became angry.

Definitely not how I saw the scene playing out in my head.

"You're only telling me you love me because you don't think you're comin' back," she finally confessed. "You know something bad is gonna happen and that's . . . that's why you said it." More tears. More short and choppy breaths. More anguish shrouding her because I knew in my heart she loved me too.

But she was terrified that I wouldn't make it back to her.

CHAPTER
THIRTY-SIX

Braylen

MY IMAGINATION RAN WILD WITH thoughts of Ryder lying on the ground. Dead. Shot. Stabbed. And nothing he could say would wipe the images from my brain. I didn't want him to leave. I had a bad feeling, had it ever since we left California, but I tried to be strong. Brave.

But him telling me he loved me, and for the first time, was like a knife to my heart when it should have made me feel elated.

"Get off me."

"No."

"Ryder, please," I begged. "I can't breathe."

"I'm not doing anything to you. The only thing I'm holding down is your hands." His body was still connected with mine, and whenever I felt him twitch inside me, he stole my breath. I knew it didn't make any sense, but I needed him to let me up. I needed distance to come to terms with what was gonna happen in a few short hours.

Ryder was gonna leave me, and there was a strong possibility he wouldn't return.

"Please," I repeated, closing my eyes briefly as my tears continued to fall. "Please."

I heard him grunt before he fell from my body, his weight disappearing altogether as he moved off the bed and stood a few feet away. The heat from his stare bored into me, and I knew there was no way he was gonna leave until I divulged everything.

A month ago he would've walked away, but not now. Not after everything we'd been through. What *he'd* been through. He needed me just as much as I needed him, and that was why hearing those three precious words cut me so deeply.

As the seconds passed with my growing vulnerability, I covered myself with the bedsheet, an action which apparently infuriated Ryder.

"Don't hide from me." Whipping off the fabric, he grabbed my ankles and pulled me toward the edge of the bed.

"What are you doing?" I shouted, struggling to move back up the mattress before my ass hit the ground.

"Come on," he urged, reaching out to grab me again. I avoided his touch.

"Just go." The words surprised me, because I didn't want him to leave. Not then. Not ever.

"You want me to go?" His voice rose a level, his face scrunching in anger. "I tell you I love you, you freak the fuck out, and now you're telling me you want me to go?" I didn't answer. "Well?" he roared. "Is that what's happenin' right now?"

"I don't know." I was scared, petrified even, but I couldn't put any of my emotions into words that would make him understand my reaction.

Running his hands down his face to try and calm himself, he finally looked at me again. There was sadness behind his eyes I hadn't seen earlier. "I do love you, Braylen. I should've told you before but I was too scared. You make me feel things I've never experienced before and that terrifies me, but I know I can't live without you." He took a step. "I'll come back. I promise."

"Don't," I said, holding up my hand to stop him from advancing. "Don't make promises you might not be able to keep."

"I'll do everything in my power to come back to you. There, is that better?" His question was sarcastic but also serious.

"What happens to me if you don't?" I cringed after the words left my mouth. I couldn't imagine not having Ryder in my life, and the mere thought I'd never see him after that day ripped me apart inside. How did the other women deal with this? I could barely handle it one time, let alone time and time again.

"Just don't go out with George. Promise me?" The corners of his lips curved up the slightest bit.

"You're an ass."

"I know. But I'm an ass who loves you." He held out his hand, and I finally accepted, taking hold and allowing him to pull me up to stand in front of him.

I cupped his cheek, then slowly trailed my fingers over his neck and down his chest, coming to rest my hand over his heart. The man was it for me, and I'd regret never telling him in case something did happen.

"I love you too. I fought against it at first because I refused to fall for you when you were so guarded, but my heart won out in the end." There was so much more I wanted to tell him, but I didn't even know where to begin.

Instead of choosing to keep it serious, an uncharacteristic trait of Ryder's that was slowly becoming more frequent, he tried to make light of my freak-out. "By the way, I knew you loved me." A cocky look took hold before he continued. "I mean, come on, how could you not?"

———◦———

AS WE ALL TOOK TIME saying goodbye to our men, I couldn't help the emotions which flowed freely once more. Only that time I wasn't the only one.

Kena hugged Jagger extra tight, breaking away briefly to sign that she loved him, and that she'd kill him if he got hurt. She smiled through her anguish before he pulled her back toward him, kissing her over and over before whispering something in her ear.

Tripp and Reece huddled near one of the trucks, talking low amongst themselves before embracing for long moments. Tripp was turned toward me, and I could see how sad and worried he looked leaving his woman.

Stone and Adelaide, along with their daughter, Riley, were having a family moment when Marek, Sully, and Kaden joined them. Anyone looking at the small group could tell they were close, closer than anyone else in the club. Other than my sister and me, of course. Both children must have sensed the sadness of the moment, because they broke out in cries simultaneously. Adelaide and Sully rocked them, trying their best to soothe them while they themselves were distraught.

Right or wrong, I took comfort in not being the only one who was visibly upset.

Ryder wrapped his arm around my waist. "It's gonna be okay, babe. You'll see." He leaned down and gave me a kiss, and just before he pulled away, I latched on to him for dear life. Lacing my fingers in his hair, I pulled him as close as I could and kissed him like I never have before. As we tasted each other, I poured every bit of love I could inside him, stealing his breath for my own to keep until he came back.

Only then could I breathe again.

CHAPTER
THIRTY-SEVEN

Ryder

TWO DAYS HAD PASSED SINCE we'd left, and every second away from Braylen was agonizing. Even though the rest of the guys were bothered by the departure, they seemed used to it. I didn't think I'd ever become accustomed to leaving her behind, crying and worried out of her mind that she was never gonna see me again. Christ! Every tear she shed tore away a piece of me, and there wasn't a damn thing I could do to comfort her, other than tell her how I felt and promise to come back.

Neither of which she initially took very well.

I talked to Braylen every time we stopped, and her voice gutted me. I knew she was going through it, but so was I. Something I had to remind her of. During our last call, she told me she loved me and not to worry about her. Truth be told, my jealous streak spiked with the thought that she was spending time with one of the guys at the club, taking her mind off her worry for me. When I voiced as much, she called me crazy, then reminded me that she didn't want to be a distraction for whatever I had to do. She just wanted me back safe and sound, and in one piece.

As planned, Etch, Smiley, and Miles joined us, taking turns with the rest of us driving back to California. I learned that Smiley—who was constantly grinning, hence the name—was twenty-six, had two baby mamas and a whole lot of drama. Minus the kids, he reminded me a lot of Hawke, or at least who Hawke was a year back. Personality-wise only. Physically, he was the exact opposite with his bright blond hair and heavy facial scruff. He seemed to be a good guy, telling us that he was honored to wear the KC cut.

Miles had a serious look plastered on his face at all times. He was older than Smiley, closer to my thirty-four years, although he seemed like he might even be older. Hard life. That was what I thought of when I looked at him, and in some ways, he kind of reminded me of myself. Before Braylen.

His light brown hair came to his shoulders, thick and wavy. I over-heard Adelaide and Sully whispering about how lucky he was to have such hair, a conversation I definitely wouldn't be mentioning to either Marek or Stone.

———◆———

"YOU GUYS CAN SET UP in these rooms." Marek showed our Texas brothers to some of the empty rooms at the club, since we wouldn't be needing them during their visit. He'd contemplated setting them up at Zip's house, where Reece had initially stayed before moving in with Tripp, because it was so close to the clubhouse, but decided against it at the last minute.

Zip was one of our fallen brothers. He was a good kid, loyal as hell. Unfortunately he'd been killed when some of the Reapers had run his vehicle off the road, snatching Adelaide and Kena per Psych's request. We paid him homage by burying him on the compound since our club meant everything to him.

"Get situated, then meet us in Chambers," Stone announced, checking to see if they needed anything before joining the rest of us.

Before long we were all gathered around the wooden table, our guests leaning against the wall much like we'd done when at their place.

"Okay," Marek started, "the trackers are still live, and it looks like they're are at the docks."

"No doubt waiting on some sort of shipment," Trigger offered. "We ambush them there. Quick and unexpected."

The ol' man was anxious to move on our enemy, just like the rest of us, but we had to be cautious. Like I'd mentioned before . . . it could be a trap.

"All of 'em?" Stone asked, frowning at how easy this all seemed.

"Enough of 'em."

"You all know what I think," I said, leaning back in my chair and crossing my arms over my chest. Everyone remained quiet, too busy processing all of the what-ifs, I was sure.

"What seems to be the problem?" Etch inquired after several moments passed without another word from any of us.

"The trackers were placed on some of the Reapers bikes a while ago. They shouldn't still be active, but they are. It might be some sort of trap," Marek gritted, obviously annoyed it was taking us so long to figure out what to do.

"Then why don't we hunt them?" Smiley asked, grinning like he'd just asked the most obvious question.

"What?" Breck chimed in, seemingly annoyed that Smiley even put in his two cents.

Even though Breck looked pissed off, it didn't stop Smiley from explaining. "Scope 'em out. Take a couple trips to where you think they are and watch 'em. See if they're even there. If they are, probably not a trap. If there's no sign of life, then figure something else out." He nodded before adding, "Oh and by the way, I've used a tracker on one of my exes, and the fucker lasted for two months. Just sayin'."

Funny how it took someone new to point out the obvious. The majority of us were dealing with our own personal issues, and because the Reapers had threatened us through our women, we weren't seeing things the way we should've. Blinded with the need for revenge, we ignored what could've essentially been right in front of our faces.

If we indeed weren't walking into a trap, we could've taken care of business much sooner. The thought alone angered me; the war with our enemy could've been over by now.

"Anyone opposed to what Smiley suggested, raise your hand," Marek said. I looked around the room and not one man raised his arm. We were all on the same page in that we wanted to do something . . . anything.

"Okay, then." He slammed down the gavel before pushing away from the table.

I was one of the last to leave Chambers, too distracted thinking about Braylen to realize only Jagger remained.

"You okay, man?"

"I guess. It's just . . . there are so many things that can go wrong. And now that I. . . ."

"Have something to lose?" he finished for me. He slid out a chair and took a seat next to me. "Listen, every time I step into that ring, there's always a chance someone is gonna get the best of me."

"I'm not talkin' about losing a fuckin' cage fight," I seethed. "This is so much more than that."

"Let me finish." Jagger was only silent for a moment. "If you remember, I killed someone in that ring." *That fact had slipped my mind.* "All I did was hit him in the wrong spot."

"Wasn't that guy a drug addict? Somethin' was gonna get him sooner or later," I mumbled, growing impatient with our conversation.

"That's not the point."

"Then what is?"

"That I take risks every time I fight. We, as a club, take risks every time we leave this compound, our reputation preceding us, angering our enemies. And we take risks when we fall in love with someone. All of a sudden nothing else matters but the woman holding our heart. It's like the thought of something happening to Kena physically hurts, so I try not to let those images in, but sometimes I can't help it." Jagger took a deep breath, reclining in his seat to give me the time to digest his words.

"When did you get so damn philosophical?"

"I'm an old soul." He laughed, slapping the table and rising to his feet. "Now let's go find out when we're leavin'."

CHAPTER
THIRTY-EIGHT

Braylen

SALZAR HAS BEEN EXTREMELY ACCOMMODATING to all of us. He's not much for words but has made sure we're comfortable and have everything we need. Marek left strict instructions that we're not allowed off the compound, even with some of the men accompanying us.

"It's been four days," Reece complained. "When are they coming back for us? I'm going out of my mind, thinking the worst." She sat on the edge of the bed, biting her lower lip in nervousness, a sentiment all of us shared. Her long chestnut-colored hair flowed down her back, her blue-gray eyes rather stunning. She'd been a stripper at Indulge, but not for long, not after Tripp had met her. He'd saved her from being attacked by one of the customers, and the rest, as they say, was history. They seemed to be smitten with each other, and although I was still getting to know Reece, I knew Tripp even less. In fact, the only men of the club I really knew were Jagger and Ryder. I'd been around the rest of them at gatherings here and there, but they were still a bit of a mystery to me. Although they all seemed to have things in common, such as loyalty and being overbearing—"protective," as Ryder would often correct.

"Someone will call soon, sweetie," Adelaide promised. "They're just not done yet." She seemed so sure everything was going to work out, I couldn't help but think she had some sort of inside information. Or maybe she just didn't want all of us to freak out at the same time. Lord knew, she had her hands full with Riley and her unborn little one.

After putting her daughter in the playpen next to Kaden, Adelaide took a seat next to Reece. "Listen, you need to calm down and focus on your baby," she instructed, gently rubbing Reece's belly.

"I know. I just can't help it." Adelaide gave her a sympathetic look before turning her attention to me. "So, Braylen"—she smirked—"things seem to be going much better with Ryder. He finally wise up?"

"For the most part." I smiled, thinking how far Ryder had come in such a short span of time. Don't get me wrong, he fought the majority of the time to let me in, but thankfully he'd come to his senses. Thinking about him just then sent a shiver of unease through me. If I dwelled on it too long, I'd start to become even more depressed about our current situation than I already was. "Hey, why don't we go out to the bar and have a drink. We can pretend like it's a girls' night out and that we're not really stuck inside this place."

"Sounds good to me," Reece agreed, swooping all of her hair to one side and adjusting her shirt once she stood. "Although I'm just having soda."

"Same here." Adelaide laughed. "Christ! I never thought I'd be pregnant *and* breastfeeding at the same time."

Sully and Kena came into the room, laughing and signing to each other, completely engaged in their conversation. I was thrilled Kena had finally opened up after all these years. Before she met Jagger, I was the only one she hung out with, but since him, she'd really blossomed, coming into her own and not being such an introvert. Sully was the one who taught Jagger how to sign so he could communicate with my sister, so I figured I owed her one as well for Kena's social successes.

"What you are two laughing at?" Reece asked, looking into the mirror to glance at her reflection. Tucking a strand of hair behind her ear, she turned to the two women who'd just joined us.

"I think Kena has an admirer," Sully teased, bumping her shoulder into Kena's.

My sister shook her head. *Sully's crazy. All he did was offer me some of his pizza.*

"Oh yeah? Who?" I asked after translating for Reece and Adelaide, who knew some sign language but not enough to keep up with the flowing conversation.

Kena tried to playfully cover Sully's mouth, but she sidestepped my sister and blurted, "Nash."

I knew exactly who they were referring to because Salzar had briefly introduced us to everyone, Nash being the one who stuck out from the rest. He was certainly handsome with his long black hair and dark blue eyes. He was tall and broad shouldered, slender but muscular. The shirt he wore left little to the imagination, fitting him like a glove.

I know, I know. I'm not supposed to notice other men, but I'm not dead. None of us were interested in anyone but the men who held our hearts, but we also knew a handsome bastard when we saw one. But we weren't stupid either—girl talk stayed between us. Besides, causing tension between any of the guys just for looking was the last thing we wanted to do.

"I'm sure he was just being polite." I gave Kena a wink. "We're gonna grab a drink and try to forget for a little while. Wanna come?"

Please.

We all filed out and headed toward the small bar. It wasn't anywhere near the size the guys had back home at their clubhouse, but I counted five seats. *Yep, it'll do.*

Nash had been standing around talking to a few of the other guys, but as soon as he saw us take a seat, he rushed over and walked behind the bar.

"What can I get you, ladies?" He looked at all of us and smiled, but afterward his attention moved to Kena. He tried not to be obvious, taking all of our orders, but his eyes kept drifting back to my little sister. Maybe he did have a little crush on her.

Over the course of the next two hours, I'd been able to relax a little, doing my best to focus on bonding with the incredible women stuck in the same position as me. For the most part, they seemed to be handling it well, but how much of that was a façade? If I had to guess, I'd say the majority.

Salazar checked in on us a few times, at one point even pulling Nash aside to talk to him before disappearing to his room. He'd been staying in one of the back bedrooms, seemingly taking his promise to keep us safe very seriously.

---◆---

"WELL, THAT'S IT FOR ME." Sully stretched her arms above her head, her white tank top exposing a small amount of skin, enough to where I saw a scar above the waistband of her shorts. My eyes flicked to hers and I prayed she hadn't noticed. The last thing I wanted to do was make her feel uncomfortable.

Ryder had told me a few things about her past, enough for me to realize what a strong woman Sully actually was to have gone through what she had and come out the survivor she was today.

"Me too," Reece yawned, finishing her soda before hopping off her barstool. "You coming?" she asked Kena, squeezing her shoulder.

My sister took another sip and placed her glass on the bar, pushing it toward Nash who was beaming at her. *Jagger better not get wind of this.*

Someone must've filled Nash in on the fact that Kena wasn't deaf, that she just couldn't speak, because a few times he asked her a question, then passed her a notepad and pen. His attention toward her wasn't pushy, but I definitely picked up that he was interested, even though I knew he wasn't stupid enough to make an actual move on her. He knew better. In fact, Ryder had mentioned that he warned everyone. What exactly that meant, I had no idea, but I could take a guess, especially if it came out of Ryder's mouth.

I'm ready too, Kena signed, smiling politely at Nash before standing.

"Yep, I'm ready for bed," Adelaide announced, stifling a yawn as she rose to her feet.

"I guess I am as well," I agreed, walking behind Kena and whispering in her ear. "You *definitely* have an admirer." She looked at the man behind the bar, then back to me.

You're gonna get me in trouble.

"Not me, lil' sis. Not me."

"Good night, ladies," Nash called out as we disappeared down the hallway.

We'd been assigned two of the bedrooms. Sully and Adelaide shared one with the children, and Reece, Kena and I shared the other, my sister and I sharing a bed while Reece occupied the spare one. Grateful not to have to sleep alone, lost in thoughts of what Ryder was doing at that exact moment, I found solace falling asleep next to Kena. Just like when we were kids and one of us had a nightmare.

CHAPTER THIRTY-NINE

Ryder

TWO DAYS AFTER WE'D ARRIVED back in California, we finally decided to take a drive out to where we believed some of the Reapers were gathered. An hour away from our stomping ground. We planned on exacting a few recon missions, so to speak, before doing anything, but lo and behold, the very first ride we took, we saw a few of our enemy unloading crates from a secluded and otherwise abandoned shipyard.

Maybe Smiley was right after all. Maybe the devices we'd placed on some of their bikes were still active, and they had no clue they were even being tracked. However, extremely cautious and aware it could still be a trap, we never made a move. Not that first time. Instead we returned to the clubhouse to discuss exactly how we wanted to proceed.

Most of the Reapers weren't the smartest tools in the shed, which had always worked to our advantage when dealing with them, but we did a thorough sweep of our rides, as well as the cages, just to make sure they hadn't returned the favor and popped some of their own trackers on our vehicles.

When we were satisfied we still had the upper hand, we strapped as many weapons to our bodies as we could, as well as filling up the backs of the cages with enough artillery and ammo to end a war. Which was exactly what we planned to do.

We wanted the other bastard who'd threatened some of the women, but more than that, we needed to take out as many of the Reapers as we could, setting our sights on Rabid more than anyone else. We had to take out the new man in charge before he even had a chance to rally his men. And if Koritz just happened to be there, then we'd make sure he got his as well.

Two days after the first secret visit we'd made, we decided to finally make our move. Marek, Stone, Breck and Jagger rode out in one of the cages, while Tripp, Etch, Smiley, Miles and I occupied the second one. The rest of the guys stayed back at the club per request of our fearless leader. Cutter wanted to go with his son, but in the end he followed orders, remaining on standby along with Trigger and Hawke.

By the time we'd arrived, the sun had long since dipped behind the horizon. Darkness shielded us as we parked half a mile away from the shipyard, the various dilapidated buildings offering us shelter while we cautiously snuck closer to some of the men hanging around the back of one of their trucks. There looked to be six of them, but there could've been more inside the building they were extracting the wooden boxes from.

"Too bad we aren't still in the business," Etch whispered. "Can you imagine how much fuckin' money is in those crates?"

"You don't even know what's in them," Tripp replied, pressing his back against a concrete wall when one of the Reapers passed by fifty feet ahead of where we were all huddled.

"Still," Etch finished, shrugging before following Marek around the corner, disappearing so fast we almost lost both of them.

"Fuck, it's dark out here," I mumbled, resting my hand on the handle of my gun just in case anything popped off unexpectedly. Turning a few more corners and hurrying across the yard, hiding now and again to ensure our attack was truly a surprise, we finally came to a place where we could see all the action. Action we were gonna be a part of soon enough.

When my eyes landed on the sight in front of me, I smiled. A two-birds-one-stone kind of smile. Not only had Rabid just exited the building, but Koritz followed directly behind him. They were still too far away to hear their conversation, but whatever they were talking about, neither of them looked too happy. The only light provided came from the full moon and the building, but it was enough for us to see how many people we had to contend with whenever we decided to show ourselves. The desolation of the area couldn't have been more perfect for executing these bastards and then hiding their bodies in any number of places.

Finally, Koritz threw up his hands, said something incoherent, then walked away. My eyes flicked to Rabid, and with the little I could make out of him, he looked pleased, clasping his hands together one time before walking back toward the building with a cocky gait. As if he'd just been told something he'd wanted to hear.

"You guys ready?" Marek asked, looking at each of us before continuing. "Be fuckin' careful and watch your back." I took a step forward, but he stopped me, shaking his head. "Ryder, you go with Jagger, Etch, and Tripp. That way." He pointed to our right. "Get behind that building as fast as you can." Turning to look at Breck, Miles, and Smiley, he instructed, "You guys come with Stone and me. We're gonna surround them on the other side."

With a lift of his hand, we began to move into position, creeping around the sides of the crumbling structures to get to the one we needed, when a shrill sound rang out, making us all stop dead in our tracks.

"What the fuck was that?" we heard one of the Reapers shout, looking all around until a few of them started yelling to each other. I closed my eyes and took a deep breath, knowing our plan was goin' right down the shitter because someone left their goddamn phone on. Some asinine song that just put us all in more danger.

"Fuck!" I heard Smiley whisper-shout, trying to silence his cell through his cut, but it kept ringing. The shouting in front of us increased, and we knew we had to make a decision to attack head-on or scatter to the sides like Marek had originally planned. Either way, our enemy knew they had company.

"Shut that thing off," Stone demanded, grabbing Smiley and pulling him behind the rest of us. Slamming him against the wall of the building, Stone reached into Smiley's vest, pulled out the device and threw it to the ground, stomping it to pieces at the exact moment it started ringing again. It was probably the first time since I'd met Smiley where he didn't have a grin kicking up the corners of his mouth.

"Sorry," Smiley apologized, keeping his distance from the rest of us because he knew he'd just fucked up. Royally. I thought for sure Stone was gonna knock him out, but instead, our VP walked back toward Marek, mumbling something under his breath.

As we took a step to disband, I heard Koritz shout, "Knights!"

CHAPTER
FORTY

Ryder

A SPRAY OF BULLETS SLICED through the air the closer we moved toward the men scrambling to hide behind whatever was in front of them, seeking cover anywhere they could find. Although they were just putting off the inevitable. There was a lot of shouting, from us and from them, instructions becoming jumbled until I barely knew who was speaking.

Moving slightly to the left to peer around the corner of the building I was hidden behind, a bullet struck the concrete beside my head, missing me by millimeters. I knew there was a good chance I wasn't gonna make it out of there alive, so I decided to push fate's hand and retaliate.

Just as I was about to move into the open, a hand shoved me to the ground, dirt going up my nose I'd been so surprised by the attack. Only it wasn't an attack at all—it was Marek. Before I could say a word, though, I saw him spin around and fire off two rounds, followed by a thump. Someone falling to the ground not twenty feet behind us.

"Thanks, man" was all I could say. What other response was appropriate?

"Tripp and Jagger made it around back. When I tell you to, I want you to stand and fire. There are three men in front of us, another two off to the left." How he could see a damn thing with the clouds passing in front of the moon was beyond me, but I had to trust him. And I did. Wholeheartedly.

"Ready?"

"Yeah." My heart crashed into my chest as a bead of sweat trickled down the side of my face.

"Go!" he yelled, pushing past my body as he barreled forth and fired shot after shot into the night air. With all of the commotion and bullets whizzing past my head, my adrenaline kicked into overdrive, pushing my feet with every step I hadn't even realized I was taking. "Behind the building. Your left!" Marek shouted before disappearing.

When I'd finally made it to the building, I indeed found Tripp and Jagger. The light from inside the warehouse allowed me to see much more than I could moments before.

"Where're the rest of the guys?"

"Fuck if I know," Tripp griped, carefully peering through the window to check things out.

"Anyone in there?" Jagger asked. When he turned to face me, I saw a streak of blood on his neck.

"You get hit?" I moved closer to try and inspect it, but he shook his head.

"Just grazed my skin. Nothing serious."

"Jesus, what the fuck is goin' on?" I asked to no one in particular. It seemed like I was drifting through a nightmare, one where all of our lives could be snuffed out in a split second. Only it wasn't a nightmare at all.

I saw movement to my left and when I turned, gun locked and loaded with my arm outstretched, index finger playing with the trigger, I was two seconds away from firing. Then I saw it was Marek running at us.

"I almost fuckin' shot you."

"Good thing you didn't." Marek was calm, calmer than he should've been in those circumstances. Then again, if he freaked out, where would that leave the rest of us?

"Hey, look who just snuck inside," Jagger interrupted, glancing from the window to us and back again. When we all turned to look at who he was referring to, we saw Koritz rifling around inside the back of some ol' truck, seemingly oblivious that there were four of us watching his every movement. All he had to do was look up and he'd see us, but like always, the crooked DEA agent was only worried about himself.

As I pried my eyes away from that bastard, I caught a glimpse of Stone hovering close to the side of the building. He appeared to be hurrying in our direction, but then he stopped, his feet seemingly frozen in place. The popping sounds of guns being fired were still prevalent, so I was baffled as to why he wasn't seeking cover.

Is he looking for us?

Why isn't he moving?

I swore the man had no fear, even when he should, and I was sure it all stemmed back to him not being able to feel pain. He could still be killed, however, and the sight of him just standing there pissed me off. Not only for him, but for us in case we bore witness to a sight that would haunt us forever.

Him being taken out.

"What the hell is he doin'?" Marek asked, shouting a barrage of obscenities before moving past us and toward his best friend.

But he was too late.

My mouth wouldn't open to warn him. I couldn't move, frozen in place much like Stone. Time slowed but didn't allow me the ability to do a goddamn thing other than watch. My heart skipped a beat and my vision blurred.

A man came out of the brush and walked up behind Stone, standing a few feet from him and pointing the gun at the back of his head. He was unaware that our leader was rushing toward him, and right before Marek tackled him, the light from the gun flashed brightly.

Stone's head jerked forward before he was thrown to the ground, his lifeless body sprawled out in front of us. As soon as Marek saw what happened, he went crazy, jamming his gun into the man's mouth and pulling the trigger. When he finally rose to his feet, his right shoulder jerked backward, his feet stumbling to keep him upright.

At that point, I'd come unglued and raced past Jagger and Tripp, intent on running right into the crosshairs of the bullets still relentlessly being fired.

I was feet from Marek when a pain sliced through my thigh, my leg locking up and suddenly becoming dead weight. I lurched forward, my arms reaching out to find something solid to brace me, but there was nothing. I'd made it to the edge of the building and unfortunately had a clear view of the scene continuing to unfold in front of me.

Another bullet pierced Marek, that time in the chest. He was thrown backward, his gun falling to his side and not in front of him to ward off another attack.

As my legs gave out and I fell to the ground, Tripp and Jagger were next to me. Jagger threw off his cut, ripped off his shirt and made quick work of tying it around my thigh, instinctively knowing where I'd been hit. Did they see it happen?

"Did you really think you'd win, you piece of shit," Koritz shouted, stepping from the building with his weapon raised to finish off our president. He spit on the ground near Marek's head. "You made a big mistake making Carrillo cut off all ties with the Reapers. That decision affected me too, ya know." Koritz's foot connected with Marek's wounded shoulder. "Now you'll finally get what you deserve." Laughing, he turned and looked toward Stone's body. "Looks like you'll be joining your VP soon enough," he threatened, stepping forward to snatch Marek's life.

"I don't think so," a gruff voice said, walking up behind the DEA agent and shoving a gun into his back. Whoever it was remained in the shadows, hiding so I couldn't get a good look at him. His voice sounded familiar, though.

Koritz whipped around, lowering his gun because he obviously knew the man; otherwise, he would've fired on him. It was then that Tripp made a move toward Marek, but before he got too far, I grabbed his leg. If he had any chance of not getting shot himself, he needed to assess the situation.

Thankfully Koritz was engaged at the moment, but how long would that last? Who was he even talking to?

"Be careful," I urged, releasing him and wincing as Jagger tied the material tighter around my wound. Seconds later my vision started to tunnel, but I fought like hell to stay alert.

"What are you doin'? We're on the same side," Koritz said, lifting his weapon back in front of him.

The mystery man laughed. "No we aren't."

Koritz wasted no time in pulling his trigger, but nothing happened. Two more clicks sounded before he tossed his weapon to the ground at the man's feet. He knew he was out of ammo and there wasn't a damn thing he could do to defend himself, so he started spouting off at the mouth instead.

My attention flicked to Tripp, who'd been able to sneak up next to Marek, but as soon as he looked toward the two men in front of him, he froze.

"Oh, so now that I gave you my contact's name, you're gonna kill me?" When the man remained silent, it was clear that was exactly what was goin' down. Koritz started bargaining for his life the split second he realized he was expendable. "I'll give ya whatever you want. Half of my take. What do ya say?"

The shadowed man finally stepped forward.

It was Rabid.

The Savage Reaper's VP himself.

"I'm gonna have to decline," he said before putting a bullet through Koritz's head. The agent was dead before his body hit the ground.

The last thing I saw before I blacked out was Rabid walking toward Tripp and Marek, muttering something as he raised his gun toward them.

CHAPTER FORTY-ONE

Braylen

ASTONISHINGLY, I WAS LOST TO the deepest realms of sleep when a loud bang woke me. Then I heard shouting followed by a bright light. Kena stirred beside me.

"What the hell?" I grumbled, disoriented and annoyed that someone woke me up in such a way. Covering my face with my pillow, it took me several seconds to remember where I was, although I'd been in the same place for days. Hearing a distressed voice, I unshielded my eyes and saw Adelaide rushing toward me.

"Get up," she yelled. "We have to go." She was frantic as she glanced around the room, the wild look in her eyes frightening me. I had no idea what she was doing because she wasn't looking at either of us, or Reece, who'd also shot up in her bed in a panic.

Then just as swiftly as Adelaide had arrived, she left.

"What's going on?" I'd already hopped out of bed and run behind her out into the hallway when it dawned on me that maybe the club was under attack. Catching up to her before she entered the large common space, I grabbed her arm and spun her around. "What's happening? Are we in danger?"

She shook her head before tears fell and painted her cheeks. "He's dead," she wailed, pulling her hair as she retreated, hitting the wall which finally kept her in place.

I had no idea who she was referring to, but it had to be one of our men.

Before I could get any answers, I joined in her anguish, crying right along with her. Kena hurried toward us, signing to me while terror stole her reserve.

What's wrong?

"I don . . . don't know," I blubbered, wiping my face with the back of my hand. "Adelaide said 'He's dead,' but I don't know who she's talking about." My lungs worked feverishly, pulling in air faster than I could expel it.

Just when I thought I was going to hyperventilate, Salzar ran toward us.

"We gotta go," he urged, moving quickly but seemingly calmer than the three of us. A flurry of bodies passed, men spouting out instructions while I stood there in the midst of the tornado. I saw Reece and Sully carrying Riley and Kaden, followed by Nash and a few others holding our suitcases.

Next thing I knew we were all loaded into two vehicles and speeding out of the clubhouse lot as if someone had been chasing us.

Apparently, time had been the culprit.

———— ◆ ————

I KEPT HEARING ADELAIDE SAYING "He's dead," but who was she talking about? Furthermore, who had given her the news? She never mentioned that someone had called her. Did one of the guys at the club we were staying at tell her something? If so, why had they chosen to keep the rest of us in the dark?

We'd been driving for three hours when my cell abruptly rang. I'd made sure it was charged, waiting for the moment when Ryder would call me. *Praying* he would call me.

Fumbling with the phone and almost dropping it, I managed to swipe the screen before the ringing ceased. "Hello," I hurriedly answered. "Ryder?"

"No, it's me." Jagger's voice sounded strained.

"Where's Ryder?"

"He can't. . . ." He trailed off, short spurts of air hitting my ear as I listened to him trying to control his breathing. "I don't even know what to say. It's so bad. So bad," he repeated. I swore he was crying, but I couldn't be sure. Either way, something terrible happened, and if I thought I was gonna lose my mind before, I was surely gonna go mental if Jagger didn't start talking.

"You need to tell me what happened, Jagger. Please." Kena whipped her head toward me, and the look on her face was priceless. Like she'd been given the best gift, and in a sense she had. At least she knew her man was alive, well enough to make a phone call.

I remained on the line, the seconds passing in silence until I heard the first syllable of his first word.

"They didn't make it."

I swore my heart stopped beating right before the line went dead. I immediately dialed Jagger's number back, but it went straight to voice mail. I tried five more times, but each time I heard his automated message telling me to leave a message after the beep. Clutching my phone tightly, I willed it to ring, my internal voice screaming at the top of her lungs for the damn thing to burst out in sound.

I hadn't even realized that I'd been crying until Kena unbuckled her seat belt and crawled next to me, pulling me into her embrace. She tried to comfort me, and I loved her dearly for her attempt, but nothing in the world would make me feel better except for Ryder's voice.

Right before I was about to lose it, my screams bubbling inside my throat, I heard one of the men's phones ring. Nash was driving our SUV while one of his buddies sat next to him—I believed his name was Cass.

"Yeah," Nash answered in a hurry. "Fuck. Okay. Yeah. I know. I'm drivin' as fast as I can." Nothing else was said before he hung up, tossing his phone into the center console.

"Who was that?" Reece asked from behind us. I'd completely forgotten she was in the vehicle with us, she'd been so quiet. When Nash didn't answer, she leaned forward in her seat. "Who was that?" That time her voice was louder, and there was no way our driver didn't hear her.

"No one."

"No one?" she screeched, followed by the click of her seat belt coming undone as she tried to crawl over the seat to where Kena and I were sitting, all the while careful of her small pregnant belly. It seemed as if Reece had finally snapped, joining the rest of us in our fear. When she'd managed to clear the seat, she lunged toward the front, hitting Nash on his arm so frantically I feared he was going to veer off the road and crash.

"What the hell? Sit down," he demanded, the gravel in his voice leaving no doubt that he was serious. And extremely angry. But Reece ignored him, her hair flying wildly around her as she continued to slap him. He tried to dodge her hits but he was trapped, trying to keep his eyes on the road while attempting to get away from her flailing arms.

"You need to calm down, sweetheart," Cass coaxed, grabbing her hands and holding them together in front of her, cautious not to injure her. His voice was eerily calm, especially after having witnessed her break with reality. "We're following orders. We're not to give you ladies any info until we know for sure what we're dealin' with, so no amount of yelling and hitting will make us talk." Cass faced not only Reece but Kena and me as well, his dark green eyes flicking to each of us to drive home his point. "Now go back and sit down," he instructed.

He released Reece's hands and turned back around to face front, not even waiting for her to comply, which she did almost right away. Kena and I moved so she could sit between us.

"Can you at least tell us where we're going?" I asked, waiting not so patiently for his answer.

"California," Nash replied. He took a breath. "We're takin' you back home."

CHAPTER
FORTY-TWO

Ryder

A FLURRY OF ACTIVITY DREW me back into consciousness, albeit briefly. My eyes were heavy, lifting them a feat I wanted to give up, but the incessant talking around me increased in volume. After raising my arm toward my face, another task I found rather difficult, I managed to open my eyes, my sight hampered by a bright light. When my pupils had finally adjusted, my vision contorted. Blurry. I saw shapes and witnessed movement, but that was all. Before long, I drifted back into the darkness, Braylen's face greeting me as I relished the comfort of the unknown.

———— ◆ ————

AN INTENSE BURNING SENSATION TRAVELED up my thigh and shoved me from sleep, scrambling toward awareness so rapidly I barely had any time to decipher where I was or who was around me.

"Uhhh," I groaned, trying to move my leg. I clutched the table I was lying on just so I had somewhere to focus my energy; otherwise, I feared I'd tear at my flesh just to try and stop the pain.

"He's awake," I heard someone say. My eyes fluttered open, then closed. Open. Closed. Open. I slowly looked around the room but still didn't know where I was.

"Ryder," the rough voice greeted. "Can you hear me?" Whoever stood over me shook my arm before waving his hand in front of my face. "Ryder!" he shouted. "Look at me."

"Fuck, man," I grated. "Shut up." It was then I recognized the voice. Jagger. "What is that awful smell?" A pungent aroma wafted up my nose until I could barely catch my breath. I turned my head to the side and the smell lessened, although I swore it was trapped inside my nostrils.

"Smelling salts," Jagger answered. "Gotta get you up and back in the land of the living."

"You wait till I get up," I threatened, knowing damn well it would be quite some time before my body would finally decide to cooperate with my brain.

"He's fine," Jagger shouted to someone, walking away from me as my eyes drifted shut once more. Slow and steady breaths calmed me as I rode back into unconsciousness. I didn't make it, however, that god-awful, borderline-painful smell filling my nose again. "Nope. You gotta get up, Ryder."

I swatted the air in front of my face, thankful to have mobility of my arm. It was a start. Now all I had to do was move my leg, enough to chop off the goddamn thing so I could rid myself of the excruciating agony.

"What happened?" I tried to sit up but found the effort laughable.

"Don't move. I need you awake, but don't try and get up. Not until he sees you." Jagger stood by my head, prepared to shove me back down if I made another attempt.

"Who? Until who sees me?"

"The guy Rabid brought in to tend to you guys." His words were so matter of fact, I almost missed the name he'd spoken.

Rabid.

The Savage Reaper's VP.

Memories hit me like a sledgehammer, assaulting my brain until all I could do was live through the horrific events all over again, as if it was the very first time.

My next attempt to get up was successful, albeit strained and half-assed. At least I'd managed to swing my good leg over the table and grip the sides of the metal slab I'd been lying on, essentially anchoring myself in place.

"Whoa," a new voice said that time. When I looked up, my vision swiftly crystal clear, I saw Tripp walking toward me. He looked larger than life, his big form striding with ease until he stood by my side. His shirt was covered in blood, but it didn't appear as if any of it was his.

As I continued to stare at the blood on him, scattered images flashed through my brain, pictures forming to piece together a forgotten story. One of Tripp standing near me after a bullet ripped through my leg. Then one of our nomad hovering over Marek. He'd gone to save him after our prez had been shot. Twice. Then my memory flipped to one of watching Stone. Witnessing the way his head jerked forward right before he fell to the ground.

"Fuck!" My eyes found Tripp's before my vision blurred once more, that time filled with unbelievable grief. "Are they dead?"

"Yeah, they are." Tripp's eyes were red-rimmed, indicating he'd already begun to deal with the catastrophe that had landed at our feet, ripping apart all who'd known them.

"I can't believe it. I just can't. . . ." Shaking my head, a tear fell down my cheek for the loss of my friends.

My brothers.

My family.

CHAPTER
FORTY-THREE

Ryder

"I CAN'T BELIEVE THEY'RE DEAD." I threw my hands over my face, shielding my anguish from Tripp as best I could, although I knew he shared in my grief. Still, there was something about hiding my emotions that allowed me a private moment of sorts to deal with the news.

"I'm upset too, but I didn't know you'd take it *this* hard," Tripp grumbled. "Didn't even think you liked them all that much."

Drawing my hands back, I stared at him in confusion. "What the hell does that mean?" I tried to move, but the pain radiating through my leg stopped me. "Marek and Stone were like my family. I know I was an asshole sometimes, but they saw past my fuckups and accepted me for who I was." My tears built, but I needed to man up and accept what had happened. I had to learn to move on; otherwise, I'd allow the sadness to fester and rot me from the inside out.

"What are *you* talking about?" Before I could respond, Tripp blurted, "Marek and Stone aren't dead. Yeah, it was a close call, for both of them, but they're alive. They're gonna have some scars, for sure, but they're still breathin'."

After my astonishment finally subsided, Tripp filled me in on what happened after I'd passed out from my own gunshot wound. Apparently, when Marek tackled the Reaper who'd shot Stone, he'd managed to change the trajectory of the bullet intended for our VP. Stone had been shot but the bullet had pierced his ear, tearing off the tip of it. I'd seen him fall forward and it'd appeared as if he was dead, but Tripp explained that the force of the bullet had pushed him forward and when Stone hit the ground, he'd been knocked unconscious. Although Stone hadn't experienced any pain when he awoke, he was pissed he was missing a piece of his ear.

I smiled at the thought of Stone's reaction, but then my thoughts went right to Marek. Whereas Stone's injury ended up not to be life-threatening, our leader's wounds were just that. Not necessarily the one to his shoulder, but the bullet that'd pierced his chest had caused a part of his breastbone to slice a section of his lung before exiting his body.

It was touch and go for a while, but thankfully Marek had pulled through, although he definitely had to take it easy and allow his body to heal properly. I had no doubt Sully would chain him to their bed if he caused too much trouble.

I'd been so lost in the news of my brothers that I'd completely forgotten Jagger had mentioned Rabid.

Psych's right-hand bastard.

As if sensing my impending barrage of questions, Jagger appeared behind Tripp. And when they both moved to the side, Rabid walked up next to me, staring down at me with a look of worry.

What the fuck is goin' on?

Anticipating my struggle, Jagger and Tripp moved to stand on either side of me, holding me down so I didn't further injure myself.

"Calm down," Jagger instructed, putting more pressure on my shoulder until he felt some of the fight leave my overly tired body. Seconds ticked by before anyone spoke, and that time it was the enemy.

Or so I thought.

"I'm not who you think I am," Rabid confessed, running his hands over his bald head in what appeared to be uncertainty. The last time I saw him, other than a couple nights prior, he'd showed up with Kortiz at our club, threatening to rain down holy hell on our club if we didn't tell him where Psych was.

I parted my lips to speak but fell silent when I couldn't decide what to ask first. Rabid saw my hesitancy and took the lead instead. "I won't tell you my real name, but I'm sure at some point you'll find out. I have no doubt you men are resourceful. But until then, I can tell you that I've been undercover, investigating the Savage Reapers. Sam Koritz ended up being icing on the cake."

As he talked about ties with not only the Los Zappas cartel, but links to terrorist groups, sex trafficking and gun running, my mind tried to comprehend everything, pinging back and forth between memories and trying to understand what he was telling us.

" . . . he up and vanished."

"What?" I asked, doing my best to focus.

Rabid, or whatever his name was, stepped closer to repeat himself, my mind temporarily blanking on what he'd just said.

"Just as I was about to take down Psych, he up and disappeared."

Tripp shoved his hands in his jeans pockets. "Yeah, we heard about that." Our nomad smiled, even though it was brief.

"Yeah, I'm sure you did."

"Don't worry, you won't ever find anything." Tripp took a moment before finishing his thought. "Tying us to it." His smirk reappeared, essentially telling the man Psych was indeed dead.

"Well, if we ever find him, just know I'll be payin' your club a little visit. I do have a job to do, after all."

"Like I said. . . ." Tripp rocked back and forth on his heels as he entered a visual showdown with the guy.

An image pushed its way to the forefront of my memory, and before I could think better of it, I blurted, "But I saw you shoot Koritz."

"He finally gave me the name I was after, the one in charge." He was so matter of fact, it was unexpected.

"Who are you undercover with that would legally allow you to shoot someone?" Jagger asked the question that time, his confusion rivaling my own.

"Doesn't matter," he replied. "Maybe I was under too long, the darkness the Reapers existing in affecting me more than I care to acknowledge." Shrugging, he said, "Or maybe I shot him in self-defense." He smirked, and I knew right then he wasn't sorry for killing that sonofabitch, and would probably do it again if given the chance. Koritz certainly wouldn't be missed, and I was only too happy that he'd finally been dealt with. And who better than from the man Koritz most likely thought was on his side the entire time.

"Why help us, though?" I asked, looking to Tripp and Jagger and then back to the essential stranger standing next to all of us.

"Because even though your club was on our radar, you guys weren't even in the same league as the Reapers. And once I found out your president had cut all ties with the cartel, I focused all of my time, energy and resources on the group I'd infiltrated all those years ago. We have enough to dismantle the club and put away the rest of 'em for a very long time."

He moved aside as I saw several strangers approach—two men and a woman dressed in scrubs. Apparently, they were who'd been called in to help. As they made quick work in checking on my leg, I couldn't help but be thankful the war was finally over between the Knights Corruption and the Savage Reapers.

CHAPTER FORTY-FOUR

Braylen

AT SOME POINT DURING THE trip home, I'd fallen asleep dreaming of Ryder. The images conjured from my subconscious helped keep me locked in my slumber. The man I loved smiled at me, his gentle touch trying to rouse me from sleep, but I refused to open my eyes even though I could hear him calling my name. Then everything changed, the sudden urgency in his voice alarming me. His mouth opened and his lips were moving, but I couldn't hear anything. Even though my lids were squeezed shut, I could see him. A worried expression pained his features. Then I saw blood. So much blood. The next thing I knew, his face morphed into a blank slate before his body turned into a whirlwind of dust circling above me.

"Braylen. Wake up."

My eyes flew open and I clutched my chest, my lungs on fire due to lack of oxygen. Apparently I'd been holding my breath while locked in my dream. No, my nightmare. My vision blurred as I tried to adjust my sight. The first person I saw was Nash, confusion wrapping its ugly arms around me and squeezing the remnants of sleep from me.

"We're here," he announced, cocking his head before shifting back into the driver seat.

"Where?"

"Home. Well, not home exactly, but close enough, I suppose." He was facing front now, fiddling with his phone while I tried to come to grips with my new reality. I still hadn't talked to Ryder, my conversation with Jagger cut short during the only phone call I'd received.

Looking out the window, I saw the sun shining brightly, although the tint on the vehicle helped to dull the effect. As I glanced around, however, I became confused. Nothing looked familiar.

"Where are we?"

Without answering me, Nash opened his door and disappeared outside. I turned my head to the side and noticed I was all alone.

Where are Kena and Reece? Where is Cass?

Where the hell are we?

Slowly opening my door, I tentatively stepped outside the SUV, closing the door behind me when I realized I wasn't in any sort of danger. Up ahead I saw Kena talking to Jagger, her hands frantically signing before he crushed her to him. Only when I shuffled my feet across the dirt separating us did they look in my direction. Jagger released my sister and she ran toward me, drawing me into a tight hug before stepping back. Jagger was slow to approach, the sight of him causing me to tremble. He looked like he'd been through hell, but from what I could tell he wasn't physically injured, other than a scrape on the side of his neck.

"Hi," he greeted, squeezing my hand briefly before releasing it. "Sorry my phone went dead, but I had other things I had to deal with." He kept his eyes on me, his stare starting to freak me out. Before I lost it, though, he lifted his chin toward the building behind him, flashing me a tight smile. "Let's go. Someone wants to see you."

I reached for his arm to stop his retreat. "Wait." A deep inhalation of air coated my lungs. "He's alive?"

"Yeah, and he's waiting to see you."

"Why didn't you tell me that as soon as you came up to me?" All of my fear morphed into anger, everything hitting me like a goddamn freight train. "I thought he was dead," I screamed, hitting his chest. "Do you have any idea what I've been through?" I raised my hands to strike him again but Jagger caught them and pulled me close.

"I'm sorry." Looking a little guilty, he said, "So much shit happened.

I'm still trying to deal with everything." We stared at each other while I calmed down, his hold lessening until he finally released me. "Now let's go." He grabbed Kena's hand and pulled her behind him as he walked away.

Once inside the building, still unaware as to where exactly we were, I followed Jagger and my sister as he led us through two empty rooms, down a short flight of steps and down a narrowed hallway. When Jagger pushed open a door and I saw what was inside, I knew we'd reached our destination.

To my left, there were two bodies lying on the ground with leather vests covering their faces. Their clothes were soaked with blood, the image of who that could be instantly causing a rush of panic. Then I remembered that Ryder was alive and my heart slowed to its normal beat. Barely.

Taking one more glance at the dead bodies, I couldn't help but wonder who they'd lost.

"Braylen," Jagger called. "Let's go." He pulled me away from the carnage, knowing I was about to lose it even though my man was still alive, although I had no idea what condition I'd find him in.

Walking farther into the large space, I saw Tripp leaning over a table talking to someone, their voices hushed. It wasn't until he moved to the side that I recognized the man laying down.

Ryder.

I rushed forward, shoving Tripp to the side and launching myself into Ryder's arms, my body partly covering his.

"Uhhh," he groaned. "Careful, baby," he warned, a pained look telling me he was injured. Before I could pull back, his lips found mine and he poured everything into our brief kiss. Our joined fear and uncertainty disappeared as our breaths mingled, a piece of our souls joining and relishing in the moment. "I love you so much," he whispered, breaking the kiss to look into my eyes.

"I love you," I replied, giving him another quick kiss before standing up to look at him. His shirt was ripped and bloody, but it was his left leg that was bandaged—his thigh, to be more exact. When my eyes found his to ask what happened, I saw the distress. Whatever happened had rocked him, and I vowed right then and there to do whatever I needed—what *he* needed—to help him through it.

Gingerly touching his leg, careful not to put any pressure on the bandage, I asked, "What happened?" Tears fell down my cheeks before I could stop them, my body finally releasing the shock I'd been trapped in and starting to tremble.

Instead of answering me, Ryder clutched my hand in his and pulled me close. He tried to sit up, and when Tripp saw him struggling, he rushed over and helped him. Swinging his legs over the edge of the table, Ryder spread them and tugged me between them, my chest hitting his as he took my face in his hands.

"I got shot." Before I started to break down even more, he said, "Don't." He wiped my tears as they continued to fall. "I'm fine. Nothing that won't heal. Trust me." His mouth covered mine, the kiss soft and light, his lips lingering without urgency. I savored his comfort even though I was the one who should've been soothing him.

After several minutes, I sat next to him on top of the metal table, our fingers linked and resting in my lap. "Can you tell me what happened?" Reservation painted his rugged face, his fingers squeezing mine tighter before he shook his head. "I have a right to know," I whispered, not wanting to upset him but still trying to urge him to fill me in on what had transpired.

"I'm sorry, but I can't really get into it. One day maybe, but not now." He grimaced when he shifted his weight, his free hand gently moving his injured leg.

"Can I at least ask who died?" The breath in my lungs froze while I waited to see if he'd answer. I swore time stood still while I witnessed a plethora of emotions contorting his expression.

"Breck and Smiley."

CHAPTER
FORTY-FIVE

Ryder

I REFUSED TO RELIVE THE brief moment in time when I believed that my prez and VP were dead. So instead of delaying my answer to Braylen's simple yet devastating question, I answered. Her face fell because she knew what a blow to all of us Breck's death had been.

Smiley, on the other hand, while upsetting that he'd died during the fight because he was a Knight, wasn't as devastating to me. Not only because we didn't really know the guy, but because I harbored a lot of anger toward him, even in his death. It was because of him and his phone that our initial plan of action had been ripped apart in the first place. Although, when I found out he'd jumped in front of Breck to try and save him being shot, a feat which ultimately hadn't worked, my anger subsided a little.

We all knew the risks, each of us signing up to defend our club against all costs. Unfortunately, two members of Knights Corruption wouldn't make it back to see their loved ones. Tripp called Cutter to tell him that his son had died, and he promised to bring his body back home for a proper burial. The nomad had filled me in on their phone call, although it'd been brief. Cutter hadn't said much, but that wasn't uncommon. He was a man of few words, but we all knew he loved his son and was undoubtedly shredded by the news.

———◆———

"ARE YOU READY TO GO?" Jagger asked, helping me to stand before I even uttered a reply. "We gotta get back and take care of everything." He mumbled something else before propping me up with his shoulder under my arm, moving slowly toward the edge of the room we'd been staying in for the past two days. Braylen shrouded my other side, ready to assist me if I needed her help as well. Kena followed behind all of us.

As we walked, I was able to finally lay eyes on the rest of the guys. Stone was leaning against the wall, fiddling with the bandage wrapped around his ear. Adelaide was beside him, slapping his hand away and yelling at him not to touch it. A few feet to the left, I saw Marek lying on a steel table, much like the one I'd been resting on. As I hobbled along, I saw Sully hunching over him and crying.

"Are we sure he's gonna be okay?" I asked Jagger, pointing toward Marek.

"Yeah. The doc Rabid, or whoever he is, brought in said he's gonna need some time to heal but he'll pull through."

Still walking slowly, we rounded the corner and down a hallway too narrow for the three of us to walk side by side, so Braylen stayed close behind, walking with her sister. A short flight of steps and two empty rooms later, we finally hit the outdoors, the California sun doing its best to offer some warmth.

"Where the fuck are we?"

"A twenty-minute ride from where all hell broke loose. Rabid had us load everyone up and come here. I don't know whose it is or what the place is used for, but it did the job, so I'm not complaining."

The guy who'd essentially saved our lives had taken off shortly after he'd revealed who he was, sort of. He never said another word to any of us before he disappeared. Months later, we'd come to find out that Michael Chase, aka Rabid, was an undercover NSA agent assigned to dismantle what was later referred to as one of the biggest cases the organization had ever been involved in.

Hey, what can I say? They had their informants and we had ours.

Up ahead, Tripp and Reece were leaning inside one of the other vehicles. As we passed by, I saw they were keeping watch over Riley and Kaden. No doubt Reece had volunteered for the job, and I knew there was no way Tripp would leave her side, not after everything that had happened. When he backed out, holding a crying Riley in his arms, he saw me and shrugged. Sully and Adelaide were still in the basement of the building, but they wouldn't leave their children for long, so I had no doubt they'd be appearing soon enough. Until then, Reece tried to soothe Kaden, who had also started to fuss.

When we finally made it to the SUV I'd be traveling back home in, Kena opened the back door while Jagger propped me against the side of it. Braylen took over and helped to brace me so I wouldn't fall. I put all of my weight on my good leg because I had no doubt my woman wouldn't be able to hold me up otherwise. I'd crush her.

As I was trying to carefully situate myself in the back seat, I saw Salzar, Etch, and Stone carrying Marek the best they could. Sully was right behind them being comforted by Adelaide. That poor woman had been through enough, we all had, and I prayed this was the end of the fuckin' danger surrounding all of us. After the men had laid Marek across the back seat of another SUV, Sully said something to Miles before walking toward Tripp and Reece.

Once Kaden was placed in Sully's arms, he calmed, and she seemed to do the same. Miles had apparently been asked to grab one of the car seats and transfer it to the truck that her husband had been placed in. And because Stone refused to leave his best friend's side, Miles made another trip back to grab the other car seat for Riley, Adelaide refusing to leave her fiancé's side.

Nash and Cass, two of Salzar's other men, the ones who had driven Braylen, Kena, and Reece to us, helped carry Breck's and Smiley's bodies. Even though the men were dead, they made sure to treat them both with the utmost respect as they carefully laid them in the back of the vehicle they'd be riding in. It was their job to transport the fallen Knights back with us.

Everyone was en route back to our clubhouse, which thankfully wasn't too far away. Our Laredo brothers would only be staying with us until the morning, making sure to get the rest they needed before making the long drive back to Texas, transporting Smiley back with them and taking care of his burial.

Cutter had been the first one in the lot as we all pulled in. As I managed to climb out of our truck, I watched everything unfold as Nash opened the back of the SUV where Breck's body was lain, stepping aside to allow Cutter the space he needed to see his son. Trigger and Hawke exited the building and gathered around Cutter, offering him solace as they helped him carry Breck toward a patch of land behind the clubhouse, the same place where we ended up burying Zip. Cutter had already arranged for a coffin while he waited for us to return, and he laid his son to rest that evening. Whoever was well enough to attend, which was everyone except Marek, paid their respects before Cutter put him in the ground.

Over the course of the following week, Adelaide checked on Marek, who had been set up in the room designated for him whenever he had to stay at the club. She watched over him to ensure he was healing properly and staving off any sort of infection. And because his woman was keeping close watch over the Knights' leader, Stone set up in his room, caring for Riley whenever Adelaide's attentions were otherwise diverted.

I'd chosen to stay with my brothers, not completely convinced we were out of harm's way. But after countless nights passed without retaliation or the police knocking down our gates, I'd made the decision to recoup back at my house with my woman.

Finally putting the last piece of the puzzle into place, completing the picture of the future I wanted.

No . . . the future Braylen deserved.

EPILOGUE

Ryder

One year later

"DAD, I DON'T WANNA GO," I heard as I rounded the corner into our guest bedroom. Zoe was standing in the middle of the room, fidgeting with her dress. "Dad . . . ," she whined, throwing her hands on her hips and entering a stare-down with me.

"Zoe," I countered, leaning against the doorframe. "What's wrong? You look beautiful."

"You know I hate dresses." She continued to fiddle with the white and black polka-dotted material. "And my hair won't go the right way," she complained. Oh Lord, I could only imagine how she'd be once she became a teenager the following year. Puberty was gonna be the death of me, I already knew it. And boys . . . I wasn't gonna do well with boys lurking around my little girl. Zoe was already a looker, and I feared for my sanity as she grew up.

Now that the threat toward our club had finally been eliminated, Rose and I had agreed on increased visitation with Zoe. While they still lived in Illinois, we both made the effort so that my daughter and I could get to know each other more. I also wanted to test the waters between Braylen and Zoe as well, seeing how well they got along before I revealed that I was thinking about having another kid. Thing was, Braylen had told me she wasn't ready for a baby, but maybe if I put the thought in her head, she'd come around sooner rather than later.

"Here, honey, let me help you with that," Braylen said, bouncing into the room to save the day. "Do you want your hair up or down?" She pulled Zoe's shoulder-length red hair off her shoulders, then released it, giving my daughter a visual of different hairdos. I honestly had no idea where Zoe inherited the red hair from; both Rose and I have dark brown. I believe my ex mentioned someone on her mother's side being a redhead, but I couldn't really remember. Other than the color of her strands, there was no mistaking Zoe was mine, although she was looking more like her mother as the years passed.

Zoe smiled, looking at Braylen's reflection in the mirror. "Um . . . how about up?"

"Up it is." Braylen described everything she was doing while she set up her tools, Zoe enthralled with the fact that Braylen was a hair stylist. And a very talented one at that. She'd mentioned that one day she wanted to start her own salon, but she just wasn't ready yet. Little did she know I had a surprise waiting for her, whenever she decided to make the leap.

Money wasn't an issue for me. I never had to think about it because I had plenty of it stocked away—mostly from the club's activities before Marek turned us legit. And because of my smart investments, I was set for ten lifetimes. Braylen knew I was wealthy, but she never asked for a figure. She didn't care, wanted to make her own way, and I respected her more for it, even though I showered her with gifts as often as I could.

Upgrading her car, for one. The day I'd picked her up in a shiny new Mercedes, her dream car, she'd thrown herself into my arms, accepting the vehicle without an issue. She'd known I'd only force it on her anyway. Besides, she'd given me the best head of my life later that evening as thanks.

Win-win for the both of us.

"Sweetheart, you need to get ready yourself or we're gonna be late," I urged, pulling Braylen close the second she finished Zoe's hair.

Furrowing her brows, she turned my wrist toward her and looked at my watch.

"But we still have two hours before it starts."

Retreating to the other side of the room so Zoe wouldn't hear me, I leaned in and nipped her lobe before whispering, "But I need some time to fuck you first."

A pink flush tickled her skin, and I knew she wanted me almost as much as I wanted her.

"Gross, Dad," Zoe admonished.

There was no way she heard what I just said. "What?" I feigned ignorance.

"I know you just said something about sex." She casually toyed with her dress, smiling now that she liked her hair.

Braylen laughed, but there wasn't a goddamn thing funny about what Zoe said. I cleared my throat to get her attention. "What do you know about sex?" I probably should've corrected her assumption, but I was too caught up with the fact that she knew anything at all about the topic. She was only twelve, for Christ's sake.

"I've heard about it." She rolled her eyes, and I thought I was gonna lose it for sure. Every muscle in my body locked up tight, but thankfully Braylen stepped in before I gave myself a heart attack.

"I'll talk to her, find out what she really knows," Braylen said quietly. "Sometimes kids say things but have no idea what they mean." I relaxed, if only slightly. "Now why don't you go wait for us in the living room?

"But. . . ." I swore I pouted like a little bitch. "I thought . . . you know." I waved my index finger back and forth between us.

She leaned up on her tippy toes and pressed her lips to mine. "I'm not letting you ruin my hair." She playfully slapped my chest. "Now go get ready, and I'll do the same." Braylen tapped her foot while she pointed toward the doorway. Unfortunately, I knew I'd have to wait to ravage my woman, but I hoped she knew she was in for it once the opportunity presented itself.

As she shut the door behind me, I saw her say something to Zoe, and they both laughed, the sound making me extremely happy. She might just be more receptive to the idea of having my kid after all.

Brutus came barreling toward me as I entered the living room, hopping up on me as soon as I sat down. It wouldn't take me long to get dressed, so I decided to spend some time with my buddy. I loved that damn dog, more than I thought I'd love any animal.

"She knows what she's missin'," I mumbled, patting Brutus's head as if he had any clue what I was talkin' about. He wagged his tail and gave me a sloppy kiss, licking the side of my face when I made a move to roughhouse with him. Jumping off the couch, Brutus ran toward the door, letting me know that while he wanted to play, he needed to go to the bathroom.

It was rather kismet if I did say so myself. Watching after my three-legged friend as he circled the same patch of grass before taking care of business, I realized that we had both been discarded during the early years of our life. Sure, no one had thrown me out of a moving vehicle, but I'd been tossed around from foster home to foster home until I aged out at eighteen, finding my real family when I became a member of the Knights Corruption years later. I'd been working at a garage when Marek had swung by to pick up a part for a bike he'd been working on. We got to talking and within an hour he'd offered me a job at the club's garage. The rest was history.

Both Brutus and I had reaped a sliver of justice for the wrongs done in our lives as well. About a month prior, I'd been out for a drive when I'd spotted a familiar lookin' piece-of-shit car: an Oldsmobile Cutlass with faded blue paint peeling everywhere on the body and a bumper held on by duct tape.

The vehicle was parked outside a liquor store, and when a man emerged and walked toward the Oldsmobile, I made my move. With his hand resting on the handle of the driver side, I walked up behind him and spun him around. When I'd asked if he was the fucker who tossed a puppy from the car, wanting to make sure I had the right person, he smirked and asked me what business it was of mine. In other words, he was the offender. Breaking his nose didn't satisfy my need for revenge, so I shattered his arm, the one used to discard Brutus like he meant nothing at all.

Much like the payback I'd sought for my dog, fate had done the same with Richard. Although I wanted to put that chapter of my life behind me and remember my mother as she was before her death, wonderful and loving, I still chose to keep tabs on her murderer. It was close to four months after I'd gone to his house that I learned he'd had too much to drink one night and ended up crashing his car into a tree, killing only himself in the accident.

His death brought the final closure to a life of misery, Braylen helping to heal the rest of me with her unconditional love and support. I was one lucky bastard, something she was sure to remind me of whenever she found the opportunity.

------•------

Braylen

ON THE RIDE OVER, I couldn't stop staring at the man who'd flipped my world upside down, in more ways than one. Everything from his occasional arrogance to his infuriating protectiveness, to the sweet words he whispered while he buried himself inside me. Ryder was the man of my dreams. It'd been a bumpy road, and there were still some potholes in our future, I was sure, but I knew we could get through anything as long as we loved each other.

And we did.

Fiercely.

For the occasion, he'd chosen to dress up. Not in a complete suit, because that just wasn't him, but a crisp white button-up, sans tie, and a pair of dark blue dress pants, brown shoes completing his dressy yet casual look.

As we sat at a stoplight, Zoe in the back seat with her earbuds in, singing along to whatever pop song was on, Ryder unbuttoned his sleeves and rolled them repeatedly until his entire forearms were exposed, the muscles jumping with each movement he made. He caught me looking and said, "I have another muscle you can stare at. Taste, even."

My eyes widened as I glanced back at his daughter, but she hadn't heard a thing he'd said. The rest of the trip was done so in silence, other than the radio, for fear that I'd lose control and jump over the console and into his lap. Which would be highly inappropriate with a child present.

So instead, I chose to keep my eyes away from all things Ryder and stare out the window as the world passed us by.

After we arrived and took our seats under the tent that had been erected on the lawn behind the clubhouse, Ryder on my right and Zoe on my left, I couldn't help but be extremely grateful for all the gifts I'd been given. My thankful thoughts were interrupted, however, when my sex-on-a-stick of a man leaned closer and started saying things in my ear that got me all hot and bothered, all sorts of sordid images flashing through my brain and causing me to twitch in my seat.

"Since you wouldn't let me do it at home, I'm gonna get my way we leave here. I'm gonna hike up your dress and bury my face between your legs. You know I'm addicted to that pussy, baby," Ryder professed, kissing my cheek like he hadn't just threatened me with a good fucking. I kept my eyes straight ahead and smiled, not wanting Zoe to think her father was whispering about sex again.

After Ryder had left the bedroom, allowing me to have a talk with Zoe, I'd discovered that she had indeed learned about sex, although some of it was still confusing. I told her it only got worse, to which she gave me the funniest look. After answering a few basic questions, I told her that if she had any more, she should really talk to her mother about them. I'd also warned her not to ask her father, not until she was much older, like around thirty. We both laughed at that one, although she thought I was joking. I wasn't.

Ryder's daughter had been staying at our house for the past week, scheduled to leave the next morning, and while our time together had been short, we'd bonded rather quickly. She thought I had a cool job, and I thought she was a pretty amazing kid. I definitely looked forward to her next visit, which was only a few months away.

As we waited for everyone to arrive, my thoughts drifted to the people who'd become like family, the tragedy bringing us all closer together. When I wasn't working, or hanging out with Kena or Sia, I was shopping with Adelaide, Sully or Reece, or hitting the town for a girls' night out, although one of the guys always attended. They said it was for our safety, but since there was no more viable threat to their club, I'd chalked up their hovering as just being overprotective.

I shifted in my seat, trying to see who'd just pulled into the lot, when

Ryder's fingertips trailed up my leg, my blue dress riding up my thigh when I'd turned around. Zoe's head was turned the other way so she hadn't noticed, but I needed to nip his advance in the bud before he became really brave. Under normal circumstances, I knew he had no qualms about throwing me over his shoulder and disappearing somewhere more private. And while he might be more reserved because of why we were there that day, I still didn't completely trust him not to act . . . like himself.

"What are you doing?" I whispered, turning my head more toward him so as not to draw the attention of his daughter. His fingers were still ghosting over the top of my leg, the heat from his touch driving me insane.

Keep it together.

"Just touching you." He smirked, knowing he was playing a dirty game.

"Well, stop it," I gritted. When his hand trailed farther up my leg, my body shifted completely toward him so only I knew what he was doing.

He gripped my thigh and leaned in. "Meet me inside the clubhouse. I'm gonna fuck you quick before they get started." He hurriedly rose from his seat, then cursed when he saw Kena and Jagger walking toward us. No way in hell we were going anywhere now, and we both knew it. A few more expletives fell from his mouth, but he'd been sure to keep his voice low so as not to have Zoe hear everything. He'd learned to curb his language whenever she was around, although right then he was certainly struggling.

I laughed as I rose to my feet, hugging my sister and then Jagger before engaging them in small talk.

"It's not funny," Ryder growled in my ear, briefly interrupting my conversation.

"It kind of is," I retorted, reaching for his hand which he readily accepted, squeezing a little too hard before I slapped his arm to loosen his grip. A smug grin spread across his face as he continued to hold onto me.

"Can you believe this is finally happening?" Jagger asked, looking first at Ryder and then shooting a glance at Kena, and not his usual smitten expression either. The silent communication was something more, but I didn't have time to dissect it because Zoe was unexpectedly behind us.

"Dad, I have to go to the bathroom," she announced, tugging on his free hand while hopping from one foot to the next.

"I'll take her," I offered, yanking my hand from Ryder's. Or should I say tried to? "You have to let me go."

He leaned down and nipped my bottom lip before swiping his tongue through my mouth. The kiss was quick yet it made my heart race.

"Never," he whispered before pulling back.

"Gross, Dad." Zoe made a face but smiled when I did. Then her expression was back to one of annoyance. "I have to pee. Hello?" She walked off toward the clubhouse and Ryder finally released my hand.

"Should I come with you?" He took a step forward and I stopped him with a hand on his chest. His very muscular, chiseled, hard chest. I lost myself in the moment until I felt his heart thumping harder against my fingertips. Breaking the brief spell of lust, I gave him a quick kiss before taking a step back.

"Later."

He caught on to my meaning and laughed, shaking his head before turning his attentions back to Jagger. The two of them chatted as I caught up with Zoe. Once I stood beside her, we walked in perfect rhythm, her hand reaching out to connect with mine. I looked down at her and she smiled as she wrapped her fingers around my hand, the gesture signifying she'd accepted me, telling me I was welcome in her world without words.

The way her pale green eyes smiled at me made my womb hurt with longing, something I hadn't experienced until right then. She was a part of the man I loved, and I wanted nothing more than to give him back a piece of myself.

A little one that was half of me and half of Ryder.

A baby.

The only thing to do now was decide when to let him in on my plans.

—◦—

Marek

"I CAN'T FIND IT," I shouted, searching under the couch, then all over the living room. "Where did you say it was?" My frustration level increased as I continued to look for the goddamn stuffed animal Kaden had apparently thrown somewhere and was now causing a fit over because he didn't have it.

Silence greeted me. Either my wife was ignoring me or she hadn't heard me. My bet was the first option, so I flipped over cushions until I found the bunny wedged in the back of the couch. "Ha!" I yelled, shaking the toy back and forth in the air as if I'd just found lost treasure. But anyone who had small children knew what a win the find was for me.

Reflecting back on where I'd been a couple years before and where I found myself right then, my life couldn't have been more different. Yes, I was still the president of my club, my vote the deciding one on most topics, although I always took the men's concerns and comments into deep consideration. We weren't only a club—we were family. A unit that had seen the worst in life, but a group that had also reveled in the gifts life had to offer.

I'd been staring off into space when Sully appeared in the doorway. "Did you find it?" she asked, cradling a very sleepy Kaden in her arms. Apparently his freak-out had worn him out.

The boy was attached to my wife, and normally I found it sweet. Then there were other times when he was a little cock-blocker. Plain and simple. I called it like I saw it. But I loved the little guy, more than I thought I ever would any child. Don't get me wrong, I had a special place in my heart for my goddaughter, Riley, and would protect her until my last breath, but it was small in comparison to the way my heart swelled watching Kaden smile when he saw me.

I'd finally come to understand why Stone turned into a pile of mush when he held his baby girl, ignoring the razzing from his brothers and focusing on the little one who'd turned him from a hotheaded pain in the ass to a doting father. Wait, never mind. He was still a hotheaded pain in the ass, only now there was another, softer side to him we were able to witness.

Much like I'd become whenever Kaden was around.

"Yeah." I passed her the stuffed animal, and in exchange she handed me the little boy, his hand resting on the side of my face as his blue eyes fluttered open for a moment before closing them and essentially passing out. "Did he go to sleep late? Why is he so tired?"

"I don't know," she answered, shrugging before walking out of the room. Sully was frustrated, and I didn't have a clue as to why. I followed her, careful not to wake Kaden because I had a feeling whatever was bothering her wasn't gonna be a quick fix.

After putting him down in his own room, I continued to our bedroom, finding my wife rifling through the closet. I didn't say a word as I wrapped my arms around her and unknotted the silk belt of her robe, parting the material before my hands roamed over her naked body. Her long, jet-black hair was fixed in a fancy updo of sorts, so I made sure not to mess up the style because I knew she'd be pissed at me if I made her redo it.

Spinning her around to face me, I kissed her as I backed her against the wall, my teeth latching on to her bottom lip before she opened for me. Sully wasn't gonna tell me what was wrong, but if I fucked her senseless, maybe that would help relieve some of the tension and uncertainty trapping her.

It wasn't that long ago when the thought of touching Sully killed me because there was a possibility that she was my half-sister. A parting gift from her evil father, Psych, right before I destroyed what was left of him, stealing his last breath as I sent him to hell. It felt like the longest span of time before I found out the truth, but in the meantime, I'd also done my share of damage by pushing my wife away.

Ignoring her.

Choosing to stay at the clubhouse instead of at home.

Keeping her in the dark as to why I'd detached myself.

Treating her badly just so I could gain the emotional distance I needed in case the results proved to be true.

But they weren't true. I'd allowed Psych to fuck with me one last time, and instead of letting Sully know what was going on I chose a different path, one that hurt her immensely. Thankfully, she'd forgiven me, but it had taken some time. There was a part of me that still believed she was guarded when it came to me, but I had no problem proving to her just how much I loved her, and promising her I would never hurt her like that ever again.

"Lie on the bed," I ordered, pushing the robe off her shoulders until it puddled at her feet.

"I can't."

"Why?"

"Because I'm going to mess up my hair." She laughed when I gave her an annoyed look, then stopped smiling as soon as I pinched her nipple, parting her lips and moaning as she threw her head back.

"Fine. Then you're gonna ride me." I walked backward, pulling her with me until I sat in the chair in the corner, positioning her legs on either side of mine so she was straddling me. I'd showered earlier but hadn't gotten dressed yet, so the only thing between me and my wife was the thin material of my boxer briefs. Tugging down the waistband, I pulled out my cock and rubbed it between her folds. Always so wet and ready for me. She arched her back, and as her tits pushed forward, I latched on, my teeth grazing the puckered bud while my thumb pressed against her clit, rubbing slow circles and driving her insane.

"Please, Cole," she pleaded, running her fingers through my still-damp hair and clutching me to her breast. While holding me close, she rose onto her tippy toes, replaced my fingers with hers and circled my thickness. "I need you to make love to me now." Sully positioned me at her entrance then slowly took me inside her.

Fuck! The feeling was still out of this world, her warmth and tightness clenching around me and pushing me toward the edge. As my mouth found hers once more, I poured every bit of myself into her.

What had begun as a 'fuck you' to the Reapers, kidnapping the president's daughter, had turned out to be my greatest gift.

My wife was the bravest person I knew, and although she always wanted to remind me that I was the one who saved her, I believed the opposite was true.

She'd saved me.

She'd given me purpose.

She'd wrapped me in love and bathed me in light when all I'd ever known was darkness.

———•———

Sully

AFTER MY HUSBAND MADE LOVE to me, gentle and slow, a change of pace from the sometimes-aggressive sex we both rather enjoyed, we sat together in silence. He jerked inside me a few times before softening, but I didn't break the connection of our bodies.

I knew he was mine, forever and ever, but there was always a small piece of me that believed he'd be ripped from my life. So whenever I could, I stayed as close to him as possible.

Cole's fingers drifted over my skin, slowing when he reached the scars on my lower back. Burn marks my father had inflicted on me when he thought I'd talked to the cops who had raided our club. Cole's muscles stiffened as they often did whenever he felt the remnants of my previous life. I didn't think he'd ever stop becoming angry whenever he was reminded of what had happened to me before he saved me, whether by sight or by touch. I'd let it go, and hopefully one day soon he would as well.

Thankfully we were still chest to chest; otherwise, he'd undoubtedly trace the jagged scars on my lower belly, and the one higher up between my ribs, both courtesy of Vex. The demented man who'd claimed me from my father when I'd stayed at the Reapers' club. My old home. Although harsh, they were all distant memories, and I refused to linger on them for too long. Besides, every touch from my husband erased the past, for me more so than for him.

Pulling me in for another kiss, he said, "We should probably get dressed now. Otherwise we're gonna be late, and the last thing I need to deal with is Stone's mouth."

"Don't you mean Adelaide's mouth?" I stood, and he slipped from my body.

"True enough." Before I made it to the bathroom, Cole grabbed my waist. "I love you," he professed, kissing the side of my neck before slapping my ass. I shrieked in surprise, which only made him smile. I loved it when he was happy. There was an air of peace surrounding him when he lived in the moment.

Our bubble of contentment shattered when we heard the doorbell, then directly afterward an incessant pounding rattling the thick wooden door.

"What the hell?" Cole grumbled, that peace disappearing as he threw on a pair of jeans.

Even though the intrusion wasn't welcome, I couldn't help but admire my handsome, sexy man. His ass was perfection, even in the baggy jeans hanging off his hips. Intricate designs covered both of his muscled arms, drifting over his shoulders and disappearing behind his strong back, his sun-kissed skin a perfect backdrop for the designs littering his body. His club's emblem was inked in the center of his chest, the artwork shredded apart from the gunshot wound he'd endured. He had a matching wound puckering the skin on his right shoulder. I knew how lucky he was not to have died that day, and before I drove myself crazy with the what-ifs, I took a breath and pushed all thoughts of that time aside.

When Cole's piercing blue eyes met mine, he smirked, knowing damn well I'd just been ogling him. Eye-fucking him was probably a better description.

The rapping on the door crushed the moment, and as Kaden's cries joined the noise, Cole cursed before disappearing from our bedroom.

Tying my robe's belt tightly around my waist, I entered Kaden's room, finding him standing in his crib and crying. The noise had obviously startled him, but as soon as he saw me, he seemed to calm down. The tears were still spilling down his little cheeks, but his crying had all but ceased, his chest rapidly expanding to pull in air.

"It's okay, baby," I soothed, picking him up and cradling him close. He rested his head on my chest and snuggled into me. I kissed the top of his precious little head, inhaling his scent and wishing he'd stay this small forever. It was hard to believe he was already a year and a half.

"Sully. Come here," Cole shouted, the tone of his voice urgent.

With Kaden still nuzzled close, I descended the steps and soon came face-to-face with our guest. Tripp stood beside Cole, talking quietly until he saw me. My husband's eyes raked over my body. I knew he was displeased that another man was seeing me in only a robe, but I also knew Cole wouldn't say anything. He didn't have to, though, his annoyance written all over his face. If he could dress me in a potato sack, he would. He'd even admitted as much.

"What's goin' on?" The way Tripp's eyes bounced back and forth between Kaden and me raised an alarm, but I wasn't gonna freak out until he told me the reason for his visit.

"You guys know I've been looking for Rachel ever since she left, right?"

Cole and I both nodded at the same time, neither of us taking our eyes off Tripp. Rachel was Kaden's mother—well, the woman who gave birth to him. I'd managed to convince my husband to allow us to care for the little one until she could be found.

It appeared the day had unfortunately arrived.

My heart picked up its beat. I tried to prepare myself for Kaden to be ripped from my arms, but no amount of planning would make it any easier. So I remained silent.

"Well, I got word." Tripp took a few steps toward me, and when he was near he rested his hand on the top of Kaden's head. I swore I couldn't breathe, a tear streaking my cheek in preparation. Cole saw me start to unravel and rushed to my side, his arm circling my waist to hold me steady.

"Out with it," my husband seethed, his patience for the entire situation rapidly unfolding. "Where is she?"

No more hesitation from Tripp. "She's dead. An apparent overdose. I can't say I'm shocked."

"What? Are you sure?" I knew it was wrong to feel elation at such news, but I couldn't help it. "Does that mean he's ours?" I looked at Cole, then to Tripp. "Does that mean Kaden is ours?" I repeated.

A slow smile spread across Tripp's face. "It does. He was your son the first time you held him, Sully. And now it's final. No one will take him from you." He glanced at Cole. "Either of you," he confirmed.

As soon as Cole closed the door behind Tripp, he strode toward our son and me with more purpose than I'd ever seen, a huge smile on his face as he wrapped us both in his embrace.

Pride beamed from him as he affirmed my inner thoughts.

"Finally."

————•————

Tripp

"SO, HOW ARE THEY?" REECE asked, greeting me at the door with our son, Luke, on her hip. My boy was the spittin' image of me, and Reece couldn't be happier. She said it was like I was always with her, even when I wasn't.

"Pretty damn happy." My assessment was surely an understatement.

"I wish I could've been there with you when you told them," she pouted, her attention drawn back to Luke. He was fussy, had been for a few weeks. When we took him to see his pediatrician, she'd informed us that Luke had begun teething a few weeks prior, which was right within the average timeframe for a baby of seven months.

"Where's his teething ring?"

"I think it's on the counter," she answered, trying her best to calm him down. He wasn't full-on crying—not yet, at least.

Our lives had been flipped upside down the day Luke was born, but I wouldn't change a thing. The little boy was truly a gift, and I hated to think what my life would've been like without the both of them.

Even though I hated the thought of her ex-husband, Rick, and what he'd put her through, if she hadn't run away from him, I would've never met her. Her tragedy brought her into my life, and thankfully she'd been able to open her heart and trust me. She had no reason to at first—I was a stranger, after all—but I'd been able to show her that I could protect her. Love her.

"I'm going to put him in his room while I shower. Unless you want to take him."

For as much as I loved my son, I wanted to join my woman. Picturing her as she soaped her body was enough to make me explode where I stood, and even though Reece was self-conscious about the faint stretch marks she'd gained during the pregnancy, I saw her as perfect. I told her so all the time.

"I'd rather join you," I revealed, arching a brow and stalking toward her. She handed me our son, thinking he was gonna save her delectable ass. Once I took him into my arms, she quickly kissed me, then practically ran out of the room.

Taking my time walking up the steps, I talked to Luke as if he understood me. "I'm gonna put you in your room, buddy. Daddy needs to convince Mommy to give him some." Placing a kiss on his head, I lowered him into his crib and surrounded him with some of his favorite stuffed animals. He seemed content so I hurried toward our bedroom, stripping off my clothes and walking into the bathroom. Reece was already finished washing her hair. Fuck, she was fast. When I glanced at the clock by the bed, I understood why. Time was ticking by, and our presence at the clubhouse would be required shortly.

When I opened the door to the shower she turned to face me, flashing me a smile before glancing down at my dick. I took a step toward her, but she shook her head. I thought for a moment she wasn't gonna let me have her. She hadn't been in the mood for the past two weeks, between taking care of Luke and her having just gotten over a pretty nasty cold.

What I thought had been a denial turned out to be the opposite. Reece sank to her knees before I could open my mouth to say anything, the sexy gleam in her eye enough to keep me quiet and frozen in place. I slid past her lips and she worked my shaft with the perfect blend of tongue, teeth, and fingers. The closer she brought me, the harder I pumped into her mouth, anchoring her to me with the grip of her hair. She placed a hand on my stomach to steady herself and took me all the way to the back of her throat, which was quite a feat considering my size. But practice made perfect, right?

After she'd sucked every last drop from me, she pulled back, and I slipped from between her lips. "You're welcome." She chuckled, reaching out her hand so I could help her stand.

"I'm gonna be sayin' that to you in a few minutes," I promised, capturing her mouth and tasting the remnants of my release with the swipe of my tongue.

"I want to talk to you about something," she said, breaking our kiss and placing her hands on my chest, the pads of her fingers grazing over the scars from my bullet wounds, a sign she was deep in thought.

"Can't we talk after I make you scream my name?" I reached down and cupped her pussy, my finger slipping between her folds to tease her.

She groaned but stopped me, grabbing my wrist and pulling back.

"No, I need to talk to you now before you make up some excuse as to why you can't discuss it."

"This better not be about you going back to work at Indulge, because it ain't gonna happen." Reece had finally quit when she was five months along—longer than I'd wanted, her employment there having been a bone of contention between us until she'd finally left. Even though she hadn't been stripping, instead helping Carla with management duties as well as filling in to bartend, I hated the thought of her being surrounded by all of those drunk and horny men. The club had hired top-of-the-line security, and either I or one of my brothers was always present whenever she was there, but I still hated when she worked a shift.

A rush of air flew past Reece's lips and she looked angry all of a sudden, telling me Indulge was exactly what she wanted to talk to me about. I narrowed my eyes, the slight tick in my jaw indicating my stubbornness was coming out to say hello. In turn, my woman shut down, clamped her lips shut and tried to shove past me to exit the shower.

I grabbed her arm before she opened the door. "Where do you think you're goin'?" I pulled her toward me, her back resting against my chest.

"Let go, *James*." She always used my real name when she was upset with me. Although I liked my given name just fine, I hated when it came off her tongue in anger.

"No, not until you tell me what's the matter." I spun her around, reached down and grabbed her under her ass, lifting her up my body before pinning her against the wet shower wall. "Wrap your legs around me," I growled.

"No."

"Yes."

She pursed her lips and I took the invitation, although I didn't think she meant it as such. I fucked her mouth with my tongue, our mouths dueling in a heated passion only she could incite from me. Her breathy moans proved she wanted me to continue my assault, so I did.

My dick was so fucking hard, it hurt. I needed relief, and soon, so I lined myself up and gently pushed inside her, making sure to take my time. Even though we'd had sex countless times, I was rather endowed, and it took Reece's body a bit to accommodate my thickness.

Once I was fully sheathed, I broke away from her mouth. "I love you, baby. But I don't want you at that place. I'm sorry." *Thrust.* "And that's final." *Thrust. Rotate.*

"But I wanna—" Her words were clipped as soon as my thumb pressed against her clit. "Yeah," she moaned, all thoughts of arguing with me vanishing into thin air. Her fingernails dug into my shoulders as I continued to fuck her. Slow and then fast, rotating speeds until she unraveled and came on my cock.

After I quickly followed and our breathing had regulated, she unhooked her legs and slid down my body. Reece was still upset about my denial.

Several minutes later, after we finished washing up, I shut off the water and handed Reece a towel that was slung over the top of the door. I hated the despondent look on her beautiful face, her blue-gray eyes telling me everything without uttering a single word.

"Reece." She ignored me and walked out of the shower. "Babe." Wrapping a towel around my waist, I hurried after her. "Hey," I called, snagging her hand and stopping her from moving forward. "Don't be like that. I don't wanna argue. I'm doing it to keep you safe. Please understand that."

Her shoulders slumped before she turned around to face me.

"I know," she acknowledged. "I just need something to do. I love Luke with all my heart, but I need to get out of this house."

"And there's nothin' wrong with that. I have the club, so I get it."

"I have to get ready," she said, switching the topic and slowly withdrawing her hand from mine. She chose a light yellow sundress, complete with short sweater and a pair of nude sandals. Placing the items on the bed, she went to work picking out my clothes.

"What are you doing?"

"You're not wearing jeans to this." She was completely serious, and I found it adorable that she felt like she had to dress me. In all fairness, jeans had initially been on my list of attire, until I decided I'd dress up a bit for the occasion, wearing black dress pants paired with a crisp white button-down. It was a day to be celebrated, especially seeing as how close to death a few of my brothers had come.

I smiled, waving my hand and giving her a subtle nod to continue.

"I love you, baby."

"You should," she replied before flashing me a smile.

"Is that right?"

"Uh-huh."

Reece moved toward the corner of the room and sat at her vanity. I watched as she flipped her head over and dried her long locks. She'd chosen to wear her hair down and wavy, a simple yet sexy hairstyle on her.

As she was busy getting ready, a sudden thought occurred to me, a suggestion which would turn everything around. I could ensure her safety and make her happy all at the same time. I'd work out the details later with Ryder, but my idea was as good as golden.

"Hey." I caught her eyes in the reflection of the mirror. "How about this? Braylen is gonna open her own salon soon, compliments of a gift from Ryder. Why don't you work with her? I'm sure she's gonna need help setting up, then running the business. You could help manage and take care of the books."

Reece's mouth fell open. "Are you serious?"

"Yeah. It could be a little bit before everything is up and runnin', but it's definitely a viable option for you. I'm sure Braylen would love your help." As far as I knew, the two of them got on well, and I was sure it wouldn't take much at all to convince her she needed my woman's help in her new endeavor.

"Oh my God. Thank you," Reece exclaimed, jumping into my arms and kissin' the hell outta me. I took advantage of her gratitude and ravaged her mouth, my dick at full salute by the time we broke apart.

"I don't have a problem with you wanting to do something with your time," I reiterated. "Even though you don't have to. I just don't want you in that club."

"I understand. I do." Reece was happy, and I'd managed to turn things around and give her what she wanted.

But she'd given me even more.

Reece had given me her heart, a son, and an anchor I'd been missing for so long.

---·---

Reece

WE WERE EN ROUTE TO the clubhouse when Tripp blurted, "I want to tell you something." I turned around to make sure Luke was content before shifting in my seat to face him.

"What's that?" I slowed my breathing, preparing to hear something I wouldn't like. I never knew what was gonna come flyin' out of his mouth, so better to brace myself for impact.

"It not official yet, but—"He glanced at me, then back to the road ahead of him, a smile curving the corners of his full lips.

"You better tell me," I warned, mirroring his happy expression.

"I'm giving up my nomad patch for a permanent one. I'm staying around for good." Tripp being a nomad, not belonging to any one charter, had always made me uneasy. Because he had no roots tying him down, he could've disappeared at any time, even though he promised he'd never leave me. Then after the birth of our son, he'd look at me as if I had three heads whenever I voiced my fears.

I knew they were ridiculous, but my life hadn't always gone as planned, so I never fully allowed myself to feel anything except apprehension. It lessened as the time passed, but the feeling still existed.

Until right then.

I was sure I had a ridiculous grin on my face, but I couldn't help it.

"Are you happy?" he asked, looking my way when I still hadn't said anything. "You look happy, but you're quiet."

"If you weren't driving, and Luke wasn't with us, I'd show you just how happy you've made me." Clasping my hands in my lap to keep them to myself, I bit my bottom lip in giddiness.

"Don't tell me that, woman." Several seconds passed. "Damnit! Now

I'm gonna be sportin' a hard-on when we pull up." His faux-annoyed expression didn't fool me.

"Then slow down. I don't need any of the other women there staring at what's clearly mine."

I wasn't a jealous woman by nature, but when it came to Tripp, all bets were off. Did it bother me when he had business to take care of at Indulge or Flings, the club's two strip clubs? Yes. Did I trust my man around those women? Yes. Did I count the minutes until he came back home? Hell yes.

Tripp had told me on several occasions that he liked when I showed my jealous side, probably because it didn't happen too often. Not because what he did warranted a reaction, but because it made him feel wanted. Desired. The reverse was not true when the roles were switched, however. My man was typically easygoing, joking around with the best of them, but if he thought someone was hitting on me, his temper would boil over. And sometimes, although not often, he'd gotten physical. It didn't take much for Tripp to get his point across to other men, because, well . . . he was huge, towering over most people at six four.

Pulling into the lot, Tripp found a parking space readily enough, turned off the engine and exited the truck. He came around to my side first and took my hand to help me down. We opened the back door and together gathered our son, along with all of the things we'd need to keep him happy for the duration.

Up ahead, I saw Hawke, Tripp's brother, talking to a woman. It wasn't until she turned that I recognized her from a picture Hawke had shown me when he was a little more than tipsy. He was upset over her leaving him to go and stay with her sister. I'd never officially met the woman, but my heart went out to her for what she'd been through.

"I didn't know Edana was back," I blurted, holding Luke close as Tripp and I walked side by side toward the others. The sun hit her hair just so, making me a little envious of her deep red locks.

"Yeah," he answered. "He told me there was a possibility she'd show up today, that she might be moving back here." Tripp slung the baby bag over his shoulder, looking quite the specimen regardless of what he was carrying. Actually, I thought it made him even sexier, but hey, that was just me.

"Well good. I'm happy for him," I said, threading my arm through Tripp's as he led us toward our friends.

"Are we early?" Tripp asked as we walked up behind his brother and Edana, giving her a hug and kiss on the cheek before he approached his brother, doing that man-hug thingy that guys do.

"Yeah, but not by much." Hawke turned his attention to me, giving me a quick kiss before backing up. He glanced toward Edana to see her reaction, but all she did was smile. "Reece, this is Edana. Edana, this is Tripp's ol' lady, Reece."

"Ol' lady? We're still doin' that?" I laughed as I shook hands with Hawke's woman. Tripp had referred to me as such a few times, and each time I told him I didn't care for the phrasing. It made me sound . . . old. He'd shrugged off my protest as if I was being ridiculous. In the grand scheme of things, if that was the worst issue we dealt with, I really had nothing to complain about.

Lost in my thoughts, I was startled when Jagger snuck up behind us, kissing my cheek before slapping Tripp on the back. Holding out his hands, he wiggled his fingers.

"Let me see this guy," he instructed. I passed him Luke, smiling over his enthusiasm over seeing our son. "He's getting so big." He jostled him a bit until he'd positioned him just so, causing my heart to skip a beat in fear that'd he'd drop him.

"You drop my kid and I'll kick your ass. Don't care how undefeated you are."

Jagger laughed at the threat, turning his attentions away from Tripp and back on Luke.

"You wanna be a fighter like me when you grow up? Don't be like your dad. He can't throw a punch to save his life."

Jagger with my son was representative of how most of these men were. Big, tough and loud, yet they all turned into big softies whenever a baby was around.

Making funny faces at Luke, ignoring the jests of his friends, Jagger's demeanor changed as soon as Kena joined the group. The way she watched his interaction with our son was borderline hypnotic, and I could only wonder what kinds of thoughts were running through her head. When she caught me staring at her, she smiled.

He's so adorable. Jagger's eyes were glued to hers.

"Me or Luke?" he teased, moving in to give her a kiss. "Wanna hold him?" A sudden nervousness made her shake her head. "He won't bite." Still, she only stood there, extending her hand to caress the side of Luke's head. "Ya gotta get used to it sometime, babe."

Why.

"Because I'm gonna want one soon, so you might as well get some practice." He laughed but Kena found his comment anything but funny. In fact, she looked petrified. She dropped her hand to her side and took a step back, giving me a pathetic smile before she turned around and walked away.

Jagger looked puzzled, confused as to what he'd said wrong. "Here," he said, handing Luke back to me before he took off after her.

I laughed. One odd expression from her and he was practically tripping over his feet to find out why.

"Where's he goin'?" Tripp asked, and I just shrugged. When I didn't answer, he added, "Looks like he probably stuck his foot in his mouth." He leaned down and planted a loving kiss on my lips. "Been there . . . done that."

"You can say that again," I laughed.

As I turned back around to watch Jagger chase after his future, I knew mine had already arrived.

Gifting me with every possible dream I hadn't even known I'd wanted.

———•———

Jagger

"BABE, STOP." *DAMN, SHE'S QUICK.* "Kena!" I finally caught up to her right before she disappeared into one of the bedrooms in the back of the clubhouse. Spinning her around, I asked, "What's the matter? What did I say?" I tried to pull her close, but she pushed me back, her hands resting on my chest to give her some space.

When I finally retreated, she dropped her hands to her sides, looking at the ground as if she feared looking at my face. Paranoia and uncertainty swirled inside me, and instead of blowing off her odd reaction to my joke a few moments before, I continued to press her for a response.

"Are you ever going to answer me?"

She picked her head up, her beautiful eyes looking lost. The longer we stood in silence, the worse I felt, a bead of nervous sweat appearing on my brow. "If you don't answer me, I'm gonna start to think the worst, and considering I have no idea why you're upset, my mind is gonna create some off-the-wall scenarios." I tried to laugh but the sound fell short.

She lifted her hands and signed, *You want to have a baby?*

"Is that what this is all about?" Another failed laugh fell from my mouth. We'd talked about having kids in passing, more so over the past few months, but nothing serious had ever been decided. I wasn't even twenty-five yet, so there was no rush. But eventually, I'd want to start my own family, especially after seeing how happy my brothers were with their kids.

I see the way your eyes light up whenever one of our friend's kids are around.

"So?"

So, I don't want to feel rushed to get knocked up. Her expression morphed into anger, the reason for her sudden change in mood rather confusing.

"Jagger!" I turned my head to the side and saw Tripp enter the clubhouse. When he caught my eye, he said, "We're startin' in like fifteen." He jerked his head toward Kena who was standing across from me in the hallway, a frown on his face as if to ask if everything was all right. I nodded.

Grabbing her hand, I pulled her toward a bedroom, kicking the door closed behind me. I knew if I didn't get her out of her own head, whatever story she was concocting was gonna fester and turn a simple joking statement into something a lot more serious, and unnecessarily so. Advancing toward her left her no option but to back away from me, the backs of her thighs hitting a short dresser against the wall. Nothing except a few motorcycle magazines laid on top, so with a quick swipe of my hand I cleared the items, grabbed her waist and set her on top of it. Spreading her legs, her black and white striped dress riding up her thighs,

I moved in between.

"Don't do this. I don't wanna fight with you, so stop overthinkin' shit." I rested my hand on the side of her neck, her pulse thrumming under my fingertips. She licked her lips, and I did something I probably shouldn't have, considering where we were and that I had limited amount of time alone with my woman. Running my free hand up the inside of her leg, she fidgeted briefly before I pushed aside her white satin panties and teased her with my finger. Even annoyed with me, she was always wet and ready.

Kena attempted to stop me, her hand grabbing mine under her dress, but her efforts were feeble at best. When she knew I wasn't gonna give up, she leaned back on the dresser, braced herself and spread her legs farther apart.

"Let's get these off you," I coaxed, helping her to rise off the dresser before drawing her panties down her legs and tossing them to the ground. "We only have a few minutes so we have to be quick, and we need to be quiet." She looked at me and just shook her head before pointing to her throat. "Okay," I corrected. "*I* have to be quiet."

Fumbling with my belt, I unzipped my pants and pushed them down my legs, pulling her toward the edge of the dresser. The moment I thrust inside her was perfection, and seconds later her short pants of air told me she was already well on her way to exploding. Her fingers tangled in my hair as I tried to show her how much I loved her.

"I know you don't want to talk about it, but I do want kids with you." Not the sexiest of talk, but I needed her to hear me, and I knew that while Kena was in the throes of passion, she wouldn't be locked up inside her head. Her body stilled as she stared at me, her pussy clenching down on me while I tried to keep some semblance of composure. "It's gonna happen. Not today, not tomorrow. Maybe not even next year, but you will have my babies." She opened her mouth, the action pointless since she couldn't speak. When she realized what she'd done, she raised her hands in front of her, but before she could sign a single word, I grabbed them and held them to my chest. "I would never rush you," I affirmed, needing her to know that while my mind was made up, she could take the time she needed to come around to the idea.

She struggled for me to release her hands, and when I did, she signed something I hadn't expected. *I'm scared.*

"What are you scared of?"

That our child will have my 'challenge'. She used air quotes on the last word.

"You know what happened to you isn't hereditary, right?" She gave me a slow nod. "Then what's really bothering you?"

She took a moment before raising her hands.

I want to be married before I have children, Jagger. And I know we're nowhere ready for that step yet, so when you make comments about having kids, I think you just want to skip right over that part altogether.

Okay, I could honestly say I didn't expect that either.

I was still buried inside her, although we'd stopped moving in order to have our little conversation. But after what she'd just said, I knew it was as good a time as any to let her in on what I'd been thinking about for the past month. Perfect timing and all.

Pulling her hips toward me, I surprised her with the sudden movement, her hands flying to my shoulders to steady herself.

"Marry me, then. Agree to be my wife."

She looked shocked, and I couldn't say I blamed her. I hadn't planned on proposing so soon, but after what she'd said, I had no idea why I'd been waiting.

Are you asking only because of what I just told you?

"Of course not. I love you and don't want to wait anymore to start the rest of our life together."

I could tell she was thinking about my response, and for a moment I thought she was gonna turn me down. I wouldn't lie; my heart fell into my stomach waiting for her answer. But when she cradled my face in her hands and brought my mouth to hers, kissing my lips in the most tender of moments, I knew her answer in an instant.

I pulled back so I could see her beautiful face. "Was that a yes?"

Her face lit up with the biggest smile I think I'd ever seen. She mouthed "yes" at the same time she signed her answer.

It was in that moment that I knew my life would never be the same again. Yes, I knew Kena was mine, that she was the woman I couldn't live without, but her agreeing to be my wife shoved our love toward a whole other realm of happiness.

WHAT JUST HAPPENED? JUST MOMENTS ago, I'd been upset with Jagger's jokes about having kids. While I knew I'd blown the situation all out of proportion, the thought of having children with him without being married was something that bothered me. I realized I seemed old-fashioned, knowing people didn't worry about getting hitched these days in order to have kids, but it was something I wanted for me. To have babies with my husband, not my boyfriend.

I wasn't sure why my feelings on the subject were so steadfast. Maybe it had something to do with the fact that if we were married, he couldn't walk away as easily as if we weren't.

Or maybe I was scared about the whole idea in general and I was making stuff up to justify my walking away from him in front of Tripp and Reece.

Everything had changed, though.

Jagger had just asked me to marry him.

To be his wife.

And I accepted.

He started to move inside me again, his lips finding the area below my ear that he knew drove me crazy. He cradled my neck in one hand, the other grabbing my ass and pulling me toward him every time he thrust forward.

"Baby," he moaned. "You've made me so fuckin' happy." He pulled back so he could see my face. Sometimes I wished I had the ability to speak, to hear my voice say his name, or to tell him that what he did to my body drove me to the heavens and back. But all I had were facial expressions, body language and the flutter of my hands.

I love you. Those three words summed up everything for me, and I hoped they were enough.

Jagger's mouth covered mine, his tongue sweeping past my lips, the urgency in his kiss telling me his body was building toward release. The soft moans that escaped him sent my desire for him so high I feared I'd never come back down. He was certainly talented, although seeing as how he was the only man I'd ever been with I didn't have anything to compare it to. But I couldn't imagine anyone else treating me so tenderly yet laying claim to me at the same time.

Each thrust of his hips sparked a fire, my body trembling the closer I came to pure bliss. When his thumb found my clit, I rocked my hips toward him with more urgency, the bubble of ecstasy spiraling through my entire body. I wanted him to see what he did to me, to make sure he witnessed my unraveling. Twisting strands of his dark blond hair around my fingers, I stared into his beautiful amber-colored eyes, his pupils darkening the harder he fucked me, the back of the dresser banging against the wall with each twitch of his hips.

My lips parted as the all-too-familiar tingling threatened to split me apart, short pants of air fanning his face as I desperately tried to catch my breath.

"Are you gonna come?"

I was barely able to nod before my orgasm hit me with such force I threw my head back and pulled him with me, still holding onto him for dear life. He buried his face in the crook of my neck, biting my skin as he took me with wild abandon, his cock thickening and stretching me even wider. He grunted out his release, the sound amplified in the barely furnished room.

It took a few moments before Jagger composed himself enough to back away, slowly uncurling my fingers from his hair. I hadn't even realized I was still holding him.

"Damn, woman, I think you may still have some of my hair in your hands." He rubbed the sides of his head, teasing me when he made a pained expression. Gifting me another kiss, he took a step back and looked around the room for something to use to wipe away our sex. There was nothing, so he picked up my panties, wiped me clean and tucked the material inside his pants pocket.

Once he helped me to my feet, I signed, *I thought you were supposed to be quiet.*

He laughed, the tiny dimple in his cheek appearing and making me melt all over again.

"Seems like I can't control myself around you," he admitted. He took a breath to say something else but a knock at the door interrupted him.

"Kena? Jagger? You in there?" My sister. The handle jiggled but thankfully the door was locked. "Hello?"

I smoothed down my dress before opening the door. Jagger was busy tucking himself back into his pants when I came face-to-face with Braylen.

As soon as she saw me, she smiled. "They're here," she announced, briefly looking down the hallway before turning her attention back to me. She tried to look past me into the room, but I blocked her view. "Don't let Ryder find out that you guys escaped to have sex or I'll never hear the end of it."

"The end of what?" Ryder asked, appearing out of nowhere. He pushed the door open with ease, not a care that maybe his friend wasn't dressed, but somehow I doubted he cared.

"What the fuck?" Ryder shouted, shooting my sister an annoyed look. She thought the situation was rather amusing. Her laughter seemed to irritate him, although I suspected he was playing it up more than anything. "Oh, you think that's funny? That he gets to have sex while we're waitin' but I can't?"

She laughed harder, leaning up on her tippy toes to kiss him.

"Poor baby," she cooed. "I'll make it up to you later."

"You're damn right you will." Looking back toward us, more so at Jagger than at me, he said, "Let's go, brother. Time to get started." Then just as quickly as they'd appeared, they left, leaving us to assemble ourselves enough to be seen back in public. I was sure my face was flushed, but thankfully Jagger hadn't messed up my hair, the long dark strands still in perfect curls down my back.

Are you ready?

He grabbed my hand and ran the pad of his finger over the area near my knuckle. "I'll get a ring and make it official."

I don't need a ring to make it official.

"But I want you to have one. Besides, I want you to make all the other women jealous." He gave me the sweetest kiss. "And hopefully it'll spur things along with your sister and that bastard she likes to call her man."

My thoughts instantly flew to Braylen and me being engaged at the same time. How fun would that be to run ideas past each other? To go dress shopping together and drive our men nuts about the tiniest details?

Pulling me from the room, Jagger laced his fingers with mine and led me back outside to join everyone. Up ahead, I saw Sully talking to Reece and Braylen, and all of a sudden I had the sudden urge to share my news. Turning toward Jagger, I tried to tug my hand from his, but he held on tighter. It wasn't until the third try that he realized I wanted to tell him something.

"Bad habit," he admitted, flashing me the sexiest grin.

Should I tell them about the engagement?

He looked uncertain, and for a moment I thought maybe he was having second thoughts. I knew it was stupid to think that way, especially seeing as how he just told me he wanted to buy me a ring to make it official, but sometimes I couldn't help but be a woman, second-guessing and overthinking things too much.

"I would love nothing more, but how about we wait until afterward? I just don't want to steal anyone's thunder. You understand, right?"

Of course.

And I did understand. I understood that while Jagger wanted to shout from the rooftops that we were going to be man and wife, he didn't want to overshadow his friends' big day. He was always thinking about others, aware of how his friends felt. Jagger didn't look like a big softie, his tough exterior exuding the exact opposite, but the man had a heart of gold.

He'd never viewed my inability to speak as a hindrance, instead finding ways to communicate with me. Texting was the easiest, but when he'd wanted to explain himself, for me to hear the sincerity in his voice, he'd called me and asked me to press the keys on my phone so I could answer his yes or no questions.

One for yes and two for no.

The biggest sign of his interest, however, had been when he asked Sully to teach him sign language.

I never dreamed I would ever find someone like Jagger. Every day with him was special, fate's sweetest gift, and soon the world would officially know we belonged to each other.

———•———

Stone

GODDAMN, MY SOON-TO-BE WIFE LOOKED gorgeous. The way her cream-colored dress hugged her in all the right places, her sun-kissed blonde hair styled casually in loose waves. I told her not to even bother with some fancy hairstyle because I was only gonna mess it up as soon as we had a moment of privacy.

I knew people said it was bad luck to see the bride before the ceremony, but we'd already had our fair share of shitty circumstances since we'd been together.

I'd been shot while helping Marek rescue Sully from Vex, her crazy ex.

I'd been run off the road, ending up in Addy's ER so she could patch me up.

Her uncle, Trigger, had shot me in the leg when he found out we'd not only been seeing each other behind his back, but that I got her pregnant.

And most recently, I'd been shot in the head during our final battle with the Reapers. Well, the tip of my ear had been taken off, but it could've been a lot worse if Marek hadn't tackled the fucker who fired at me.

Come to think of it, I'd been shot quite a few times, but none of my close calls even compared to what Addy had dealt with when she was pregnant with Riley. Ovarian cancer. I'd almost lost her. Could've lost them both.

Shoving aside thoughts of the past and what could've happened, I turned in my seat to stare at the woman who loved me beyond reason, who I would gladly die for if the circumstance ever called for it.

"Don't even think about it, mister," Addy warned, a small smile curving her delectable lips.

"What are you talking about?" I reached over and caressed the side of her face before snaking my hand under her hair to lightly grip her neck, her rapid pulse telling me she was more than ready to give me what I wanted. What we both needed. I pulled her close but she placed her hand on my chest, my frenzied heartbeat giving away what my eyes tried to shield.

"You know what I'm talking about. Don't start something we can't finish right now."

Before I could even think of something witty and convincing to say, a rap sounded against my driver-side window. Grunting in annoyance, I turned toward the intrusion and saw Jagger's face staring back at me. The way he looked at me, as if I was the one holding him up, told me it was time to greet everyone who'd gathered to share in our day.

Our wedding day.

I'd wanted to marry Addy the day I found out she was pregnant with Riley, but she'd refused, telling me that having a child was no reason to rush into marriage. So I'd allowed her the time she needed, finally proposing at our daughter's baptism. Then when she was pregnant with our second child, our son, Lincoln, I wanted to get hitched soon after, but she wanted to wait until after she gave birth so she could fit into her dress the way she wanted. I reluctantly agreed.

It didn't take much on my part to convince her to name him after me, his need for his mother only rivaled by my need for my woman. The little one was attached to her, whereas Riley was Daddy's little girl. Don't get me wrong, she still preferred her mother for certain things—reading bedtime stories, for one—but whenever she hurt herself, it was me she came running to, crawling into my lap and resting her head on my chest.

"I guess that's our cue." Addy laughed. Once she'd exited, she popped her head back inside the SUV, that time in the back seat as she fiddled with Lincoln's car seat. Our son was sleeping, but he started to stir once Addy lifted him into her arms. He nuzzled into her and fell back asleep. *Don't blame ya, buddy.* The nine months since he'd been born flew by in a blur. I only hoped the clock ticked by slowly today so I could cherish the moments.

I got to work helping Riley from her seat, her eyes intently watching me, waiting for me to do what I always did whenever I was near her—make a funny face. Twisting my lips and sticking out my tongue, I made a noise before tickling her.

"Daddy." She giggled, her two-year-old face lighting up as she tried to wriggle away from me. Her laughter filled my ears, and I swore it was like the sun shone all day long.

"If she has an accident, you're gonna be the one to change her. And seeing as how I had a hell of a time getting her in that outfit," Addy said, pointing to Riley's purple and white flowered dress, "it's not gonna be a walk in the park." She smiled before shaking her head, knowing damn well her stern words wouldn't deter me from making my little girl laugh once more.

That was until Riley told me she had to pee. Then I withdrew my hands and finally picked her up.

Kissing her cheek a few times, she placed her tiny hand on my face. "Daddy, you hairs tickawin me."

"Your mommy likes them." I winked at Addy as she sidled up next to me, tightly holding Lincoln. She gave me a kiss before going to find our friends.

"Give me my goddaughter," Sully said, reaching for Riley before I even realized she was near. Since I had to grab a few of the kids' bags from the back seat, I handed the little girl over, Sully kissing Riley before giving her a big hug.

"Where's Kaden?" Looking around, I didn't see the little boy. Though I was certain if she was here, so was he.

"Cole has him." She pointed across the lot to where her husband was standing behind Tripp, his large body shielding parts of my best friend. "Did you hear?"

"Hear what?"

The biggest smile appeared on her face. "Kaden is ours, for good. Tripp stopped by earlier and told us." My confusion prompted her to finish, her smile briefly disappearing. "He said Rachel was found dead. Overdose."

"That's great." Sully's eyes widened at my bluntness. "Look, I'm not saying it's great that she's dead, but come on, Sully. From what Tripp told me about her, she was a train wreck. No way she could've been a good mother to Kaden." Reaching out and touching her arm, I said, "That was always your job." Unshed tears filled her brown eyes. "Oh God. Don't cry or your husband is gonna have my head." I smiled, and she laughed, wiping away the lone tear that fell down her cheek.

As we turned around, Marek approached and pulled me in for a quick hug, slapping my back in greeting. He kissed his wife before she went off to join the others, Riley's sweet laughter carrying behind them.

"You ready to do this, brother?" He looked me up and down from head to toe. "I see you pulled out all the stops today." Marek was referring to the black Armani I'd chosen for the occasion. No way was I showin' up half-assed dressed to marry the love of my life.

"I look good," I joked, laughing as I took in the scene around us. All of our friends were present, with the exception of the brothers of the club who'd passed on, Zip and Breck. Two loyal men who were ripped from this world too soon. Although the threat had finally been eliminated, it didn't take away the sting from the loss.

Seeing Cutter talking to two people I'd never seen before, I lifted my chin in his direction, Marek turning to see.

"How's he doin'?"

"As well as he can be, I suppose."

"Who's he talkin' to?"

Marek folded his arms across his chest, a satisfied grin swiftly appearing. "That's his daughter, Kalista."

"What? I thought he wasn't in contact with her." I'd heard bits and pieces about Cutter's daughter, and how he refused to have a relationship with her, but his reasons were much like the excuses we'd all used as to why we didn't want to get attached to anyone outside the club. Safety.

We'd all failed, giving in to loving our women, all the while driving ourselves insane trying to make sure no harm came to them. Unfortunately, we weren't able to stop some of the things that happened, but we were able to move on from the guilt. Mostly.

"I think Breck's death made him realize how short life really is. Besides, there's no more threat, so he's out of reasons why he should continue to keep her out of his life."

"I guess you're right." Looking back toward them, I asked, "Who's the guy?"

"Her husband, Eli. He's the lawyer I met up with a couple years ago, the one who gave me some legal advice about setting up the strip clubs. Stuff I had to know to run the businesses."

"Oh yeah. I remember you telling me about him. Did you know he was married to Cutter's daughter?"

"Not a clue. Besides, I don't think they were married when I met him. And get this—they have a son. Holden, I think his name is. Anyway, that means Cutter's a grandfather."

I made a face. "That's just weird."

"I know," Marek agreed. Although Cutter looked like he could be a sweet old grandpa, his clean-shaven face and short gray hair styled perfectly in place, he was anything but. He was ruthless when he needed to be. I'd seen that man do some shit that made me queasy. I couldn't imagine him tossing around the ball with his grandkid.

"What a small world," I said, shaking my head at the coincidence. Before we were interrupted by Jagger and Ryder who were headed our way, I bumped Marek's shoulder with mine. "I just found out about Kaden. Congrats, man."

"Yeah." A brightness shone behind my friend's blue eyes. "You should've seen Sully's face when Tripp told us. I was kinda jealous that I'd never made her heart soar like that." He laughed. "But I get it. Besides, I really shouldn't be jealous of my son, right?"

"Why not? I'm jealous of my kids. The way Addy dotes on them, ignoring me sometimes." I winked. I wasn't serious. Not completely.

"I wouldn't change a thing, though. Kaden can have all of Sully's attention as long as she continues to smile like she has been."

"When we gonna start this shindig?" Ryder interjected, fast approaching and pulling me into a half hug once he was near.

"Yeah, let's go, brother. What's the matter? You got cold feet?" Jagger was only joking. If anyone besides Marek knew that Addy was my fuckin' life, it was him.

"Funny," I responded, giving him a half hug as well. Slinging the diaper bag over my shoulder, I clapped my hands together. "Let's get me married, boys."

As I walked toward the grounds behind the clubhouse that had been set up for the ceremony, I couldn't help but think of how lucky I'd been to finally convince Addy to be mine. There were times I was sure she'd second-guessed her decision, but I couldn't've been happier that she stuck it out, giving me two healthy and beautiful children to boot.

The woman was absolutely amazing, and in no time at all, she'd legally belong to me.

To cherish and love for the rest of my undeserving life.

———•———

Adelaide

LOOKING FROM PERSON TO PERSON as my father walked me down the makeshift aisle, I smiled, my heart overflowing with happiness that everyone had made it to celebrate with Stone and me.

"You sure you want to marry him?" my father asked. At first, I thought he was serious. I turned to him to ask him why he'd said such a thing, but then I caught the gleam in his eyes. "Lincoln is a good man, honey." He refused to call him Stone, always using his given name. "I know I didn't want to see it at first, but that was only because I wanted to keep you safe. But he's proven to me that he can take care of you, and my grandchildren. I'm proud to call him my son-in-law." He smiled. "Just don't tell him."

I laughed, tears welling in my eyes as I leaned into him. "You're gonna make me ruin my makeup, Dad." He kissed my temple, neither of us breaking our stride. Catching a glance of my new stepmother, who was holding the baby, I whispered, "Camille looks beautiful. How did you get so lucky?"

"I have no idea," he confessed, a wide smile on his face as their eyes connected. My father had remarried six months before, and I couldn't be happier. She was a lovely woman who'd brought happiness back into his life, so I'd accepted her right away. She never cringed or shied away whenever my father and I spoke of my mother, instead encouraging us to share our memories of her.

I made sure to take my time walking to meet my future husband, partly because I loved to make the man sweat, but also because I wanted to take the time to appreciate the group of people who'd become so intricate in my life.

Cutter sat next to who I'd learned was his daughter, Kalista, and her husband, Eli. From what I understood, their relationship had been nonexistent. Because of the danger that had surrounded the club, he'd chosen to keep her out of his life, only coming to reveal that he was her father when she'd mistakenly walked into the club's bar, The Underground, years back. Out of all the men of the Knights Corruption, I knew the least about Cutter. He kept to himself, a quiet man, but I knew he'd suffered a great loss when Breck was killed. So the fact that he'd chosen to open up communication with his daughter made me happy.

Another two steps closer to my man and I saw Hawke and Edana cuddled close to each other, her head resting on his shoulder as he whispered something in her ear, turning his eyes back on me right afterward. He winked, and the smile that lit up his face was one I hadn't seen before. He'd been depressed over the breakdown in their relationship, the dynamics drastically changing after her attack, but now that she was back, they both looked happier.

Next was Ryder and Braylen. The two of them were made for each other. In fact, they reminded me a bit of Stone and me. He was a pain in the ass most times, and she made sure to tell him about himself. There was a great love between them, though. One that anyone could see as soon as they saw them together. His daughter, Zoe, sat at the end of the aisle, the cutest girl I'd ever seen—next to Riley, of course. I wondered if he and Braylen would have one of their own soon, the way he watched her holding Kaden for Sully making me think the answer would be yes. Then again, maybe I simply had baby fever, so in love with my own children that I wanted everyone to be blessed with them.

Smiling at my thoughts, my eyes connected with Jagger and Kena. I really liked him, and she was his perfect match. She wasn't as ballsy as her sister, but she still didn't take any crap from him. Then again, he didn't give her much to worry about. I'd been the one responsible for him learning sign language. Okay, I hadn't taught him myself, but I'd orchestrated the training to occur between him and Sully, essentially threatening Marek so he'd let it happen. I wasn't delusional; I knew if the leader of the Knights Corruption refused, the only thing I could've done was pester Stone so badly he would've had to convince Marek otherwise. The two of them smiled lovingly toward me, and it wasn't until I was closer that I noticed Jagger rubbing her left hand. Her ring finger, to be exact. When I looked up, he widened his eyes and grinned.

A few more steps and I saw Tripp and Reece, their adorable son, Luke, cuddled close to his mother. When Tripp's gaze met mine, he flashed me the biggest grin. What could I say? The man had a special place in my heart. I'd been the one who nursed him back to health after he'd been shot and left for dead in front of the club's gates. We'd formed a friendship, a special bond during that time. And although we never had any feelings toward each other, he loved to give Stone a hard time, pretending he was hitting on me. My man had finally calmed down some when Tripp met Reece, and he saw how hard his brother fell for the woman. Reece had escaped an abusive relationship, and I was beyond happy that'd she'd met someone who could love and protect her as fiercely as Tripp could.

My uncle, Trigger, was busy bouncing Riley on his lap when he turned his head to watch my father and me walking toward him. Just the sight of him made me miss my mother more so than normal, the resemblance between them uncanny. They'd shared the same almond-shaped eyes and full cheeks, along with the same shade of brown hair, although my uncle's was mostly gray these days.

Thankfully, my father and uncle had ended whatever feud had kept them apart over the years and started talking again, right after Riley was born. My mother's brother was ferociously protective over me, even going so far as shooting Stone when he'd first found out about our relationship. It took me a little while to forgive him for that, but I knew his actions had been driven by his love for me, as well as some unspoken code amongst the men of the club, a code Stone trampled all over in order to be with me. My uncle had only started to accept Stone after the birth of our daughter, although he continued to give my man a hard time every now and then.

When we'd finally made it to the front of everyone gathered, I passed my bouquet of red roses to Sully, who'd readily agreed to be my matron of honor, her husband standing next to Stone, clasping him on the shoulder while giving me a slight nod and a smile.

My soon-to-be husband took a step toward me and reached for my hand, my father kissing my cheek before releasing me. Two of the most important men in my life shook hands, mutual respect emanating from them both.

"I can't wait to get you naked," Stone whispered in my ear before ushering me to stand in front of Father Houston, the priest who'd come to marry us, the same one who'd performed Riley's baptism.

The flush of my cheeks made Stone laugh. No one had heard what he'd said to me, but one look at my face and they could surely guess.

As I faced the love of my life, barely listening to the priest as he talked, autopilot kicking in as we repeated our vows to each other, I lost myself to Stone's piercing gaze.

So much had happened during our relationship, both good and bad, but we'd persevered.

Fate could've dealt us a different hand altogether.

Cancer could've stolen my life.

Stone could've been killed, multiple times over the course of the past couple years.

But none of that happened. Instead, I was given my happily ever after—the man of my dreams, and two wonderful children I loved more than life itself.

Well, soon to be three. I had yet to tell Stone my little secret.

Fifteen years later

"COME ON, RILEY," I GROANED, chasing after her while she ran toward the back of the clubhouse. "I didn't kiss her. I swear." *Damn, she's fast.* Increasing my stride, I caught her by the wrist, spinning her around before she could fight me. A gust of wind kicked up, strands of her blonde hair shielding her angry gray eyes from me. Until she swiped them away, glaring at me in the process.

"Let go, Kaden," she whisper-shouted, trying to tug free from my hold. But I wasn't gonna let her go until she heard me out. I wanted to shout that I didn't do anything wrong, that I'd been the one who was caught off guard when Tracy Flemming planted one on me after school the day before, but I had to make sure to keep my voice low enough so no one heard me.

We were at our fathers' club. Everyone had gathered earlier for a barbecue, and the last thing I needed was for Riley's dad to catch us. The man was seriously scary when he wanted to be. I overheard him telling her that he'd shoot any boy who dared to put his hands on her.

I was too young to die.

I'd been able to convince my dad's best friend that I'd watch out for his daughter, that I would make sure no guys came near her. Little did he know I had an ulterior motive for promising such things, that I was the guy staking a claim on his daughter, albeit privately for the time being.

"Not until you let me explain. It wasn't what it looked like." The fire in her eyes turned me on, my almost seventeen-year-old hormones wreaking havoc inside my body. I risked a step closer, which only pushed her to retreat until her back was flush with the concrete wall behind her.

"I know what I saw." She threw her hands on her hips and rolled her eyes. Riley Crosswell was so damn spirited . . . and I loved it.

I loved her, and it was time I reminded her of my feelings.

I moved swiftly, slamming my mouth over hers before my tongue begged for entrance. Moments later, she groaned into the kiss, and I knew I had my opportunity to make her see the truth for what it was.

I only had eyes for her.

My heart belonged to her. Always had, ever since we were kids.

Unexpectedly, she tore her mouth from me and shoved me backward, her hands in front of her in case I tried to come too close again. "Did you sleep with her?"

"No!" I lowered my voice before I drew any unnecessary attention. "I would *never* do that. She kissed *me*, baby. I didn't kiss her back. I swear."

"Well, obviously she thought she could. Seeing as how no one even knows we're together."

"You know how your dad will react," I reminded her, feeling the anger start to bubble inside me, pissed I couldn't openly claim Riley for my own.

"I know," she conceded, looking away from me before chewing on her bottom lip, something she did right before she was about to cry.

"Don't be upset. We'll figure something out," I promised, lifting her face to mine before I kissed her once more.

———◆———

Riley

LIFE WASN'T FAIR. KADEN MAREK was the boy I'd loved my entire life, yet I couldn't tell anyone. My dad would seriously freak if he found out we'd been secretly seeing each other, and he was so damn stubborn— something my mom often complained about—that there would be no convincing him to allow the relationship.

Not only did I have my dad to contend with, but every other man in the club. I swore they made it their personal mission to make sure I grew old alone. The only exception was Kaden's dad, the president of the Knights Corruption. He smiled whenever he saw Kaden and me together. Sometimes I wondered if he suspected something, although he never said anything if he did.

"I love you," Kaden whispered into the kiss. Pulling back, he stared into my eyes, his the most expressive blues I'd ever seen. So much so I was surprised we hadn't been found out yet. Whenever we were around our families, like that day, he would stare after me, and when I'd catch him, he'd give me a sexy smirk before looking away.

"I love you more."

"Not possible," he argued, his hands going from my waist to under-neath my ass, lifting me until I wrapped my legs around his waist. He used the wall behind me as an anchor.

His biceps flexed as he held me, the corded muscles of his chest surely contracting beneath his blue T-shirt. I'd seen Kaden naked a handful of times, his body like a work of art, but it was only last month that we'd decided to finally have sex. At first it'd been a little painful, but the six times we'd been together since then were nothing short of electrifying.

Lost to teasing touches, heavy breaths and soul-scorching kisses, neither of us heard him approach.

"Whoa!" he shouted. "What the hell is goin' on here?"

I broke the kiss, unhooking my legs and planting my feet on the ground before pushing Kaden back so I could turn and face the intruder.

"Uncle Trigger," I pleaded, my eyes practically bugging out of my head. "Please don't tell my dad. I. . . . We just. . . ." I clamped my mouth shut because I couldn't think of what to say to persuade him not to rat us out.

Within moments, his expression changed from shock to amusement.

"I won't say a thing, sweetie. On one condition." His smirk made me wary.

"Anything," I promised. Kaden reached for my hand, but I batted it away, not wanting to add fuel to the fire. Although the damage had already been done; he'd seen us groping each other, practically dry humping against the back of the clubhouse.

"You have to promise that whenever you do tell your father, that I'm there to see it." He laughed, and I wasn't quite sure if he was serious or not.

"Why?" Kaden asked the question, just as baffled as I was.

"Let's just say it'll be the sweetest karma."

THE END ... OR IS IT?

NOTE TO READER

IF YOU ARE A NEW reader of my work, thank you so much for taking a chance on me. If I'm old news to you, thank you for continuing to support me. It truly means the world to me.

If you've enjoyed this book, or any of my other stories, please consider leaving a review. It doesn't have to be long at all. A sentence or two will do just fine. Of course, if you wish to elaborate, feel free to write as much as you want. ☺

Also, I mentioned Cutter's daughter, Kalista, and her husband, Eli, in this book. But did you know that they have a story of their own? *Torn* came out in December of 2015.

If you would like to be notified of my upcoming releases, cover reveals, giveaways, etc, be sure to sign up for my newsletter.

ACKNOWLEDGEMENTS

TO MY HUSBAND, THANK YOU for always holding down the fort so that I can pursue my dream. I love you!

Clarise (CT Cover Creations), you are so freakin' talented, woman! Ryder's cover is AMAZING, just like the rest of the series. You've done a brilliant job and I cannot wait to work with you on my next project.

Kristin and Becky (Hot Tree Editing), your suggestions and comments have really helped to polish the final book in the KCMC series. I couldn't have done it without you.

Kiki, and all of the amazing ladies at The Next Step PR- I don't even want to think about navigating this wonderful book world without your encouragement, knowledge and support. I'd really be lost without you.

Ruth, I'm so excited to have you in my corner. You've been extremely helpful, especially during the final stretch of Ryder's editing when I had no time for anything else. I look forward to our chats and love that you love my men as much as I do. ☺

Elmarie, thank you so much for taking the time to beta read yet another book for me, although something tells me you were looking forward to Ryder. ☺ I can't wait to chat with you about my upcoming project.

Beth, thank you for your continued support. You cheer me on when I'm nervous, and celebrate when I succeed. You rock!

To all of the bloggers who have shared my work, I'm forever indebted to you. You ladies are simply wonderful!

To all of you who have reached out to me to let me know how much you loved my stories, I am beyond humbled. Thank you so much, and I'll continue to do my best to bring you stories you can lose yourself in, even if it's only for a few hours.

And last but not least, I would like to thank you, the reader. If this is the first book you've read from me, I hope you enjoy it. If this is yet another story from me you've taken a chance on . . . THANK YOU from the bottom of my heart!

ABOUT THE AUTHOR

S. NELSON GREW UP WITH a love of reading and a very active imagination, never putting pen to paper, or fingers to keyboard until 2013.

Her passion to create was overwhelming, and within a few months she'd written her first novel, Stolen Fate. When she isn't engrossed in creating one of the many stories rattling around inside her head, she loves to read and travel as much as she can.

She lives in the Northeast with her husband and two dogs, enjoying the ever changing seasons.

If you would like to follow or contact her please do so at the following:

Website:
www.snelsonauthor.com

Email Address:
snelsonauthor8@gmail.com

Also on Facebook, Goodreads, Amazon, Instagram and Twitter

OTHER BOOKS BY
S. NELSON

STANDALONES
Stolen Fate
Redemption
Torn

THE ADDICTED TRILOGY
Addicted (Addicted Trilogy, Book 1)
Shattered (Addicted Trilogy, Book 2)
Wanted (Addicted Trilogy, Book 3)

THE KNIGHTS CORRUPTION MC SERIES
Marek
Stone
Jagger
Tripp
Ryder

18374273R00156

Printed in Poland
by Amazon Fulfillment
Poland Sp. z o.o., Wrocław